WAR CHIEF

Geronimo knew how many white men wanted all Apaches—men, women, and children—dead. The White Eyes' newspapers were full of such talk. Orders had been given to exterminate them, sell the children into slavery in Mexico, whatever it took to assure that not one Apache still drew breath in Arizona or New Mexico. Geronimo would not have believed it, but one who knew English showed him the words in the newspaper.

There was only one way to make sure that it didn't happen, and that was to strike first and to keep on striking until all the White Eyes were dead or had run for their lives. The mountains and deserts belonged to his people. The Mexicans hadn't been able to take them away, and the Americans were going to fall just as hard. If blood had to be spilled until there was no one left to bleed, that is how it would have to be. That was why he had decided to leave the reservation. Now that he was out, he intended to stay out, until he had won or until he could breathe no more.

By Bill Dugan

Duel on the Mesa

Texas Drive

Gun Play at Cross Creek

Brady's Law

Death Song

Madigan's Luck

War Chiefs

Geronimo

Chief Joseph

Crazy Horse

Quanah Parker

Sitting Bull

Published by HarperPaperbacks

Geronimo
WAR CHIEFS

BILL DUGAN

HarperPaperbacks
A Division of HarperCollins*Publishers*

HarperPaperbacks   *A Division of* HarperCollins*Publishers*
10 East 53rd Street, New York, N.Y. 10022

Cover illustration by Jim Carson

First printing: September 1991

Printed in the United States of America

HarperPaperbacks and colophon are trademarks of HarperCollins*Publishers*

10 9 8 7 6

Chapter 1 ═══════════

Fort Apache—August 1881

SAM BOWMAN SLOUCHED in a chair, conscious of the eyes drilling into him from every side. The other men were waiting for him to speak, but he wasn't sure how to say what he had to say. He only knew he had to say it. He was aware that his dark skin set him apart from the others. His hatchetlike features and dark eyes marked him as somehow different from them.

General Eugene Carr drummed his fingers impatiently on the desk. "Come on, Sam. Obviously, something happened out there. What was it?"

"I quit," Bowman said. The silence that greeted his announcement seemed to sweep toward him like a noxious, invisible cloud. It wrapped around him and started to squeeze. He was having trouble breathing.

Lieutenant Thomas Cruse was the first to break the silence. "Sam," Cruse said, "what in hell are you talking about? You can't quit."

"The hell I can't. I can and I just did."

"But why?" It was Carr now, his voice tinged with disbelief and hinting at anger barely controlled. He tugged at his white mustache, his green eyes flashing. "Sam, what did you see? What were they doing?"

1

"Dancing."

"Dancing? That's all, that's why you want to quit?" Cruse asked in disbelief. "I don't see . . ."

"Tom, I seen this kind of dancing before. It always means trouble. Always. I don't want no part of it."

J. C. Tiffany, the San Carlos agent, put in his two cents, as Sam had known he would. "Why don't we just bring in the medicine man? That'll put an end to it, won't it?" Tiffany shifted his bulk in the chair, but kept his nervous hands clasped over his substantial gut.

"I think that's a good idea," Carr said. "We'll talk to him, see what he's up to, and that'll be that."

"No," Bowman snapped. "That *won't* be that. It ain't just the medicine man. Noch-ay-del-klinne ain't the problem by hisself. It ain't even what he's tellin' them. It's what they think he means."

"And what is he telling them?" Carr asked.

"All kinds of stuff. Bullshit, mostly, gobbledygook, but they take it and run with it. All of 'em. They're comin' in from all over. There's hundreds of 'em. I never seen anything like it in my life. There's all sorts of Apaches there, bands that most times would slit each other's gullets, as like as not. But not now. Now they're all brothers. They all listen to him, then they dance, and when they're done dancin', they talk, all night sometimes. They been doin' it for near a month now. And we can't stop it. We try, there'll be hell to pay."

"What, exactly, is he telling them, Sam?" Carr leaned forward, almost halfway across his desk now, looking like he was fixing to get up, but he stayed there, as if his hands were glued to the desktop.

"He says that when the corn is all the way ripe, the

White Eyes will leave. He says they have to, because the great chiefs want to come back, the dead ones, and they can't come back until the white man leaves. There's more than a few ready to help that happen. And once it starts, there'll be no end of it. I don't need that kind of trouble. Nobody does."

"So what do you suggest?" Tiffany demanded. "Do we cut and run? Is that it? Do we just walk out of the territory, leave the land, give it back to them?"

Bowman's voice was almost a whisper when he answered. "The way they see it, it ain't ours to give. It's their land. And they mean to have it back. Plain and simple."

"But there's coal, there's silver, gold, copper, there's good timber and good ranch land. We have responsibilities to the people who've come here to settle. We can't ask them to leave their land, their possessions."

Bowman leaned back in the chair. Tiffany was getting right to it, and Bowman was ready. "You ask the Apaches to do that, don't you, Tiffany? We give the Chiricahuas a reservation in their own territory, then we rip 'em up and move them here. We tell the Warm Springs they can stay at Ojo Caliente, but they ain't in New Mexico anymore, are they, Tiffany? They're here, too. We tell 'em to learn to farm, then push 'em off the farms, make 'em leave melons rotting in the fields because somebody digs up some copper or some land company wants to run cattle. We do that. *You* do that. And you have the sand to sit there and tell me we can't make people move?" Bowman shook his head.

"You're a half-breed, aren't you, Bowman?" Tiffany asked.

"What's that got to do with anything?" Cruse said. "Sam's our chief of scouts. He knows these people a lot better than some Bible thumper with friends in high places and strings to pull."

Carr interrupted. "Lieutenant, I don't think that kind of talk serves any purpose."

Cruse ignored the admonishment and jabbed a finger at Tiffany. "I don't think *he* serves any purpose. And I don't think you disagree with that, General."

The agent started to get up, but Carr stopped him with a slap of one large palm on the desktop. "Sit down, Tiffany." Turning to Cruse, the general tried a different tack. "Tom, let's just try to forget about what any of us thinks about the rest of us. We got bigger fish to fry." He leaned back in his chair, his hands two restless crabs on the edge of the desk now.

Cruse nodded. "All right, whatever you say, General." He glared at Tiffany, but said nothing more to him. Turning to the chief of scouts, he asked, "Sam, what do you think would happen if we ignored the medicine man?"

"Hard to say."

"Would it just die away, wither like an unwatered plant?"

"Not likely."

"And if we try to bring Noch-ay-del-klinne in?"

"Trouble for sure. Most likely the Apaches would break out of the reservation. Certainly the worst of them, and I can't even guess how many. But I know what would happen next. They would rip the territory right up the middle. Wouldn't a white man be safe from here to Mexico. You all know that, except maybe Tiffany here. But then, I expect he knows it better'n most."

Tiffany bristled, looking for a moment as if he was going to argue, then stood up. "The final say is mine, General. I've already told General Willcox I want Noch-ay-del-klinne brought in to the agency. No more discussion. I want him brought in as soon as possible. On his own if he'll come, arrested if he won't."

"You're making a big mistake, Tiffany." Bowman stood himself, started to say something, then changed his mind. "But I'm out of it. Do what you want." Turning to Carr, he said, "General, I know it isn't up to you, but it ought to be. My scouts are good men, all of 'em. But they're out of control. They want passes to go up to Cibicu. If I tell 'em no, they go anyway. If I tell 'em okay, they don't come back when they're supposed to, and when they do get back, they're ornery as hell. You can't talk to 'em then."

Carr nodded his head slowly. "I understand what you're telling me, Sam. I do. But my hands are tied."

"You be careful, General. You're sitting on a keg of powder and Tiffany here's about to light the fuse."

"Thanks for the warning, Sam. I appreciate it." He watched the chief of scouts walk toward the door. When it closed behind him, Carr said, "Lieutenant, I . . ."

A trooper appeared in the doorway then, waving a sheet of paper. "Telegram, General," he said, entering the cramped room. He set the paper on the desk, saluted, and backed out.

Carr picked it up, read it through once, then again more slowly. When he was finished, he turned to Cruse again. "Lieutenant, please get Captain Hentig over here. We have to make plans. Mr. Tiffany, I'd appreciate it if you'd leave us alone now. You've made the bed, but we have to lie in it ourselves."

"I'd like to stay, General, if you don't mind," the agent said.

"I do mind, Mr. Tiffany. Very much. Excuse us, if you would, please. . . ."

The agent left, letting the screen door bang shut behind him. Cruse was already halfway to Edmund Hentig's quarters. He watched the agent over his shoulder. Hentig was standing in the doorway as Cruse reached the captain's cabin. "General Carr wants to see you right away," Cruse said.

"Trouble?"

"Probably."

The two men didn't speak as they crossed the baked earth of the parade ground. Carr nodded as they entered, directed them to chairs, then read the telegram aloud. " 'Arrest or kill Noch-ay-del-klinne immediately. Willcox.' "

"There you have it, gentlemen," Carr said. He handed the telegram to Hentig. "I want you all to read it. I will wire for confirmation, but . . ." He didn't finish. He didn't have to.

"That's Tiffany's work, the bastard!" Cruse said.

The column was a long one. Nearly a hundred and twenty officers and men. Twenty-seven miles out of Fort Apache, General Carr had called a halt for the night. Cibicu Creek was less than a day's ride. Early the next day Carr watched the column prepare for the second day, misgivings tugging at his consciousness like minnows worrying a piece of bait. He tried to ignore them, but they wouldn't go away.

Lieutenant Cruse and Captain Hentig were taking a small group of men on ahead. They had Mickey Free with them, since none of the officers spoke

Apache, and Mickey, the half-Irish half-Mexican interpreter, had spent most of his life with the Indians after being captured on a raid that had left him the only living member of his family.

Mickey, too, was nervous. He had tried not to show it, but had failed. When he had learned where they were heading, his one good eye had darted around the camp, almost as if looking for a way out. But there was none, and Mickey was a good soldier, if a little unpredictable.

Now, taking the point ahead of Cruse, he was nearly two hundred yards in the lead. The canyon leading to Cibicu was full of thunder. The drumming and dancing went on day and night, new Apaches picking it up when others fell from exhaustion. The closer the column came, the more ominous the drumming sounded. Cruse played with his dark mustache, a nervous habit he had tried and failed to break.

Ed Hentig was to his left as they entered the mouth of the last canyon before the Apache camp. "You figure Sam was right, Tom?" Hentig asked.

"He disagreed with Tiffany. That tells me all I need to know."

"I don't mind telling you, I don't like this. Not one bit."

"Long as we're careful, I think we'll be okay. Mickey and the scouts are checking every square foot of the canyon. If there's anybody there, they'll know it."

"Suppose they go over. Suppose they turn on us. What then?"

"That's a chance we'll have to take." Cruse didn't want to admit that the same thoughts had been worrying him since the meeting in Carr's office. Bowman had said they were restless. And they were Apaches before they were anything else. Usually as loyal as any troops he'd encountered, they were now caught between two powerful forces pulling them in opposite directions. Loyalty and duty were one thing, but identity was another. It wouldn't take much to push them over the edge. Nearly half the column was composed of Apache scouts. If they bolted, the remaining men would be in deep, dark water.

Cruse dispatched his sergeant of scouts, an Apache known only as Mose, to go ahead and tell the medicine man they were coming and to ask if he would come to meet the general at the Carrizo ford. The walls of the canyon were dotted on either side with silent, scowling Apaches, some half-hidden by scrub pine and oak, others, arms crossed over their chests, standing in plain view, motionless as boulders. Cruse pointed out a pair of warriors high overhead. Each man held a carbine across his chest, resting in the crook of an elbow.

"I don't like the look of it," he said. "They're stripped to the waist, and those cartridge belts show they mean business."

Hentig shook his head. "Don't worry about nothing, Tom. We can handle whatever comes up."

"You're new here, Ed. I've seen it at its worst. Unless you've been on the wrong end of an Apache rifle, you can't imagine what it's like."

They were moving cautiously, letting the scouts stay far enough in the lead to make sure they didn't ride into an ambush. The sun continued its steady climb, and Cruse kept looking up. The canyon was too tortuous in its wandering through the mountains to permit him to see very far behind him. They had gone another mile when Mose returned. The scout didn't look happy.

Cruse waved Lieutenant William Stanton over closer to hear what was said, then nodded to Mose.

"Noch-ay-del-klinne says he cannot come to meet with General Carr. He says he has a sick person to tend to. He says he is not feeling well himself, but if the general will wait two days, then he will come to Fort Apache."

"Carr won't wait," Hentig said.

"He can't wait. You saw the telegram," Cruse reminded him. "There was no mistaking what Willcox wants. Tiffany, really. That bastard's behind this mess."

"He's a pain in the ass, but that's all."

"That's not what I've heard."

Turning to Mose, Cruse said, "Go back and tell the medicine man the general is coming. Tell him we mean no harm, and there will be no trouble unless his people start it."

Mose chewed at his lower lip for a few seconds. "There are many warriors there. They are looking ugly. Everyone is nervous. They think we are coming to fight."

"Set them straight, Mose. Lives depend on it. Make sure he knows we don't mean to attack."

Mose shifted in the saddle. "Is that true?"

"Is what true?"

"That you mean no harm? There are rumors. . . ."

"Of course it's true. General Carr doesn't want trouble. But he has his orders, just like I have mine and you have yours."

"Apaches have had many promises made. They don't believe them anymore."

Cruse shook his head. "Not this time, Mose. Trust me, it'll be all right. Go ahead now. We want to give him plenty of warning. He already knows we're coming, but it'll be better if we send another message on ahead."

Mose said nothing. He turned his horse, and Cruse watched him go, taking two privates with him. He looked at Stanton then, whose face was drawn, his lips white. "Son of a bitch had a lot of nerve, challenging you like that," Stanton said.

"I don't blame him, Bill. He's got good reason."

The drumming was growing louder now, and Cruse wasn't sure whether the intensity had picked up or whether the fact of their drawing closer just made it seem that way.

It took another hour to reach Cibicu Creek. Noch-ay-del-kline's camp was upstream a way, but already it was easy to see there were hundreds of Indians. Wickiups lined both banks of the creek, filling every clearing, it seemed. Warriors, stripped to the waist and heavily armed, watched them negotiate every yard of the winding trail. Cruse sensed that something was different, but couldn't put his finger on what it was.

Stanton had dropped back to be with his own troop again, and Cruse hoisted himself in the saddle to look around. He saw a small clearing with three wickiups. Women and children stood in tight clumps among them. He waved a hand, and then realized what was different. No one waved back. Usually, reservation Indians were friendly, except for the worst of the unreconstructed hostiles, but that was no longer the case. Nobody was happy to see the soldiers.

General Carr closed with his half of the column and

called a halt. "We'll camp here. I want to talk to the medicine man," he said. Cruse wasn't sure it was a good idea, but he agreed to escort the general.

After issuing orders to establish a camp, they dismounted and approached on foot. They were still two miles downstream, and the walk was not an easy one. The handful of white men were sweating profusely. Even the Apache scouts looked winded. The canyon walls were studded with pine and piñon. And with staring Apaches.

As he reached the outer edge of the medicine man's camp, Cruse noticed several of his runaway scouts. They scowled and turned away, ignoring his raised hand. The sun was white-hot, but it was well past noon, and the heat would be letting up soon. That, at least, was something to be grateful for.

Hearing hoofbeats, Cruse turned to his left. One of the hostiles, Sanchez, charged toward him, a Winchester carbine braced across his saddle. Skidding to a halt in front of Carr's small escort, he studied them quietly for a minute. Finally, when the silence grew too heavy for them all, Sanchez said, "Go back. You are not welcome here. No white men are welcome here."

"We want to talk to Noch-ay-del-klinne," Carr said. "He knows we're here."

"Everyone knows you are here. And everyone knows why. Go back."

Carr looked at Cruse. "Lieutenant, what do you think?"

"I think we better walk very softly, General. We're in a nest of rattlers. Make sure nobody fires a gun for any reason, except self-defense."

Sanchez wheeled his mount and disappeared. Captain Hentig moved to the left of the camp with a small group of scouts. Cruse led the way toward the medicine man's wickiup. When they stepped inside, Noch-ay-del-klinne greeted the general, but stayed where he was, on a bed of skins wrapped around pine boughs. He told them he was not feeling well.

"We want to talk to you," Carr said. "You'll have to come with us."

"Can't it wait a day or two, until I'm feeling better?"

"No," Carr said, "it can't wait. I'm sorry."

The medicine man nodded. He got to his feet. It was apparent that he was under the weather, but he made no further mention of his health. As they moved back into the open Cruse felt a sudden change in the attitude. It seemed to him as if every Apache in the camp grew tense. The soldiers noticed it as well. They hiked themselves up to their full heights and fidgeted with their uniforms. The incessant drumming stopped. The dancers held their places, as if frozen, turning only their heads to look at the small group of soldiers.

A few on the inner edge of the circle of Apaches moved closer. Two of Cruse's scouts started talking to the medicine man in his own language, raising their voices to make certain everyone heard what they were saying. Cruse looked to Mickey Free for a translation.

The interpreter's one good eye kept darting around the circle of Apaches as he explained. "They are telling Noch-ay-del-klinne that no harm is meant him. He can come back in a day or so, after the general has a chance to talk to him."

Cruse was nervous, but fought the urge to unbutton

the flap on his holster. Any little mistake could be the one that would set off the explosion. He glanced at the sky, almost unconsciously calculating the time till sundown. Three hours, or thereabouts. He wondered whether that was soon enough.

Carr led the way, taking care not to push the Apache too roughly as he tried to make his way through the encirclement.

Noch-ay-del-klinne came along, a scout on either side of him. Their stumbling passage was taking too long. Nerves were drawn taut, trigger fingers on both sides were getting itchy. They were nearly back to the creek before Cruse took a breath. They were being followed by small bands of Apaches, some on the trail to the creek, others filtering through the trees on the high ground to either side.

They reached the creek without trouble. Fording the shallow water, they moved back into the base camp, still only partially established, where the rest of the scouts and troopers stood in nervous clumps, watching the general ford the Cibicu. As he reached the far bank Cruse noticed the troopers looking past him, and turned to see two dozen Apaches about to ford the stream. The sun was already slipping down, starting to redden.

"General," he said, "what about the Indians?"

Carr wheeled around. "What Indians?"

Cruse pointed toward the creek, where half a dozen warriors were already knee-deep in the middle of the fast-moving water.

"Stop them. Don't let those Indians in camp."

Hentig had overheard the exchange. He took several steps forward. *"Ucashay,"* he shouted, waving his arms. "Go away! *Ucashay!"*

Four or five Apaches stepped to the edge of a low bluff on the far side of the creek. Cruse recognized two of his renegade scouts, Dandy Bill and Juanito. He also spotted Sanchez on the left end of the short line. It reminded him of a skirmish line, then a shot cracked, and all five Apaches fired their rifles almost simultaneously, and Hentig went down on one knee. Almost immediately, fire erupted from all along the creek bank.

Bullets were digging at the dirt all around Cruse as he tried to get to Hentig. Someone grabbed him, and he turned to see Private McDonald tugging on his sleeve. "Don't do it, Lieutenant. You'll never make it," he shouted.

The troopers were firing back now, scurrying for cover as the Indians pressed their assault, but, it seemed to Cruse, only halfheartedly. From the corner of his eye he saw the medicine man start back toward the creek as his escort took cover. McDonald fired once, hitting Noch-ay-del-klinne in the back. The medicine man fell to the ground and lay still.

The sudden thunder of hooves erupted from beyond the camp. Cruse realized the Apaches had encircled them and were now running off much of their livestock. It was getting on toward sundown now, and the firing gradually tapered off. The Apaches were content to snipe at long range, knowing that after nightfall they could get in behind the column and trap it. Then it would be just a matter of time before the column was wiped out.

Carr ordered his men to pack all the ammunition they could carry and abandon the rest of the supplies. Some troopers piled supplies into barricades for cover while they gathered weapons and cartridges. Others kept up a steady covering fire.

By nightfall they were ready to pull out.

Carr sent the column on ahead, Cruse and Stanton commanding their respective troops, Cruse with his detachment of scouts leading the way.

They moved as quickly as they dared, knowing the Apaches were already filtering through the trees, ready to take up positions on either side of the Carrizo Creek canyon. If the soldiers didn't make it through before morning, they wouldn't make it at all.

Twice they almost stumbled into a group of warriors. On foot they couldn't move nearly as quickly as the Apaches, but most of their horses were gone, and the terrain was too rough for mounted men in any case.

All night long they ducked and dodged from tree to boulder to tree, stopping often to listen, and waiting for stragglers. Cruse had one wounded man on his own mount, and it slowed him considerably. By sunup he was nearly a mile behind the rest of the column.

They had made it, but Cruse knew they were far from home free. Something he didn't understand had happened, and the worst was yet to come.

Chapter 2 ═══════════

THEY BUILT the fire well away from camp. Juh and Nachite had called for the meeting, and the others didn't have to be told what it was about. They had all seen the signs, the columns of soldiers, more than anyone could remember for four or five years.

Juh sat back from the flames, his face impassive, almost ghostly at the outer fringes of flickering light. Squat and powerful, his features drawn taut under the bright red hair band, his long, black locks framing the orange countenance. Nachite was taller and younger. Over six feet, his height was the exception among his people. And his face was smoother, almost unlined. Some, including Juh, said it was because he didn't care about anything, didn't worry about the White Eyes or his people. He was not like his father, Cochise, they said. Others said it should have been he who died instead of Taza, who was not Cochise either, but who at least had tried to live up to his father's reputation.

Geronimo came last, along with Loco. Geronimo sat even farther from the flames than Juh. Loco spoke first, as befitting his station. The oldest chief still on the reservation, he had only one eye, having lost the other to a grizzly bear so long ago that no one except Loco himself could remember. The others, Nolgee, George, Mangus, sat around the fire, their faces tilted up to look at Loco, who walked back and forth, his hands behind his back.

Looking at Juh, he started with a question. "What is there to talk about, Juh? We all know we can't defeat so many soldiers. If we leave the reservation, they will come after us. Women and children will die, and so will we."

"There are too many soldiers," Juh said. "I don't know why they are here, but it can't be good."

"You know why they're here. It is the Cibicu business. Soldiers were killed. They will not let that go unpunished."

"But we had nothing to do with that," Nachite said. "No Chiricahuas shot at anyone. And still the soldiers come. They frighten the children. The women are afraid to work in the fields. Sooner or later they will come to take us away. Should we wait until that happens?"

Geronimo was restless, his face stern, almost the model of the cruel savage the newspapers were so fond of writing about. He stood up. For a moment Loco looked at him, giving Geronimo a chance to speak, but he simply moved around the circle a few feet, then sat down again.

"Peace is the only way for us to survive," Loco said. "You all know it. It is hard to accept, but it is true. I don't think the soldiers mean to harm innocent Indians. They are looking for those who caused the trouble at Cibicu."

Juh waved a hand impatiently. "It was soldiers, not Apaches, who caused the trouble. The medicine man was doing nothing wrong, but the soldiers came to take him away. Now they want to take others away. Soon it will be our turn."

"I don't think so," Loco said. The old man was only too aware that his name had been given to him because he advocated peaceful coexistence. He was nervous, too, not as nervous as Juh and Nachite, but he had seen enough promises broken to realize there was reason to be concerned.

"If we talk to the agent Tiffany, we can find out what the soldiers want."

Geronimo spoke for the first time. "Do you trust the agent Tiffany, old man? Do you trust a man who gives our land away to put money in his own pocket? Do you trust a man who sells our food and tells Washington that we have eaten it? Does that fill your children's stomachs?"

"It wouldn't hurt to ask him," Loco insisted.

Geronimo laughed. "No. But it would hurt to believe what he answers. You want to believe the Americans are different from the Mexicans. I know better."

Loco paused for a moment before answering. When he did, he deliberately used Geronimo's Apache name. "To you, Goyahkla, all White Eyes are enemies. We understand this. We know what happened to your family at Janos. But everyone here has lost a wife, a mother, child, a father, a brother. And—"

"But not everyone here has lost a family because he was foolish enough to believe a white man's promise. I was that foolish once, but not now. It is not like when the Nantan Lupan was here. Crook did not lie. But these new soldiers, I think they do lie."

They talked on into the night, the few younger warriors listening, and tending the fire while the chiefs continued to argue. Loco refused to yield to the paranoia, but he knew he was on very thin ice. His own Warm Springs people were nervous, too, but he remembered what happened to Victorio and his band. If a great warrior like Victorio could not win, what chance did the Apaches have? Even if they were able to overcome their distrust of one another, they were outnumbered ten to one, with more soldiers arriving every day.

Loco knew that troops of cavalry had come from New Mexico and California, even from far to the north. War would just bring suffering, and if the war was needless, then so would be the suffering. In the end, it was the great respect with which he was regarded that allowed him to prevail, at least for the moment.

Juh was the first to agree. "All right," he said. "Tomorrow we will go to Tiffany. We will ask him why the soldiers are here, what it means for the Chiricahuas and the Ojo Calientes. If we can believe what he says, we will stay. But if we can't believe him, then we will take our people and go to Mexico. Loco, you can do what you like."

"That is all I ask. Just give the White Eyes a chance to show they don't blame us for Cibicu."

"Maybe we should not ask Tiffany," Geronimo said. "Maybe we should ask Noch-ay-del-Klinne." There was an abrupt silence. Geronimo had ignored the prohibition against mentioning a dead Apache by his Apache name.

Loco smiled. He knew Geronimo had meant to shock them, and he had succeeded. "If you go on the warpath, Goyahkla, you might get the chance to speak to the medicine man."

Loco looked at the sky then. It was already turning gray. "I will go to Tiffany this morning. Who wants to come with me?"

"I'll go," Juh said.

"I'll go, too," Nachite said. He looked at George and Nolgee. The latter nodded. Nachite said, "Anyone else?"

There was no answer. Loco looked at Geronimo. "Goyahkla, will you come?"

Geronimo shook his head. "I already know what he will tell you. And I already know whether to believe it."

One by one, Juh, Nachite, and the others returned to their wickiups, melting into the shadows without bothering to take leave. But Loco wanted to think. He sat close enough to the fire to feel its heat and stared into the flames. When he looked at the sky, he could not see the last few stars because of the bright flames. And as the sun came up even the fire's light disappeared.

At seven o'clock the agency would open. It was Friday, ration day. They would soon know why the soldiers were on the reservation. Loco knew that Tiffany lied often, but he knew, too, that the agent only lied when it would put money in his pocket. There was no money to be made in answering a simple question one way or another, so there was no reason to lie, or so he hoped.

As the sun started to climb above the White Mountains far to the east, Loco helped two warriors who had stayed the night with him as they put out the remains of the fire. When the ashes had been drenched, he climbed a low hill and got on his horse. It was ten miles to the agency at San Carlos, and he had to leave immediately if he wanted to be there when the agent arrived at his office.

Winding his way through a narrow canyon, he looked up at its rim as a cavalry troop passed by. He saw a handful of scouts, probably Tonto Apaches, in the lead. Loco knew they were looking for the Indians from Cibicu, but he pushed his mount a little harder. It was not unknown for a lone Apache to be fired upon for no reason, though usually by prospectors or miners, not soldiers. And there hadn't been much of that in the last few years, but everyone was nervous. The soldiers' faces were hard as stone now. Even the friendly ones, like Davis and Cruse, seemed distant, as if they weren't sure who they could trust.

Loco watched the column pass out of sight along the rimrock, then kicked his mount to make up for lost time. When he reached the agency, Juh was already there. He watched passively while the old chief dismounted, walked over to join him, but said nothing.

Loco thought Juh had already made up his mind. He suspected that the visit to Tiffany was something Juh thought a useless exercise but would do because the old man had wanted it. Tiffany was not there yet, but small groups of Apaches were already beginning to straggle in. Ration day was always confusing. The old system, the one Crook had used, giving each warrior a little medal with a number on it, had been allowed to die out. Now the ration allotment took longer, sometimes all day. It seemed strange to stand in a long line, waiting like a beggar for a handful of flour and a small bag of beans. There was supposed to be meat, too, but Loco knew the cattle were starved right down to bags of bones, then allowed to bloat on water before being driven in to be weighed.

Everyone knew it, but no one seemed to care enough to stop the abuse. Loco knew the Apaches had good reason to be angry, but he knew that anger would not solve the problems. It would just make them worse.

When Nolgee and Nachite arrived, Loco led the way to Tiffany's office. The agent was already there. He looked up as they entered, almost as if he had been expecting them. Then Loco smiled to himself. There were spies everywhere. Tiffany probably did know they were coming, and probably knew why as well. He no doubt had an answer all ready for them. He would smile, and tell them just what they wanted to hear. But there was no point in leaving now.

The agent called into another room where the little Mexican Severiano worked. He was the interpreter, and Loco wondered whether he always told the agent exactly what they said. He thought not, but couldn't prove it. He was trying to learn some English, to check on the interpreter, but it was hard to find someone willing to work with him. Crook had talked of starting a school, but so far the only Apaches to receive any education had to go to the east to get it or, like the medicine man, to a religious school in California.

Loco introduced the chiefs with him, a formality only, since Tiffany knew who they were.

"What can I do for?" Tiffany asked.

Loco looked to the others. They each nodded, and he spoke for them all. "We want to know why the soldiers are here. Why so many?"

Tiffany waved a hand. "Nothing to worry about,

Chief. They are just looking for the bad Indians who killed the soldiers at Cibicu Creek. They don't care about your people. Go back to your farms and forget about it."

"It is not easy to forget. There are so many. Every day, more and more. They go past our homes. They ride through our fields. They frighten the children."

"Children frighten easily. Just tell them there is nothing to worry about."

Juh stepped past Loco. The agent stiffened. He knew there was nothing to fear from the old chief, but Juh was another matter. This was one of the most feared of all Apache warriors. Some said he was the equal of Victorio and Cochise. Even when he was placid, Juh's face carried the scars of a lifetime of battle. There was no little acid in his voice when he spoke.

"Yesterday we saw one of those they call Judge. He was riding with a man we know from Tucson, a marshal. Why were they here?"

Tiffany shrugged. "Who knows? Probably hunting."

"Here? Is there no game closer to Tucson that they have to ride a hundred miles to go hunting?"

"What are you worried about, Juh? Did they bother you, did they threaten you?"

"No."

"Then what are you worried about?"

"We know that they would like to arrest many of us. They have tried before. They want to put some of us on trial. They want to hang us."

"Some of you deserve hanging. You know that as well as I do."

"By your law. But not by ours. This was our country. We did things the way we had always done them. You can't come in here and make new laws to cover things that have already happened."

"We can do whatever we want, Juh. If you don't like it, you can complain to General Willcox, or to the commissioner in Washington. But that's the way it is, and they won't tell you any different. Just go home and stop fretting."

Juh took a step forward, but Loco grabbed him by the shoulder. The old chief raised his voice, knowing that Juh was too polite to interrupt him. "Thank you, Mr. Tiffany. We will go. But we would like to come back from time to time, if the soldiers keep coming. Our people are very upset. Perhaps you could ask the soldiers not to destroy our crops?"

Tiffany nodded his head. "I'll tell them. But they do what they want. That's how soldiers are."

Loco thanked him again and tugged Juh toward the door. When they were outside, Juh spat in disgust. "The fat man was not telling the truth. He was not even listening. He doesn't care what happens to us or our families."

"But what he says makes sense," Loco reminded him. "The soldiers do not need to bother us. They are looking for those Apaches from Cibicu. They would not have ridden past without stopping if they were looking for Chiricahua or Ojo Caliente Apaches."

"Not now, they're not. But when they don't find Sanchez and Na-ti-o-tish, they will come back. They won't be so particular then. I was at Cibicu, so was Geronimo. We saw what happened. And when they don't find the right Apache, any other Apache will do. Remember I told you that."

The lines for rationing were very long, and the

chiefs walked slowly past the shuffling double file. Juh shook his head. "Old women, standing begging for flour. That's what they want us to be."

He was about to say more when pounding hooves echoed across the open square. A moment later, a cavalry column appeared around the end of the agency building. Loco knew the commanding officer by sight. Major James Biddle dismounted and commanded his troopers to form a double line. Biddle walked along the file of waiting Apaches accompanied by two scouts.

He singled out half a dozen warriors, asking them to step aside. Each was bracketed immediately by a pair of troopers. Juh moved close to the old chief. "You see," he said. "They want to arrest people."

"You worry too much, Juh. They aren't arresting you."

"No, but they are arresting George."

Tiffany appeared in the doorway. He shouted to the major, and once more Loco wished he knew English. He watched as Tiffany came down off the porch and walked toward Biddle. Severiano came out of the agency building, and Loco called to him. "What is going on?" he asked.

Severiano listened to the major's explanation to Tiffany, then said, "The major wants to arrest those men he has pulled out of line."

"Now?" Loco asked. "What about their rations? What will their families eat?"

"That's what they say. They say they will go with him but to please let them get the rations for their families."

"What does the agent say?"

"Tiffany says that is fair. He says the men will

come in. He will move them to the head of the line. He says the troopers can escort them to their wicki-ups after they receive the food."

Loco nodded. It didn't seem that bad. He knew the men being singled out had been at Cibicu. He knew, too, that the men had done nothing but watch. All the Apaches knew who the bad Indians were. The men being arrested were not bad Indians.

"It is as I said," Juh whispered. "We should not wait for them to come for us. The soldiers will come soon. If we leave now, we can be in Mexico in two or three days. Then let them come look for us if they want."

"Don't be a fool, Juh. If you run, they will think you have reason."

"I want to live, and to keep my family safe. That *is* reason to me, even if not for you, old man."

"Watch your tongue, Juh. I have but one eye, but I can see some things better than you. I am not so old that I won't make you take back your words."

"You are an old man, and I respect you, but it is not for nothing that they call you Loco." He turned on his heel and was gone. Loco watched as Nachite and the others followed him without looking back.

The old chief was worried, but he knew Juh liked to talk. He knew there was still time to convince him to stay on the reservation, but it was important to make a show, and Juh had done it with his customary flair.

Loco watched while the men singled out for arrest were marched to the head of the line. When they disappeared into the agency, he mounted his horse for the long ride back to his camp. By the time he reached his *ranchería,* the people were already buzzing about the soldiers.

People surrounded him, pressing so close he had to kick at them to make room enough to dismount. "Is it true?" they asked. "Did the soldiers arrest Nolgee? George? Why were they arrested? Was there much shooting?"

Loco tried to explain what had happened, but the people were too excited to pay much attention. They were listening with their nerves and not with their ears. They were so afraid that the soldiers would come for them, too, that they could not believe it wasn't about to happen.

Ducking into his wickiup, he talked to his wife, sending the children outside to play. "Juh was here, wasn't he?"

She nodded. "Yes. And Nachite."

"What did they say?"

"They said the soldiers came to the agency and arrested some Apaches. They said they wanted to go to Mexico but that you talked them out of it."

"Did you believe them?"

"You could talk a rattlesnake out of its skin. Of course I believed them."

"You think they will stay?"

She shrugged her shoulders. "How should I know? You are all the same. You say one thing one minute and something else a minute later. They are upset. We are all upset. I think they will stay for now. But it won't take much to change their minds. I think they want their minds to be changed, and only wait for an excuse."

"Was Geronimo here, too?"

She shook her head. "No, only Juh and Nachite.

They said Mangus was going to go to Turkey Creek and tell the people there what was happening. Geronimo was going, too."

Loco took a long breath. His wife was nearly twenty years younger than he, but she had been with him a long time. She could sense that he was worried.

"There is nothing you can do about it, Loco. If they want to leave, they will leave. You can't be responsible for them."

"But the soldiers will think I *am* responsible. They don't understand us. They think a chief gives orders, like one of their generals, and all the warriors obey."

"The tan one knew better."

"Nantan Lupan is no longer here."

"Perhaps he will come back."

"I hope so, but I don't think so. This new one, this Willcox, he doesn't understand. Worse than that, he doesn't care to understand."

The old chief patted her on the arm, then walked outside. He watched the children playing on the packed earth surrounding the *ranchería*. It seemed so simple, what the White Eyes asked, but it wasn't simple at all. It was almost impossible to give up a way of life, and even harder when everyone was pushing and pulling in different directions. He wished that for just a short time everyone would tell the Apaches the same thing. Maybe then it would be possible to make them all happy by doing it. But the way it was now, that wasn't possible. If you made one white man happy, you made another unhappy.

He walked out into the flats, until he could no longer see the *ranchería*. It seemed to him that time was passing him by. Maybe Juh was right. Maybe he was too old. Maybe he was wrong, and there was no

way to live with the White Eyes. But the medicine
man had tried to tell people that he had seen the old
chiefs, and the chiefs had said to learn to live with
the whites. They wanted to rest in peace. But no one
listened. They heard what they wanted to hear.

Looking up at the sky, he watched the sun already
beginning to slip down behind the Mazatzal Mountains. It looked for a moment as if it were being swallowed whole, the jaws of the mountains opening
wide to swallow the sun the way the ground had
swallowed the old ones, and the way it was waiting
to swallow him. That would come soon enough. But
not yet.

Starting back toward the *ranchería*, he walked
quickly, with a grace uncommon to one his age. He
could hear the shouting as he drew closer to the wickiups. By the time he reached the *ranchería*, people
were milling around. He thought at first there had
been some sort of accident, or that he had been
wrong and the soldiers had come. But when he saw
no blue uniforms, he knew it was something else.

He grabbed a young buck by the arm. "What is
happening?"

"The soldiers are coming. They arrested Nolgee,
and now they are coming here to arrest us."

"No, they aren't. They told us they wouldn't."

"But Juh said so. He said they were going to arrest
Nolgee, then changed their minds. But now they have
changed again, and they have taken him away. We
are next."

"Where are you going?"

The young man shook free. "I am going with Juh,"
he said. "You should come, too. Everyone should
come."

Loco shook his head. "No, I will not come."

"You will be sorry."

"Perhaps." He watched the young warrior run for his horse, a nearly empty cartridge belt draped over one shoulder.

By morning, he knew, Juh would be gone. And Geronimo, and Nachite, and so many others. All he could do was hope to keep the others safe. But he wasn't sure. He wasn't sure of anything anymore, except that there was more trouble coming.

Chapter 3 ===============

GERONIMO SPOTTED the wagons first. He lay on the top of a low rise, training his field glasses on the lumbering mules. The wagons appeared to be unescorted. The drivers would be armed, and each of the three had a shotgun rider, but that shouldn't be a problem. The small train was nearly five miles away. There was plenty of time. Backing away from the crest of the hill, he was already planning deployment of his men.

The pass was steep on both sides, but there was little cover on the slopes. His men would have to line the ridges on both sides and move quickly, once the wagons entered the narrow draw. Dividing his men, he directed half to move to the northern ridge. He wanted two clusters, one at either end of the pass, with the balance strung out along the middle of the ridge line.

He took the southern rim with the rest of the warriors. Again, he concentrated his men in two knots, with a thin line between them. He remembered the old days, when he had a hundred men and more. Now he was down to fewer than thirty. It seemed as if no one cared anymore. Loco was a perfect example, a

31

man who once feared no one in battle and now feared only that he would upset the White Eyes.

But this was Apache country, it was *his* country, and he was not going to give it up easily. Geronimo waved a hand, and his men lay flat. Some had woven headdresses of bunchgrass so they could stay right at the ridge line to look down into the valley. From below, no one would notice them lying flat on the light brown soil.

The wagons were drawing closer now, and he risked one more look through the binoculars. It would be the last time, because he didn't want to take the chance that a stray glint of the polished glass would betray his presence. He could see the men more clearly now. The lead driver was a big man, middle-aged, a dark mustache dropping over thin lips. He seemed alert, his head whipping back and forth to check the country ahead, occasionally turning all the way around to look back over the seldom-used road to make sure the wagons weren't being followed.

The man had blue-gray eyes, like Chihuahua's eyes. Geronimo wondered if Chihuahua was Mexican, like some said, but he didn't think so. Chihuahua thought like an Apache and fought like one. No Mexican could learn to do that as well as Chihuahua, even one who had been raised by the Apaches.

Pressing himself against the ground, he waited for the first cracks of the whips to reach him on the wind. Then he would hear the wheels creaking, the springs of the wagon bed squealing like rats.

He couldn't get his mind off Loco. He didn't understand the old man. Loco had been close to Mangas Coloradas, and Mangas had been a great warrior, a man who tried the path of peace and had been whipped within an inch of his life for his troubles. Geronimo had been there, still a young man, when Mangas had come back from the mining camp at Santa Rosa. They had bound and whipped the great chief, laying his back open from shoulder to hip with ugly welts that broke the skin in so many places, Mangas was weak from loss of blood. And Mangas had learned from that betrayal. Others had learned, too. Juh had learned and Geronimo himself had learned. Why hadn't Loco learned?

And the old man knew the stories, too, about the death of Mangas. He knew how the soldiers had poked him with heated bayonet points while he lay on the ground, trying to sleep. Mangas had been captured in spite of a white flag and promises of a truce, and the white man, General West, had wanted him dead, and had told the soldiers guarding Mangas. So they baited the great man until he couldn't take it anymore and when he had gotten to his feet to protect himself, they had shot him down in cold blood.

That was bad enough, but what happened next was too much to bear, too hard to understand. They had cut off Mangas's head, and the army doctor had boiled it, peeled the skin away, and emptied the skull of its brains, for "science" he had said, then sent the great skull somewhere for others to look at it. Yet they called the Apaches savages.

Loco knew all this, and still he preached that peace was the only way for the Apaches to save themselves. Loco was a fool. The only way for the Apaches to save themselves was to be more cruel than the White Eyes. Outnumbered by hundreds to one, the Apaches had to be ruthless and brutal, capable of things that would have once turned their stomachs, tough as they were. But they were fighting for their land, and the white man planned to leave them nothing, no land, no food.

Geronimo knew how many white men wanted all Apaches—men, women, and children—dead. The White Eyes' newspapers were full of such talk. Orders had been given to exterminate them, sell the children into slavery in Mexico, whatever it took to see to it that not one Apache still drew breath in Arizona or New Mexico. He would not have believed it, but one who knew English showed him the words in the newspaper.

Still he hadn't believed, but he had taken the paper to the agent, Clum, and Clum had told him the same thing. Clum said it wouldn't happen, but Geronimo knew better. He knew that the ones who wanted the Apaches dead would do things to make sure it happened. White men like Clum would not be able to stop it, even if they wanted to, and Geronimo wasn't sure they did.

There was only one way to make sure that it didn't happen, and that was to strike first and to keep on striking until all the White Eyes were dead or had run for their lives. The mountains and the desert belonged to his people. The Mexicans hadn't been able to take it away, and the Americans were going to fall just as hard. If blood had to be spilled until there was no one left to bleed, then that is how it would have to be. That was why he had decided to leave the reservation. Now that he was out, he intended to stay out, until he had won or until he could breathe no more.

Listening to the wagons come closer and closer, he could feel the familiar rage building inside him. Every squeak of the wheels seemed to taunt him, every creak of the springs was an insult. He would take no more.

Geronimo could tell by the sound that the wagons were all in the valley now. Just a little closer, a little deeper in, and it would be time. The drivers would not be able to turn the wagons. The pass was too narrow for that. If they tried, the wagons would turn over. They were trapped, and all he could hope was that one of them carried ammunition. It was better in the old days, when food could be killed with arrows and lances. But the Mexicans had guns, and that meant the Apaches needed guns, too. Having learned to use them, the Apaches were dependent on them. But bullets were scarce. Half of his raids had been simply to obtain more ammunition.

The creaking grew louder, and it sounded as if the wagons were rolling right up the side of the draw toward him. It was time. Scampering to the top of the ridge, he opened fire. The warriors followed suit. A thunderous volley rolled and echoed through the draw, then raced across the flatlands beyond.

The first volley killed three mules. The lead wagon lost two, and the driver cracked the whip again and again, his deep voice bellowing to the surviving animals to pull, pull, pull. Firing from both sides of the draw, the Apaches had no doubt they would win this one.

The driver of the lead wagon braked, abandoned the reins, and leaped from the seat with a rifle in his hands. It was new, and glittered like silver in the bright sun. The driver and the other men, six in all, had started to fire back. All three wagons were stopped now, and the men were on the ground, firing

their rifles up toward the crest of either ridge. But
there was no place for them to hide. The big man driv-
ing the first wagon raced back to the second.

Even before the driver climbed up onto the seat,
Geronimo knew what he was going to do. Shouting
to aim for the driver, Geronimo broke into a run, his
thick legs pumping as he raced down the sandy slope.
Cactus clawed at his leggings, but he was used to
that.

The driver had the mules in motion, and the wagon
lurched, dragging the dead mule along with it.
Wounded in the shoulder, the man slumped to one
side, but jerked the reins, trying to get the second
wagon alongside the first. The other men ran forward
and formed a line beside the lead wagon, then fired
at Geronimo and the other warriors behind him.

The moving wagon lurched drunkenly, jumping
ahead in fits and starts. The driver was hit again, but
he held on to the reins, trying to get the heavy
freighter in position.

He had almost reached the lead wagon when the
driver was hit a third time. This shot was fatal,
knocking him backward over the seat, where he
sprawled on top of the canvas covering the freight.

But one of the other haulers was smart. Unwilling
to expose himself to the charging Apaches, he shot
the mules. They fell dead in the traces, and the wagon
stopped. Almost aligned, but not quite.

The men had some cover now, at least from the
worst of the firing, and they lay on the ground, firing
out from under both wagons. Geronimo could see two
men, one behind each wheel, working their rifles and
firing almost without aiming. He turned to look back

up the slope for a moment, but no one had been hit, and he plunged on.

One of the crouching freightmen howled, then rolled over onto his side. He was exposed to the left of the wheel, and Geronimo fired from his hip. He saw a puff of dust as the bullet narrowly missed, but the freightman didn't move.

Over the gunfire the piercing shrieks of the warriors seemed to swirl in the air as the Apaches charged down into the draw from both ridges. Firing from the wagons was tapering off, as if fewer men were shooting now. Two, at least, were out of action—one dead, the other at best unconscious.

As they reached the bottom of the draw the Apaches turned away from the wagons and sprinted toward either end of the narrow passage. Several bucks dropped to their stomachs and began to fire toward the wagons at the prostrate wagoneers, lying across the line of fire now.

One man, who looked as if he couldn't weigh more than a hundred and twenty pounds, climbed out from under a wagon and tried to scramble up toward the ridge. Two warriors were still up top, and both leaped over the crest and charged toward the tiny man as he half ran and half swam uphill against the loose soil. He saw the Indians coming, but it made no difference. His arms and legs flailed against the shifting footing, he went to his knees, then back up as the warriors closed on him.

Geronimo raced toward the wagons, heading for the gap between them. Only one man seemed to be firing at him, and Geronimo reached the wagons and leaped atop the one on the right. With his pistol in his right hand, he leaned out over the edge of the freighter. He could hear scrambling on the sandy ground, ducked to the other side as the men rolled out. If he fired at point-blank range, there was no way he could miss.

The man jerked as the bullet slammed into his chest, his legs twitched, then he lay still. A high-pitched howl punctuated the end of the gunfire and Geronimo turned to see the scrambling little man struggling in the grasp of four warriors. They held him, two on each leg, and were pulling him apart, as if he were a wishbone.

With a sound like tearing cloth, the man came apart, and two warriors staggered back, one leg in their hands, its bloody end sticking out of frayed denim. The remaining two warriors picked up a large rock and dropped it on the still-quivering body, then used it to crush the man's head.

The hostiles swarmed over the wagons now, slashing at the ties holding the canvas covers in place. Anything of value was thrown to one side. Two cases of cartridges were turned up. There was cloth, some strange-looking metal things he had seen used by the ones they called carpenters. A crate of repeating rifles, then another box of ammunition were found in the second wagon.

And there was food, some in cans and some in barrels. It must have been intended for one of the mining camps, where the white men dug up the yellow metal they liked so much. Not much else warranted attention.

The Apaches tore the wagons to pieces, piling the unwanted freight in mounds, then tipped the wagon beds onto their sides. Others were busy carving steaks from the dead mules. Geronimo paid attention to the real booty, the ammunition. Cracking the cases open, he ripped a canvas sheet into several pieces, then began to empty the ammunition onto the cloth scraps. He did not count the way the White Eyes did, but he made six bundles almost equal, wrapped them in the canvas, and tied them with the remains of the rope.

Next, he broke open the box of rifles. There were twelve of them, brand-new. They smelled of oil. He unwrapped each one, tossing the oily cloths wrapping each one into a pile. Some of his people had ancient Mexican guns, single-shot rifles that were no match for the repeaters some of the soldiers were using. The new guns would make them very happy. Geronimo called several of the men over and directed them to take the rifles and the bundles of bullets back to the *ranchería*. When the men had left, he turned back to the wagons.

Four of the dead freightmen were spread-eagled on wagon wheels. They had been cut from the belt line to the breastbone, their thighs laid open from hip to knee. They dangled, heads down, over mounds of cloth and wood. One warrior. Nan-ti-klay, was already torching the first mound. Geronimo watched impassively as the flames began to lick upward. The four men would be charred hulks, their brains roasted in their heads, by the time they were found. The little man who had been dismembered and crushed lay on the hillside where he had been killed.

The big man, the driver of the first wagon, had been left alone. He had done a brave thing trying to save his friends. That was courage worthy of great respect, and they would not mutilate him. The White Eyes didn't understand. They would find the mutilated bodies and would think they had been tortured, but it wasn't always like that. They didn't know that in the Happy Place, your body was the same as it was here. If you had one eye, then in the Happy Place you had one eye. If your legs had been cut off, then you had no legs in the Happy Place, just as Mangas Coloradas would spend eternity in the Happy Place without his head, thanks to the soldiers' medicine man.

The smoke began to blacken and grow thick as one mound of useless goods after another caught fire. When all four were blazing, Geronimo backed away, then started up the slope. He didn't issue a command. He didn't have to. The men would follow him because they had no one else to follow, and because none of them had anyplace else to go.

Chapter 4 =====

LOCO SAT in the sun, his back resting against the back wall of his wickiup. Rubbing one ancient hand against his left cheek, he felt the thick bands of scar tissue, left behind by a bear claw. He had killed the bear, but it had cost him the use of the left eye. It still worked, but the flesh was so distorted by the bear's assault, the muscle ripped loose by the razor claw, that the eye would no longer stay open. That had happened a long time ago, but he could see it so clearly he sometimes still woke in the night, his heart pounding and his throat dry from his labored breathing. He had killed the grizzly using only a knife, but that meant little to him now. He knew others still talked about the incident, but he wished it had never happened. It wasn't so much the loss of vision that bothered him, but the way people looked at him when they met him for the first time, especially the children.

Loco had lived a long time, and he had seen things much worse than the razor claw of the bear sweeping past his bobbing head. He had seen the bodies of women and children, their scalps lifted by the bounty hunters. He had seen Mangas's headless corpse lying in the dirt, food for the coyotes. He had seen his peo-

41

ple sold into slavery, and seen some, though very few, when they returned. Compared with that, the bear was nothing.

He had learned a great deal, too, from what he had seen. The one painful thing he saw more clearly with his one eye than the others—Juh, Geronimo, Nachite—saw with two was that there was no way to defeat the White Eyes. There were far too many of them, and they had weapons the Apaches could only dream of. He remembered the first time they had been attacked by the fieldpieces. The great guns on their huge wheels, with barrels like tree trunks and muzzles like the maws of bears, had thrown shells enormous distances, and the shells exploded when they hit something. No one could be expected to withstand that kind of attack, not even a man who killed a grizzly with his bare hands.

And since that is what he saw, that is what he said, whenever he got the chance. The others, the hotheads and the dreamers, waved him off. They respected him, and they knew too much to think him a coward, but they refused to understand that his truth, as painful as it might be, could not be ignored, so they tried. They beat their heads against stone walls until their brows were bloody pulp, their bones splintered, their brains bruised in their bony boxes. And still they saw nothing.

It was terrible on the reservation, having to wear the medal around his neck, instead of coming and going as he pleased. He hated not being able to feed his family without going like a beggar to the agency for the pitiful cup of bug-infested flour and bag of rotting beans. But he believed it was better for all Apaches if they would invest their energy in learning to live with the White Eyes instead of trying to drive them away. Only no one wanted to listen. It was too easy to shake your fist against the dome of the wick-iup when no one could see you, and whisper how you would have your revenge. But the secret that Loco knew, and that he wished were not a secret at all, was that there *was* no revenge. The war was already over. It was now simply a matter of deciding when to stop the killing and the dying.

He heard the footsteps approaching his wickiup, but chose not to move. Anyone who wanted to see him would find him. If he were too lazy to walk around the wickiup, he was no warrior, or it was not urgent. He recognized the moccasins when they appeared on his right. Warriors always approached him from the right, out of respect, knowing that he could not see them from the left side.

Tzo-ay sat beside him, but said nothing. Loco reached into the pouch on his belt, took out some tobacco and an oak leaf. He rolled the tobacco into a fat cigarette. He had a box of the White Eyes matches, and struck one with his thumbnail. Lighting the cigarette, he took a long puff of the smoke, held it in his lungs for a bit, then let it go in small rings of rich white, like snow.

Without looking at the younger man, Loco offered the cigarette. Tzo-ay took it with thanks, permitted himself a single small puff, then handed it back, again with thanks.

"What is it?" Loco asked.

"They are coming," Tzo-ay said.

"Who is coming?"

"Geronimo, Juh, Chatto, many others."

"Why?"

"They want you to join them."

"I won't. They already know that."

"They sent me to ask you again."

"Tell them no. Again."

"They knew you'd say that. . . ."

Loco nodded. "Of course they did. I told them before."

"No, that's not what I mean. They expected you to refuse. . . ."

"So you have a message for the old man, is that it?"

Tzo-ay nodded. Loco turned then to look at him more closely. "And what is the message?"

"They say if you will not join them on your own, they will force you, and the women and children. They say they will shoot those who don't come with them."

Loco took another long puff on the oak-leaf cigarette. He held the smoke in until he had to cough, then let it out in one shapeless cloud. "It has come to that, has it? Apaches killing Apaches . . . doing the work of the White Eyes . . . will they collect the bounty from the Mexicans, too?"

Tzo-ay shrugged. "I'm sorry to be the one to bring the message. It was not my doing."

"I don't blame you, Tzo-ay. I don't think I really blame them, either. They are desperate men. They know how it used to be, they remember too well the freedom. I am an old man. I remember many things they do not. I remember a freedom they could only dream of, but that freedom is gone now. It is dead, like Co—like the great chiefs." The old man almost forgot himself, and violated the custom of not mentioning the names of the dead ones. He understood the taboo, knowing that the shade of the one named would have to stop whatever it was doing and come to see why his name was mentioned. It was impolite to cause such a thing, disrespectful.

"I didn't want to come. I . . ."

"You did what your chiefs told you. They are older than you, and are supposed to be wiser. Don't blame yourself for a decision another man made."

"I am not happy with it. I don't think it is right."

"No, it isn't right. But it is my problem, not yours. Thank you for telling me."

"You won't come, will you?"

"No," Loco said, letting his breath out in a long sigh. He puffed again on the cigarette. "I won't come."

"They mean what they say."

Loco nodded. "Maybe they do."

"Geronimo was very angry. He said you pay too much attention to promises that are not kept."

"I know. He has felt that way for a long time. But Geronimo does not always think things through. He is too angry. But I don't blame him for that. I know what happened at Janos. It is a terrible thing to lose your family. And when you come home to find your mother, a young wife, and three tiny children dead, it changes you in a way that can never be undone. I understand him. He is a great man, in his way. Not like Victorio was, or Mangas Coloradas, but . . ." The Spanish names of the dead, although acceptable, never sat comfortably on Loco's tongue. They always seemed to him to be lies of a peculiar kind; calling someone by the name his enemies gave him seemed almost to be taking sides.

"I have to go now."

Loco nodded. "I understand. When will they come?"

"Soon, I think. They are not far away. Tonight, maybe tomorrow, although I think sooner. They want to move quickly, before the army knows they are here. You should know they are serious. They mean to do it."

"Of course they do. But I have lived with much worse. I can live with that." He said it in such a way as to let the younger man know the conversation was over.

Tzo-ay reached out to clap the old chief on the shoulder. "You have been like an uncle to me." A moment later, he was gone. Loco did not get up quickly. There was much to think about. He looked at the remains of the oak leaf, its end no longer red, but a cylinder of light gray ash. Tossing it away, he leaned back again and watched the people of the *ranchería* go about their usual business. The children were playing, making noise the way children did when they were nervous. The women prepared food and some worked in the pitiful fields, tending crops that made too many demands on the stingy soil.

After a long time the old man got to his feet and went inside. He wanted to think, and to rest. There was much to think about, and he was very tired. And if Tzo-ay was right, it would be a busy night. He lay down in a deerskin robe and closed his eyes. He could hear the sounds of the camp for a while, but they faded as his tiredness overtook him.

He did not sleep well. His wife woke him twice to ask if he was ill. He patted her arm and told her no, then tried again to sleep, where sometimes he could see things more clearly than when he was awake.

The third time he woke, it was pitch-black. The camp was quiet. But something had changed. They had come, he was sure of it. He sat up and strained to hear something in the deathly stillness. Not even a dog barked. Then he realized why. The dogs, of course, would have been killed to keep them quiet. So, he thought, they have come already.

He went outside. Everything looked normal, but that wouldn't last. He heard something behind him and turned as a hand descended onto his shoulder.

He wasn't startled. Turning slowly, he saw Geronimo, a finger to his lips. "Have you made up your mind to join us?"

"No. It is a mistake."

Geronimo shook his head angrily. "No! It is a mistake to stay here. How long will you wait—until the ground shrinks away beneath you, and you cannot stand on your feet without stepping on another man's land? Is that what you want? Is that the peace the White Eyes offer you?"

"There is no point in continuing to fight against them. We can't win. Better to save what few Apache lives there are, save the women and the children."

"Save them for what? To live like cattle, and pay another man for the right to breathe?"

"No."

"That's what it is. You must come with us."

"No."

"We will make you come."

"I know what you plan. Tzo-ay gave me the message."

Loco waited for an answer, but it was long in coming. Already people were slipping out of the other wickiups. Almost instinctively, they drifted toward

Loco's wickiup. Soon there was a tight circle around the two men. It was growing thicker and thicker as more and more people pressed in behind. Geronimo's men were going from one shelter to the next, rousing the occupants and telling them to go outside.

Someone stirred the embers of the fire and threw some pine branches on them. The dry needles exploded into flame, sending a wash of yellow light over the heart of the camp, casting strange shadows on the worried faces of the other Apaches.

When the needles had burned away, the fire settled down, but the branches were ablaze now, and the light was full and steady. "I ask you once more," Geronimo said.

"No," Loco said.

Geronimo shook his head. The fire brightened his long, black hair, making him look older somehow, as if the hair were gray. He barked a command, and several of his warriors started pushing through the crowd.

"You want us to destroy this *ranchería* and all the people in it?"

"What would that accomplish?"

"It would save the White Eyes the trouble. And it would save you the torment of waiting. Let it end now as it must end soon in any case."

"I think—"

There was a shout then, in English. "What was that?" Geronimo hissed.

A gunshot cracked, then more shots, a volley. No one was hit, so whoever fired must have been shooting into the air, but the *ranchería* erupted into a swirl of running bodies. The children started to wail, and the women dragged them away, trying to hush them and comfort them by turns. Loco looked at Geronimo. "This is what comes of your madness," he said.

A second later, Albert Sterling, the chief of the Indian police, pushed through the rapidly thinning crowd. He saw Geronimo and reached for his sidearm. Before he had a chance to clear the holster, a rifle cracked, and both chiefs saw the splatter of blood as a bullet passed through Sterling from behind. More firing erupted, and some of Sterling's police charged forward to rescue their chief. But it was too late for that, and Loco knew it.

The gunfire exploded on all sides now. "All right," he said, "we will go."

"Pack your things, old man," Geronimo said, then disappeared into the darkness.

Loco went into his wickiup. He told his wife what was happening and urged her to take only what they could carry on a long march. Now that Sterling had been killed, he knew there would be much trouble.

When he ducked back outside, the firing had already stopped. The bodies of four Apache police were stacked beside the fire. Some of Geronimo's warriors were standing in a circle, laughing and shouting. At first Loco couldn't see what they were doing. As he walked closer he realized they were playing a game, kicking a ball around the inside of the circle. Then he stepped into the ring, and the warriors melted away, leaving the ball behind.

Loco bent to retrieve it, then stopped. It was Albert Sterling's head.

Chapter 5 ⟰⟰⟰

March 1882—San Carlos Agency

LIEUTENANT BRITTON DAVIS WOKE with a distant hum filling the room, the sound bouncing off the log walls. He stared at the canvas ceiling for a long time, trying to place the sound, but nothing came to mind. He glanced at the calendar on the wall near the fireplace. Friday. For some reason that was supposed to mean something to him.

He sat up, shivering in the chilliness of the morning. He forced his eyes to open wide, then shook his head to clear it of the last vestiges of sleep.

Davis got up and walked to the window. It was fogged over, and he rubbed the pane with the flat of his hand. He could feel the cold glass, hear it squeak under his palm, and finally he could see. And it all came home to him. There must have been five hundred Apaches out there.

It was ration day. In the old days, under General Crook, on demand, the reservation Apaches were required to report in to the agency building, show their medals, each stamped with a number that applied to one and only one adult male Apache. For purposes of realism, boys old enough to carry weapons in combat were given numbers, and medals, but women and children were exempted. But that system had been allowed to fall into disuse. Instead of a roll call, it was just ration day.

And ration day meant the families of the braves crowding around the main agency building were not far away. Davis dressed hurriedly and walked outside, still hitching his suspender straps over his shoulders. Despite the chill he opted for a heavy shirt instead of a coat. One advantage of being on detached service was that he needn't wear his uniform. It had reached the point where he was more comfortable out of it than in it, something that did not bode well for his return to regular service, the only realistic future for a man who wanted to build a service career.

The Apaches clustered around the two-story log headquarters building, small groups of the Indians talking among themselves and keeping one eye on the front door of the agency.

Davis glanced at his watch, then at the sky. It was gray and overcast, which made it seem earlier than it actually was. He noticed the Apaches watching him as he moved toward the front door. Sutcliff should already be there. It was customary for a rough count to be taken at dawn, and ad hoc numbers assigned, so the people could go on about their business. But Sutcliff was new, and maybe no one bothered to tell him about the custom. It was a cinch Tiffany hadn't told him anything that would make his job easier.

Rapping on the door, Davis turned his back to it and scrutinized the Indians, man by man, face by impassive face. Most of them knew little or no English, which meant their conversation would be in their own tongue or Spanish. Davis had some Spanish, but was just now working on his Apache. Mickey Free was working with him, but Mickey had only imperfect English and a kind of pidgin Spanish to complement his Apache. It made for less than perfect understanding in the best of circumstances. Davis wondered how, under pressure, communication was even possible.

The door rattled behind him, and he turned to see a tall, gangling man with a dreary mustache hitching his trousers and snapping his broad brown suspenders. The man's face looked as if he had borrowed the eyes of a much smaller man, and the whole face seemed to pinch in around the tiny eyes. His hatchet-like nose was pink, and not from the cold, Davis guessed.

"What the hell you want?" Sutcliff asked.

"You Stewart Sutcliff?"

"Who wants to know?"

"Are you Sutcliff or not?"

"What if I am?"

"If you aren't you should be, and if you are, you're late. Don't you know that—"

"Hold on, bub. What gives you the right to be talking to me like that?"

"I'm Lieutenant Davis. I'm in charge of the police on this reservation."

"What are you messing around with me for? I got work to do."

"Why do you keep these people waiting? You're supposed to see to it that they get their rations on time."

"People did you say? They're Apaches. They ain't people. And I don't take my orders from you. I take my orders from Mr. Tiffany, and he gets his from Washington. You got a complaint, put it in writing. Now get out of my way and let me do my job."

Davis waited until Sutcliff went inside, then followed him in. He stood near the counter, his eyes boring into the back of Sutcliff's head, but the assistant agent didn't seem to notice. He set up a scale on one end of the counter, then put a stack of paper sacks next to it. Davis leaned over to peer behind the counter.

The scrutiny was getting to Sutcliff and he finally whirled around. "Look, Lieutenant, why don't you tell me what you want? Maybe I can save us both some trouble, all right?"

"I don't want anything in particular. I just want to watch you awhile, see how it's done."

Sutcliff shrugged. "You got nothing better to do then watch a man weigh flour and beans, be my guest. Just don't get in the way."

Davis nodded. When it was apparent that he meant to say nothing else, Sutcliff went to the front door and opened it again. Davis could hear the shuffling feet as the first Apaches stepped onto the wooden walk in front of the agency building. The doorway grew dark as the first of the men filed inside.

Davis watched quietly as Sutcliff checked the paper in the first man's hand, then turned to a handwritten list on a clipboard. He put a check next to the Indian's name, then moved to the scale. "Ulzana," he said. "Three, right?"

The Apache wrinkled his brow a moment, until Sutcliff held up three fingers, then he nodded.

"Two pounds of flour, two pounds of corn, three pounds of beans." Sutcliff was talking louder than normal, as if volume could bridge the language gap between him and the Apache.

Davis watched while Sutcliff dug a metal scoop into an open sack of corn. The rattle of the grains on the metal tray of the scale sounded like hailstones on a tin roof. Davis looked a little more closely as Sutcliff dipped back into the sack, brought out another scoop, and poured it into the tray. The needle on the scale's dial wavered, then settled down just under the black "2." Sutcliff brought a partial scoop out, let a few kernels of the dried corn trickle onto the tray. When the needle was dead center on the "2," he shoved the scoop into the sack.

Opening a bag, Sutcliff poured the corn inside, rolled the top, then repeated the process with pinto beans. For flour, he did the same, this time setting an open bag in the tray and pouring the flour directly into it. Davis saw black flecks in the grayish-white flour, but didn't say anything.

One by one, the Apache men filed in. Sutcliff worked hard, checking each numbered paper, referring to his list for the allotments, and parceling out the supplies. But Davis was uneasy. It looked as if the amounts were too small. The scale didn't lie. Or did it?

Not wanting to make a scene in front of the Apaches, he watched awhile longer, then drifted out. Four scouts were already running the makeshift count, checking each Apache brave against the master list. The roll was supposed to be called weekly, although it required most of the Indians to travel miles from their *rancherías* into the agency and often took half a day or better. It disrupted their work, what little they had, and did little to engender trust, without which, Davis knew, the simmering resentments would continue to bubble just under the superficial tranquillity. That suited some folks, including one J. C. Tiffany, just fine. But the system was a sham and a shambles.

Nobody knew for sure how many Indians were on the reservation, but Davis knew the number changed almost daily. Since the big breakout in January, Apaches had been coming and going. Some, tired of the constant pressure of the warpath, drifted back to the reservation to recoup. Others, fed up with the constant humiliation and the cheating that Davis was anatomizing in a report, drifted away to join Geronimo, Juh, Chatto, and Loco down in the Sierra Madre Mountains.

He would have to change things, provided General Crook would agree, and there was little doubt of that. The last time Crook had been assigned to Arizona Territory, the general's attitude, which was sane and civilized, had led to continuing conflict between the whites in the territory and the army on one side, and the army and the Indian Bureau on another. But it had been peaceful. With Willcox gone and Crook coming back, though it seemed to be taking forever, Davis hoped some peaceful settlement would be possible, one that would last. But he wouldn't bet on it. Crook had too many enemies, men who made a good, fat living out of the conflict. They would not be happy to see peace descend on the territory.

Davis watched the pointless roll call, noting the wooden faces and the stiff backs of the men as they shuffled forward to show their rumpled papers. From there it was on to another line to come under the unfriendly stare of Stewart Sutcliff, who made his living handing out food to people he despised. It was no way to live, and it was a wonder things ran as smoothly as they did. Some of the cynics said it was because all the troublemakers were in Mexico, but Davis was a gnat's eyelash away from concluding that the majority of troublemakers were on Washington's payroll. And the chief troublemaker seemed to be Tiffany himself. All Davis needed was another couple of nails for the coffin. And he'd already decided he'd like to build the box himself.

Back at his quarters, Davis finished dressing and saddled a pony. He wanted to get out away from the agency, see what things were like in the *rancherías*. It wouldn't hurt, either, to talk to a few of the Apaches. Their point of view was given short shrift, and it might help ease the tension if they thought someone was finally paying attention to them.

He headed toward Turkey Creek, where several of the more infamous of the Apaches had settled. The Chiricahuas had been the last to come in. The White Mountain and Warm Springs bands had had more time to settle in, or to be beaten down, depending on which point of view best suited your perspective on the matter.

Rumors about breakouts were constant, but things had been quiet for three months, since Loco and his people had been forcibly conscripted by Geronimo and Juh. Maybe the new rumors were just that. But most white men lived with one ear on the door and slept with one eye open. There was reason for it, but there was reason on the other side, too, it seemed.

The rocky terrain reminded him all too clearly of scouts into the mountains when the Apaches were out. It sometimes seemed as if he'd climbed every damn mountain from Mexico City to Colorado chasing after the same people whose rations he now worried over. They were mountain people, the Apaches. They knew them inside and out, every wash and canyon, every hill and every spring.

There were times when five thousand men on horseback had been chasing fifty men on foot, or on horseback when the Apaches could manage to steal some. There was nothing like them on the continent. They could travel for days without sleep, covering a hundred miles a day and more. They would ride horses into the ground, then get off and run.

And they had done it for a reason. This was their land. Or it had been. And they had been told over and over by an endless parade of beards and spectacles from Washington that it would always be their land. All they had to do was toe the line, stop stealing horses, and stop killing the white man.

But somehow it always ended up badly. The last man often knew little of what the man before him had said, and cared even less. If coal was discovered, move the Apaches. Did somebody want the land for development? Very well, move the Apaches. Discover copper, and you move them again. Then shoot them when they couldn't take it anymore and went back to the old way of life.

Davis knew he was in danger of romanticizing a people who were as brutal as the land they once roamed at will. But whose fault was that? They had been driven into the mountains by warlike tribes to the north and the east. They became ruthless because they had no choice. Their children were stolen and made into slaves by the Mexicans. Their women and old men were murdered by Americans who had no use for anything with a red skin. Being peaceful, it seemed, was a one-way street. Chivington had proved that at Sand Creek, and Custer had reaped the whirlwind.

Davis knew his ideas were viewed with more than a little jaundice by some of his fellow officers. Orlando Willcox had been anything but pacific when it came to Apaches, and had never been able to find it within himself to admit there just might be a little tilt to the scales, one that did not work in the Apaches' favor. But Davis was used to sticking to his guns, and came by it naturally. His father had opposed the secession of Texas in '61, and gone to live in Mexico. It was comforting that he had had more than a few Unionist friends come join him.

There were no grand confrontations out here. The terrain wouldn't permit it, and the Apaches were too few in any case. Unlike the tribes of the plains, the Apaches were more democratic. They had chiefs, great ones like Cochise and Mangas Coloradas and Victorio. But if you were an Apache warrior, you made up your own mind. If you wanted to fight, you fought. If you wanted to go home, or go hunting, that's what you did.

And the white man didn't seem to understand. Until George Crook came along. Davis looked up to his soon-to-be commander the way Isaac looked up to Abraham. Crook was a wise man, and a brave one. And unlike most military men who had made reputations as Indian fighters, he tried to understand his foe and had come to respect him. That put him in a distinct minority. But Davis understood, too, that some of the other commanders, Howard and Sheridan, and even Sherman himself, knew the fault was not all on one side. But they were professionals, they had a job to do, and they tried to do it efficiently.

It all rolled around in his head like so many rough stones slowly being polished in a tumbler. And when the first *ranchería* came into sight, he stopped for a moment to look at it. The wickiups seemed so feeble in the pale late-winter light. It was hard to understand a man being attached to so fragile a way of life.

But they were attached, and it was their life. He would see to it that it was respected. Or there would be hell to pay.

Chapter 6

July 1882—San Carlos

RUMORS FILTERED IN from every corner of the territory. Ranches were being attacked so often, and in so many distant places, General Carr had two men assigned full-time just to sort out the reports. The white citizens of the territory were given to seeing Apaches behind every rock. But despite the exaggerations, the newspaper hysteria, and the fervent hope on the part of those who continued to grow fat on army contracts, some of the carnage was real.

Geronimo was gone. Juh was gone. No one knew for sure how many warriors had gone with them. Since Crook's system of tagging and counting had been allowed to fall into disuse, an accurate tally was out of the question. Lieutenant Cruse was one of the two officers assigned to processing the deluge of horror stories, sorting the real from the imagined, and trying to get a fix on the location of the marauding bands.

One rumor that warranted exploration concerned a warrior named Na-ti-o-tish. Not a chief, and not a seasoned warrior either, he had been preaching fire and brimstone with the panache worthy of a Mather. The disaffection among the reservation Indians was

real enough, and Na-ti-o-tish seemed to have found
a way to tap into it. But Na-ti-o-tish kept on the move.
Keeping his own camp a secret, he would slip into
one or another of the *rancherías,* try to rouse a few
warriors to join him, then slip away before the army
could find him.

Cruse's scouts had more than a dozen sightings to
check out, and Cruse was worried that another
breakout would lead to a general uprising. Carr was
even more concerned. He had already requested reinforcements from General Willcox, and nearly a half-
dozen cavalry troops were on their way from New
Mexico and forts in the southern part of the territory.
But even with all the troops available, they were
spread thinly.

The tracks of the Southern Pacific had to be protected, and that meant stringing detachments all
across the southern part of the territory. These troops
could protect the railroad, and also be in a position
to intercept any renegades coming up from Mexico.
Or so the theory went.

But word kept coming in of a ranch torched and its
residents roasted over open fires near Palominas, a
freighter captured and its handlers mutilated beyond
recognition outside of Willcox. Horses were disappearing by the dozen as the raiders rode their own
mounts into the ground then stole new ones.

On the morning of July 13, the new chief of the Indian police, "Cibicu Charley" Colvig, stepped into
Cruse's office. The two men had been staying in close
touch as they tried to sift useful intelligence from the
flood of hysteria.

"Got word on Na-ti-o-tish, Tom," Colvig said.

"Reliable?"

Colvig shrugged. "Supposed to have a bunch of broncos with him over near Cedar Creek. Thought I'd check it out. Want to come along?"

"I'd like to, Charley, but I got more to do than I know how."

"Folks do like to carry on, don't they?" Colvig said, laughing that dry laugh of his that sounded more like a cough than anything else. "Seems like they actually *like* the notion of renegades slitting their gullets, like it gives them something to think about or I don't know what-all."

"They'd think twice if they'd seen those miners we buried down near Willcox, or that football game they played with Al Sterling's head," Cruse said.

"That's just what they like, Tom. A little spice."

"You be careful, Charley. I don't know how many bucks Na-ti-o-tish has, but the number gets bigger all the time. Even if you figure it's exaggerated, there's a bunch of 'em."

"I'm not lookin' to gun him, Tom. Just want to find out where he is. The rest will be up to you army boys. I figure I'll spend a day or two, see can we pin him down a little. I get in trouble, I'll send a courier. You think Carr'll come runnin'?"

"Hell, he'd crawl through a prairie fire on hands and knees to win one for a change."

Colvig laughed. "Shows what's wrong with him, that does. After you been here awhile, you cross your fingers and just hope not to lose."

"They didn't teach us that at the Point," Cruse said, laughing.

"That's the trouble with you soldier boys. You forget Arizona's different. Come on, walk me to my horse."

Cruse got up and circled his desk. He turned to look at the pile of papers on it, shook his head, and Colvig laughed. "If papers'd whip them redskins, the war'd already be over, Tommy."

Outside, it was already hot. The sky was that washed-out blue color it got whenever the sun threatened to boil it away to get at the bare bones of the earth more easily. Colvig's unit was already waiting by the corral. "Bringing eight of the best damn Apache police I got. If Na-ti-o-tish is out there, they'll find 'im."

"He's out there, all right, Charley. You just make sure you see him before he sees you."

"Could be worse, Tommy. Least I'm not looking for Geronimo or Juh, somebody who knows what he's doin'. Then I'd worry."

"I'll worry for you, then, Charley."

Colvig nodded to his men and swung up into the saddle. "You do that, Lieutenant. You just do that. And if you're a prayin' man, fold your hands one time for old Charley. The Good Lord don't know me from Adam, so I expect a word from somebody on speakin' terms with Him might be useful."

Colvig clucked to his mount and headed across the parade ground. He turned to look back once, waved a hand, then fixed his eyes on the shimmering sawtooth of the Pinal Mountains. He was heading out past Globe, hoping he didn't get any interference from the miners. They were a rowdy bunch and, if the truth be known, more disreputable than any Apache. They liked a good fight and thought nothing of bashing one another over the skull with pick handles and shovels. A little rotgut in their bellies, and they'd take out after a shadow, claiming it was an Apache.

Colvig didn't want to worry about a bunch of drunks, if he could help it. He headed up into the Pinals, knowing Apaches liked to follow the crests of mountains, unlike the whites, who preferred to follow creek beds and river bottoms, winding in and out among the peaks. The Apaches were outnumbered, and survival depended on seeing trouble before it saw them. Sticking a plug of tobacco into his mouth, he gnawed it until it was wet enough to shape, then tucked it into his cheek with the tip of his tongue.

The men with him had been handpicked. All Apaches, they had done a good job for him in the past, and Al Sterling had spoken highly of them when he had been police chief. Colvig crossed his fingers, hoping he didn't end up the same way as Sterling.

Only one of the policemen spoke English, and that broken, so Colvig kept Kan-ya at his right hand. Keeping single file, they threaded through a narrow canyon, then headed partway up to get on top of a small mesa. It would be a while before they had a chance of cutting the trail left by Na-ti-o-tish and his band, if the rumors were anywhere near accurate.

By noon they were on the mesa, the peaks of the Pinals jutting up all around them. Colvig dismounted and walked to the edge of the mesa, binoculars dangling from his left hand. Standing as close to the rim as he dared, he swept the valleys on all sides, looking for a puff of smoke, a cloud of dust, or better yet, the Apaches themselves. But there was nothing to be seen.

Kan-ya had his own field glasses, as did the others. It seemed no Apache could do without them, and fights had started over a pair of the army-issue glasses more times than Colvig could count.

"Over there," Kan-ya said, jabbing a finger to the north. "See?"

Colvig fixed his own binoculars on the distant point. He was looking toward Aztec Peak. To its right, he knew, Cherry Creek wound down out of the Sierra Anchas toward the Salt River. The trail to Navajo country was out there, and Colvig knew Carr and Willcox were concerned that Na-ti-o-tish might make a break to the Navajos, possibly trying to stir them up and get them to join the rebellion.

He swept the glasses closer in, following the open space from Aztec Peak back toward the mesa on which he stood. He saw then what Kan-ya had pointed out, a small band of mounted men. They were too far away for him to identify. "Who the hell is it?"

Kan-ya shook his head. "Apaches."

"Na-ti-o-tish?"

"Don't know."

"They're heading this way, whoever they are. But there ain't many. Maybe we should go take a look."

"Better to wait. See who it is."

"No time, Kan-ya. If it is Na-ti-o-tish, we got to know it now."

The scout shrugged. He was used to Colvig's breakneck decisions. There was never a wasted moment when they were on a scout. Colvig liked to move fast, get in tight, and do what he had to do. The Apaches moved so quickly, they could vanish into the barren mountains in the wink of an eye. With the thick pine forests blanketing the area to the west, the horsemen could disappear almost at will. If that happened, it would be as if they had never been seen at all.

Colvig was troubled by the direction. If it was Na-ti-o-tish, why was he heading toward San Carlos instead of away from it? The rumor was that he was leading his band to the Navajos. The way the horsemen were heading was taking them away, not toward the Painted Desert and the Navajo reservation beyond it.

The nine men mounted their horses and moved across the tabletop of the mesa toward the descending trail. It would take them nearly an hour to get down the six hundred feet. There was a risk in going down on the front edge. If the Apaches spotted them, they'd run like rabbits, but going the back way would take twice as long, giving the horsemen even more time to vanish.

The trail was a tricky one, and the men dismounted again at the head of it. They'd have to lead their horses, leaving plenty of room between, in case of an accident. Colvig had seen more than one man, horse and all, plummet hundreds of feet to his death from the precipitous trails in this rugged country. He had no desire to emulate them.

It was nearly two by the time he reached the base of the mesa. Colvig swung back into the saddle to watch the scouts, the last of whom was still only a third of the way down, picking their way over the narrow trail, switching back where the trail doubled on itself. An occasional loose rock skipped away from a probing hoof and arched out and down, landing with a clatter on the pile of broken rock at the bottom.

From the valley floor it was no longer possible to see the approaching horsemen. Kan-ya was on the ground, looking up, when he snapped his head around.

"What is it?" Colvig asked.

Kan-ya held a finger to his lips, and Colvig reached for his rifle.

He was climbing down from the saddle when the first rifle barked. One of the scouts low on the trail, second from the bottom, hit the ground as a puff of dust drifted from the rock wall just inches from where he'd been standing.

"They know we're here," Kan-ya said, tugging his mount toward the base of the wall.

Three more shots in quick succession shattered the quiet. Echoes slapped at the wall and bounced back. The topmost man fell, swinging awkwardly from the reins of his mount for a second. The tug spooked the horse, who reared up, lost its footing, and followed its rider over the edge. The scout let go of the reins, and his arms windmilled in an awkward swimming motion as he tried to control himself in midair.

The wounded man hit the trail fifty or sixty feet below where he'd been standing, bounced once, then swung around as he latched onto the trunk of a scrub oak canted away from the rock wall. He managed to right himself just long enough to regain control, then scrambled back toward the trail, his left arm hanging limply, a bright red stain widening on the beige cloth.

"We're in for it now," Colvig muttered as he sprinted toward the base of the mesa. Three men were still on the trail, and they left their horses to fend for themselves as they raced down the rocky ledge toward the bottom.

Several more rifle shots cracked and echoed, but Colvig could see no one. The firing stopped when the scouts reached the bottom. The wounded man, Garcia, ripped off his bloody sleeve and Colvig wrapped it around the wound, which appeared to be no more than a deep furrow plowed through the meat of the upper arm.

"They know where we are," Colvig said. "I reckon we might as well see can we find where they're at."

As if in answer, another volley of rifle fire exploded. Bullets whined off the rocks and sent a shower of stony fragments cascading down off the wall a few feet above them.

"Kan-ya, we got to get out where we can maneuver a little. We stay here, they'll cut us to pieces. Pass the word. I'm going first, over toward them trees. . . ." He pointed toward a stand of pines about two hundred yards away. The Apaches were in there somewhere, but it was better to hit them head-on than to wait around. As near as he could tell, there were no more than five or six. The longer they waited, the bigger the size of the enemy band. It was now or never. "When I break for it, everybody cover me. When I get to the trees, send them over one by one. Got it?"

Kan-ya nodded. He passed the word along the line. The Apaches were used to oral relay, and he had never known them to make a mistake. They seemed to remember things perfectly on one hearing.

Colvig waited until the last scout raised a hand to signal that he knew what to do, then ducked out from behind the rock and broke for the pine forest. He hadn't gone thirty yards when another volley clawed the ground all around him. Unharmed, he continued his zigzag as the scouts laid down covering fire from their Winchester repeaters.

Chapter 7 ===========

July 1882—Fort Apache

KAN-YA RACED across the parade ground, his horse worked to a lather, stumbling as it charged toward the administrative office. Lieutenant Cruse heard a commotion through the open door and ran out as Kan-ya skidded to a halt. Trying to climb out of the saddle, the policeman lost his balance and fell heavily.

"What happened?" Cruse shouted as he ran off the porch. Kan-ya lay there gasping. Cruse saw blood on the back of the scout's shirt and turned him over slowly. It was through and through, and the front of Kan-ya's shirt was soaked, most of it dried to a dirty reddish brown, but some fresh blood was seeping through the ugly crust.

Gasping for air, the scout started to explain, but lost consciousness. Troopers were sprinting across the ground from every direction. Two of them helped Cruse lift the wounded scout. He sent another for the surgeon, then helped lug Kan-ya to the infirmary.

The post surgeon, Captain Milton Armbrister, burst through the door just as Cruse pulled a blanket up over the unconscious man.

Cruse dismissed the troopers, then paced while

Armbrister went to work. Glancing over the surgeon's shoulder, he saw the ugly wound, bigger than a silver dollar, obviously one of exit. Armbrister kept mumbling to himself as he worked, first cutting away the bloody shirt then cleansing the wound.

"Look's bad. Lord, it looks bad."

"Is he gonna make it?" Cruse asked.

Armbrister shook his head. "I just don't know, Lieutenant. He's strong, but this is bad. It probably punctured a lung. He's lucky the bullet squeezed between ribs without breaking them. My guess is he was hit from long range, and the bullet was about out of steam when he got hit, so it skipped along the bone instead of breaking it."

"But will he make it?"

"That's up to the Good Lord, Lieutenant. He has to be watched . . . constantly. There might be infection, fever. I'll do what I can, but . . ." He shrugged then, turning to look at Cruse with a gloomy expression. The surgeon's drooping mustache and thick, shaggy eyebrows just added to the look of despair.

"I'll assign someone to stay with him."

Armbrister nodded. "I'll stay awhile, see if he stabilizes. The next twelve hours will make all the difference. If he gets through them, he's got a chance."

Cruse moved toward the door, stepped into the bright sunlight. Where the hell is Cibicu Charley? he wondered. What in hell happened? Kan-ya had been Colvig's interpreter. He was a good man, and a brave one. In the back of the lieutenant's mind was the thought that Kan-ya might have important intelligence about the whereabouts of Na-ti-o-tish. That made him valuable, but it was the human concern that was foremost in his mind. He knew the scout and

liked him. It was always hard to lose a man, but w̶
he was a good man, one you admired, it was almo⸺
unbearable.

In the meantime there was work to be done. Colonel Evans had to be told. Cruse hotfooted it back to the administration building. Evans wasn't there, but his orderly was, and he would know where to reach him. Cruse fought the urge to telegraph the other posts in the vicinity, but he knew nothing, and a vague report of a wounded Indian policeman would just feed the rumor mill. That was the last thing he wanted to happen, so he resolved to wait and see whether Kan-ya regained consciousness.

He directed the orderly, a young corporal, to send a trooper to sit with Armbrister and Kan-ya, and to see that the trooper came for him as soon as the scout came to. That done, he went to Colonel Evans's quarters to tell him what had happened so far as he knew, which wasn't much.

Evans was eating lunch and invited Cruse to join him, but the Lieutenant declined, saying he'd wait at the office.

"You let me know if you hear anything before I get there, Lieutenant."

Cruse said he would, saluted, and walked back to the office. He wished Al Sieber were there, because the old chief of scouts knew more about the Apaches than anyone he'd encountered. But Sieber was working for Colonel Forsyth now, and it would take a day or two to find him, assuming he wasn't out in the mountains somewhere. Sifting through the reports on his desk, he sorted them with half an eye. Something had gone very wrong, and he couldn't concentrate on anything but trying to guess how bad it was going to get before it got better.

The colonel showed up twenty minutes later, and by then Cruse was no longer even trying to work. Evans noticed his distraction. "Try not to worry about anything, Lieutenant. We can handle anything that comes along here."

"With Na-ti-o-tish, maybe. But suppose it's Geronimo, or Juh? What then?"

"Apaches are men, Tom. They die when you shoot them. Even Geronimo."

"But how many others will die before that happens?"

"If I have my way, none."

Cruse shook his head. "I don't think . . ."

A shadow darkened the doorway before he could finish the thought. It was McGuire, a new private in Evans's Troop F, and his thick brogue didn't obscure what he was saying. "The injun's awake, Lieutenant. Captain Armbrister sent me to get you."

Cruse was up and running. Already out the door before he realized he hadn't waited for Evans to decide whether to go himself, he shrugged off the indecision and sprinted across the parade ground to the infirmary.

Kan-ya was sitting up when Cruse burst in. He looked drawn and weak, his eyes drooping, but he tried to smile. "What happened?" Cruse asked.

"We saw some warriors. We were coming down off Macon's Mesa when others ambushed us."

"Colvig?"

"Dead. All the others, too. I crawled into some rocks, and they looked for me, but Ussen wasn't ready for me in the Happy Place yet."

"My God! How many?"

Kan-ya shrugged. "Many. Not sure how many."

"Na-ti-o-tish?"

Kan-ya, trying to spare his wounded lung, nodded. His voice was very weak, and he stopped frequently to cough. There was a hollow burbling in his chest with every hack. "They go to San Carlos to get bullets and horses."

"You sure?"

"Heard them when I was hiding."

"When did this happen?"

"Yesterday afternoon."

Cruse looked at his pocket watch. "They could be there already. I have to tell the colonel." He was already moving toward the door. To Armbrister he said, "Take good care of him, doctor."

Armbrister nodded. "That's my job. He's a strong man. I think he'll make it, if he listens to me and doesn't push himself."

To Kan-ya Cruse said, "You do what he tells you, you hear?"

The scout nodded, then sank back on his bunk. He nodded again, then closed his eyes. Cruse looked at Armbrister, who shook his head. He followed Cruse out onto the porch. "I don't know whether he'll make it or not. He's lost a lot of blood. He's still bleeding internally, I think, although not much. It's a toss-up."

"Do what you can for him."

Armbrister went back inside as Cruse started for Evans's office. The colonel was standing in the doorway when he got there.

"What did you learn?"

"Colvig's dead, so are all his men, except for Kan-ya. Na-ti-o-tish found him."

"Jesus!"

"That's not the worst of it. They're heading into San Carlos to steal horses and ammunition."

"We've got to telegraph San Carlos."

"If they haven't cut the line."

"Let's find out."

Evans led the way to the telegraph office. As both men knew, the Apaches had gotten very adept at sabotaging the telegraph lines. Originally, when they realized the talking wire allowed information to be passed from post to post at lightning speed, they had settled for just cutting the line. A cavalry patrol could usually find the break in a matter of hours and make repairs. More recently, they had taken to making a cut, then tying the ends together with rawhide, in the crook of a tree branch if possible, to hide the break. Minute scrutiny was then necessary, often taking days before a break could be found and repaired. Since the Apaches could cover seventy miles a day with regularity, and even more than that when the situation required, a day was often all they needed as a head start.

If they had gotten the lines down, they would be able to hit San Carlos and be on the move before any other post learned of the raid. They might already have made their raid, since Kan-ya said the attack on Colvig had taken place the previous day.

Evans stood over the telegraph operator dictating his message. The operator jotted it down, reduced it for transmission, then started tapping the key. "Make sure they respond immediately," Evans said. "Tell them to signal on receipt."

The operator nodded, finished his metallic clicking, then waited for a response. After five minutes of dead silence, in which each man could hear nothing but his own breathing and that of the other two, Evans barked, "Send it again!"

"Yes, sir. But I don't think it's getting through."

"Don't think. Send it!"

When the operator started to resend, Evans said, "Tom, you'll have to send a unit to San Carlos. Half a dozen men, at least. If the Apaches are breaking out, I don't want anybody out there alone."

"Yes, sir."

"God, I wish Crook were here."

"When's he due?"

"Not till September. In the meantime I guess it's time to put a column together. We can't wait. I think it's best to assume they'll head for Mexico, but maybe not. There were all those rumors about Navajo country. We'll have to guard against that, too."

Cruse looked at the telegraph key. It was deathly quiet.

Chapter 8

July 1882—Fort Apache

WORD OF CIBICU CHARLEY'S MURDER SPREAD across the reservation like kerosene creeping slowly toward an open flame. Na-ti-o-tish was no longer a joke. As near as anybody knew, he had seventy-five warriors with him. He might not have been the experienced tactician that Juh was, or the heart-stopping ogre Geronimo was believed to be, but the murder sent shock waves throughout the territory.

Colonel Evans was ready to move. Scouts had brought back word that Na-ti-o-tish was, indeed, headed north. He had swept past Globe, killing several miners on the way, and was back in the forest north of that mining town. The mountainous terrain was a great advantage for even the most ordinary Apache, and several of the warriors accompanying the renegade Tonto were seasoned veterans.

At the head of four troops of cavalry and Cruse's company of Apache scouts, Evans was heading toward the Salt River. His column was one of several, as troops all over the territory were on the move. Nothing much could be done about getting reinforcements from the south, or from New Mexico, because Juh, Geronimo, and the impressed band of Loco were still on the loose in the Dragoons or Mexico or the Chiricahaus, depending on which report you happened to read last.

Approaching the Salt River where it received the less impressive flow of Tonto Creek, one of Evans's scouts spotted a rider pushing toward them. It was a bluecoat, the scout said. Evans had called a halt the previous day, and his troops had established their bivouac. As they broke camp Evans waited for the lone cavalryman to make contact. Captain Adna Chaffee materialized out of the shimmering haze an hour later. Commanding Troop I of the Sixth Cavalry, a white-horse unit, Chaffee had been scouring the mountains accompanied by Al Sieber at the head of a detachment of Apache scouts.

Na-ti-o-tish was ahead of them, Chaffee reported. "Sieber thinks they're headed for Navajo country. Maybe a day's ride ahead."

"Has he spotted you?" Evans asked.

"Probably. But they didn't seem worried. A handful of cavalry doesn't seem like much of a threat to them, I'd imagine. If he realizes you're here, though, he'll likely bolt."

"Where are they camped?"

"Not far from Canyon Diablo."

"You go on back. Now that we know they're not far, we'll be careful coming up. We'll try to stay out of sight until we can join up."

"Very good, Colonel. My guess is he'll lay for us, try to trap us, maybe at the canyon, so we'll see if we can't hold him without engaging him until you get there. If he thinks we're going to walk into his ambush, he'll be patient."

Chaffee saluted, remounted, and kicked his white

stallion. They watched him disappear in the morning haze, then saw him again, climbing the trail up to a gigantic mesa two miles ahead. In the bright sun it wasn't hard to pick out the white horse against the dark rock.

Evans had another white-horse troop, under the command of Thomas Converse. He put Converse out front, hoping that Na-ti-o-tish would get sloppy. If he saw the second white-horse unit, he might not realize there was a much larger force after him.

It was the middle of the afternoon when Evans heard some scattered firing. Closing on the sound, trying to stay out of sight, he found Chaffee's unit exchanging fire with the Apache band across the yawning abyss that was Canyon Diablo. Seven hundred yards wide, the canyon was a jagged slash in the earth a thousand feet deep. Far below, a branch of Chevelon Creek wound through the middle. Small pines lined both sides of the fork, and the sparkling sand of the canyon floor made it look almost idyllic. But the canyon itself was another matter. Thousand-foot walls dropped straight down, in some places even overhanging the canyon floor. Only a few trails led down the walls, and the Apaches were in position to cover the trail dead ahead, as well as the canyon floor and the trail ascending the opposite wall.

Evans knew that if he sent his men down the trail, they would be under Apache guns every inch of the way. They would be forced to move slowly down the treacherous and narrow ledges, where even a sudden dodging of a bullet might send a man plummeting to his death.

Chaffee came back to confer, and Evans, after listening to the captain's summary of the Apache de-

ployment, gave him command of the engagement and
sent Converse ahead to join up with Chaffee's men.
Ira Morgan, commanding D Troop of the Third Cavalry, was sent to the left with instructions to look for
another way down into the canyon. A third descent
lay a mile or so to the right, and Lieutenant Cruse and
his Apache scouts were sent that way.

As they drew up their plans the Apaches on the far
side spotted Michael Conn, a sergeant they remembered from the reservation. They called him "Coche
Sergeant," because he had been in charge of livestock at San Carlos. They started to yell, almost teas-
ingly. "Coche Sergeant, nyah, nyah. Come and get us,
Hog Sergeant." Conn started to swear back at them,
his thick Irish brogue making him sound almost as un-
intelligible as his antagonists. He rose up when a bullet narrowly missed him, and shook a fist. As he
started to drop down, another slug pierced his throat.
No one could get to him, but the bloody mess under
his chin convinced the troopers Conn was a goner.

Evans hoped that both units would be able to cross
and flank the Apaches. It was a risk, but one that
should work if Chaffee and Converse were able to pin
the Apaches down while the other units negotiated
the hazardous canyon crossing.

Firing across the chasm was steady as the units
began to move out. Cruse and his men found their
trail and started down. They could hear the constant
volleying as they worked their way down a few yards
at a time. They had to go on foot, since horses could
never make the descent.

It took nearly two hours to reach the bottom of the
canyon. To Cruse it looked like a separate world, almost like paradise. The brilliant sand, the burbling

of the Chevelon Fork, its cold, clear water meandering among the stunted trees, gave the canyon a kind of beauty unlike any he had ever seen.

Only the distant echoing of gunfire disrupted the serenity. In the shadows of the canyon wall Cruse looked up, and was amazed when he realized he could see the stars. So deep it kept even the sunlight at bay, the canyon made the sky seem dark as night. Cruse had to pat his pocket watch through his pocket to remind himself it was just after noon.

The ascent was no less treacherous. Cruse found himself wondering whether they would make it. He was near the head of the string of men dwarfed into insignificance by the imposing walls. Glancing back over his shoulder, he could barely pick out the men at the end of the line. They were like so many ants climbing a tree to the top of the world.

The Apache scouts moved easily up the sheer face, but it was harder on Cruse, who had still not gotten used to how perfectly adapted the Apaches were to the worst excesses of the terrain.

The gash in the earth split a huge flat-topped mesa in two. Cruse knew there would be good cover on top, if only he and his scouts could manage to gain the top of the trail. He was keeping one ear peeled for gunfire from Morgan's men. Too far away to see them, he would have to hope that they were having the same luck he had so far encountered.

The top of the mesa was covered with a pine forest. He knew there was little in the way of undergrowth, and the trees would offer the only cover once they managed to reach the plateau. As he climbed, the sound of the firing grew louder. It was difficult to tell whether it was coming toward him or not.

The point man was just fifty yards below the rim-rock now. Cruse could feel the anticipation of his men. They were so close. All they needed was for their luck to hold just a little longer. He saw the lead man emerge into brilliant sunlight, which slashed across the canyon wall.

Picking up speed, he had to keep telling himself not to get careless. Another scout appeared, then a third. That meant one more man ahead of him. He watched as one by one they climbed up and over the edge of the canyon and disappeared. His mouth was dry, and his breathing scraping away at the inside of his throat.

Cruse didn't want to look down, but couldn't help himself. Glancing back over his shoulder, he could make out a couple of the men behind him, but the rest of his unit was still lost in the towering shadows. His head began to spin. He was so high, he couldn't see the ground, and didn't dare try to look for it for fear he would lose his balance and fall off the wall.

The rim was within his grasp now and he scrambled over the stony ledge, threw both hands up to steady himself, and climbed the last couple of feet. The lead scouts were waiting for him. He sent one ahead to check out the forest between the trail and the location of Na-ti-o-tish and his warriors.

The distant firing continued as more of his scouts attained the rim and formed a broad semicircle facing toward the sound of the fighting. As the last three or four men climbed onto the top of the mesa, Cruse walked to the edge and looked down. He could just make out the stream a thousand feet below, its rippling water picking up glints of reflected sunlight.

The advance scout was heading back at a run. Too

well drilled by their own culture to make any noise, the remaining scouts watched quietly. Cruse saw the coiled steel in their backs and shoulders tighten another turn. Something was up, and they knew it. He moved through the scouts. The man he'd sent ahead, an Apache by the name of Roderigo, headed straight toward him. Despite his long sprint, Roderigo was breathing normally as he relayed his information.

"Horses, maybe a hundred. And Apaches coming."

Cruse snapped out of the hypnotic reverie induced by the long climb. "Where?"

Roderigo pointed back toward the sound of the gunfire. Without having to be told, the scouts were already melting into the forest, taking up positions behind the stouter trees. Thirty seconds later, the first Apache warrior drifted out of the trees, his moccasins silent on the thick carpet of pine needles.

Right behind him, without a trace of their customary wariness, a dozen more in scattered file took shape. They must have been trying the same thing we are, Cruse thought. Never dreaming their pursuers had managed to get across the canyon, they were moving carelessly, as if on a Sunday stroll.

Cruse waited until they were close. Before he could give the word to fire, he heard the sudden sharp eruption of rifle fire far ahead. He realized Morgan and his men must have made it across the canyon, too. A second later, he gave the command to fire, and the ambush took all but one of the warriors in the first volley. The remaining warrior scrambled back into the trees, but Roderigo brought him down with a single shot from his breech-loading Springfield.

Cruse and Roderigo led the way to the Apache herd and cut the horses loose, dispatching a handful of men to move them farther away. Cruse and the rest of his men sprinted through the trees. The gunfire was getting more intense now as Chaffee and his men continued to fire across Canyon Diablo. Morgan was pressing forward from his vantage point. Conscious of the danger of getting cut down by Morgan's bullets, Cruse circled his unit to the right, planning to come in on Na-ti-o-tish from the rear.

The gunfire was spreading out now. In the parklike forest, the echoes of the rifles seemed to come from everywhere at once. Cruse and his men moved slowly, trying to avoid tipping off the hostiles to their presence until they were in a position to bring heavy fire to bear. He knew it was a slim hope, because Na-ti-o-tish would almost certainly have heard the brief but furious volley that brought down the flanking party. But if the hostiles spotted them too soon, they would be almost useless to Morgan and Chaffee.

Moving from tree to tree, leapfrogging through the shadows, the Apache scouts moved closer and closer. Cruse stayed right up front, always within one or two men of the lead. It was one of the things the scouts respected about him. He remembered a conversation with Geronimo, who scorned the American and Mexican military leaders' habit of directing their troops from the rear. "An Apache leads his men into battle," Geronimo had said, "he does not send them. Your White Eyes officers are afraid of bullets, they are afraid of pain. They think their lives are too precious to lose. It is only the soldiers who die when the White Eyes fight."

Cruse was in sympathy more than he had realized. The truth of the supposed savage's words had haunted him that night, and he had lost a good deal of sleep since, thinking about it. It made him a little reckless, he knew, but it seemed only fair that a man willing to lead others to their deaths take the same chances he asked his men to take.

Now, dodging through a pristine pine forest, a place more appropriate to a family outing than a bloodletting, he found it ironic that he was more concerned about his enemy's opinion than he was about his own life. Part of him wished the Apache war chief were there to see him, to see how unlike most White Eyes officers he was.

The gunfire continued to widen, as if the hostiles were beginning to fall back away from the canyon rim. So far he hadn't had a glimpse of them, and he couldn't tell whether Morgan's assault was having any effect. He knew that the canyon was wide enough that the exchanges of gunfire across the abyss were nearly at the limits of a rifle's effective range. The Apaches had had time to dig in, and they could stand off an army for days or weeks unless an effective attack were mounted from this side of the Big Dry Wash.

Drawing even closer, he was near enough now to hear the occasional whine of a stray bullet as it sailed among the trees off to his left, its flight parallel to the canyon. That could only mean Morgan was pressing his advantage, and that Cruse and his scouts were getting close to the hostiles' position.

He looked for Roderigo, spotted him up ahead, and darted across an open space to skid in behind the scout. A bullet ripped a chunk of pine bark off Roderigo's tree, and Cruse ducked instinctively.

"They see us now," the scout said, without turning around.

Cruse could smell the burned powder hanging in the air. A thin pall of gauzy smoke hovered among the trees above his head, like a cloud trapped under the crowns of the enormous pines.

"How many?" Cruse asked.

Roderigo shook his head.

"All right, then, we'll have to be more cautious. I'm going to try to get closer to see if I can get a fix on their positions."

He scanned the forest ahead of him. There had not been a second shot, and still he had not seen a trace of the hostile warriors. Snatching at the binoculars draped around his neck, he trained them on the forest ahead. Resolving one thick, rough trunk after another through the glasses, he scanned up and down, then panned across. Adjusting the focus to peer more deeply into the woods, he still did not manage to find the least sign.

Roderigo, aware of the difficulty, stabbed a finger off toward the left. "There," he said, "behind that rock."

Cruse homed in with the glasses, braced them against the tree trunk, and fine-tuned the focus. He could see the rock clearly, a humpbacked gray mass like the shell of an enormous turtle burrowing through the carpet of pine needles. Still seeing nothing, he shook his head. Roderigo sensed his failure. "Wait," he said. Raising his rifle, the scout fired at the rock, sending a shower of granite chips sparking in every direction. Almost immediately, Cruse saw a red headband materialize. He was staring right into the warrior's eyes, saw the rifle come up, then ducked away as he saw the Apache aim. Bark flew off the big pine, slivers stinging Cruse on the right cheek.

"Did you see?" Roderigo asked.

Cruse didn't bother to answer. The Apaches loved to tease their officers, particularly about their superiority in eyesight and tracking ability. About the only area where the scouts would concede white superiority was marksmanship, and at least some of the difference there was attributed to the inferior quality of Apache weapons.

Plunging onward, Cruse could see a few of the hostiles now. Some were still prostrate behind rocks, firing across the canyon, but many had begun to fall back under Morgan's pressure. As the pincers closed, most of the hostiles squirted out from between the jaws, falling back into the forest away from the canyon.

Al Sieber was with Morgan, and he made a dash across the open space, firing as he went, then dived to the ground beside Cruse, who was crouched behind a broad, flat rock.

"I think we got them on the run now," Sieber said. His voice sounded almost gleeful, more like a child at play than a man exchanging rifle fire with hostile Indians. Sieber got up on one knee, facing the canyon. He shouldered his rifle. "There he goes," he grunted. Cruse looked but saw nothing until Sieber squeezed the trigger. The crack of the rifle sounded, and a split second later an Apache, caught by Sieber's bullet while in the act of getting to his knees, pitched forward onto his face.

"I didn't even see him," Cruse said, marveling.

"He saw you, Tommy." Sieber laughed.

Cruse started to answer, but Sieber shushed him, squeezed off another shot, and a second hostile curved in the air, his body bowed like that of a landed trout. For a moment the warrior seemed to hang in the air, motionless, silent as a puff of gunsmoke, then he dropped, his arms spread out like a diver's, and he was gone. The man never uttered a sound. Cruse could see him for several moments over the curving lip of the canyon, then the falling buck disappeared behind the stone. Straining his ears, Cruse waited to hear one last desperate yell, but the warrior, obviously still alive, did not give him the satisfaction. The young lieutenant could only imagine the wreckage of a human body after the thousand-foot plunge. He suppressed a shudder as Sieber bagged a third warrior the same way.

The rimrock had been swept clean now. Back away from the canyon rim, small knots of hostile warriors were exchanging shots with Cruse's scouts. The lieutenant started to move away from the rock, bent over in a crouch. "Where the hell you going, Tommy?" Sieber demanded.

"I want to get to that little ravine up there."

Sieber shook his head. "Don't do it. There's Apaches all over there. You'll get your ass shot."

Cruse ignored the advice. Grabbing two of his scouts and a couple of Morgan's men, he charged toward the ravine. Sieber watched as a hostile reared up as if out of the ground, his rifle swinging toward the charging lieutenant, no more than three or four yards away from Cruse. Cruse saw the warrior at the same instant. He started to bring his sidearm to bear and twisted his body. The Apache was young, not more than a kid really, and he looked more nervous than fierce. Cruse heard the Apache's gun go off at the same moment he squeezed his own trigger.

The Indian's shot went wide, but Cruse heard a

grunt just to his left and a little behind. He hit the deck and saw the Apache fall then, almost forgetting that he had expected his own death. He twisted to see one of his men lying on the ground behind him, a bloodstain spreading across his shirt. Cruse grabbed the wounded man and hauled him bodily toward the only cover within reach, the shallow ravine. Dropping the wounded man over the edge, he jumped in himself. The small water-carved arroyo was little more than six or seven feet deep, and Cruse managed to crawl up the far side. Banging away as fast as he could fire and reload, he watched as the Apaches continued to fall back, leaving more and more dead and wounded sprawled across the thick carpet of rust-colored needles.

Troopers under Morgan were racing through the trees now, and Cruse's scouts pushed in from the right. The hostiles had expended most of their ammunition. As they tried to fall back through the forest more and more of the warriors turned to run, but the merciless firing from their pursuers chewed them to pieces.

It was beginning to get dark. Cruse glanced at the sky, estimated there was only a little over two hours' daylight left. He dragooned a group of scouts and organized a search for the wounded. Getting them down the canyon wall would be nearly impossible in broad daylight. If the sun set, they would have to wait over night.

The firing dwindled away, shots less and less frequently breaking the stillness of the forest. The pall of gunsmoke was still there, but it had begun to thin under a gentle breeze. Bending over a wounded private, he exchanged a few words with the thin-faced

man, reached down to wipe a trickle of blood away
from the corner of the trooper's mouth. The kid closed
his eyes, his chest rising and falling sporadically.
Breath whistling through his nostrils inflated a pink-
ish bubble the size of a grape. Cruse watched it,
tempted to reach down to break the bubble, but it
swirled in the fading sunlight then vanished with a
barely audible pop.

Cruse got to his feet as Al Sieber ambled out of the
trees. The chief of scouts waved a hand. When he got
closer, Sieber smiled. "When you went down, I
thought it was all up with you, Tommy."

"Too tough to kill, Al."

Sieber shook his head. Waving a hand toward the
forest behind him, he said, "Ain't nobody too tough
to kill, Tommy."

"Na-ti-o-tish?"

Sieber shrugged. "It's over, Mr. Cruse. It's all over."

"Anybody else with him, significant, I mean? Juh?
Geronimo?"

"No such luck."

Chapter 9

September 1882—Fort Apache

THE TALL, severe-looking man with a swatch of biblical whiskers draped over his muscular chest climbed out of the saddle. Dressed in duck with a severe cut, his graying hair covered by an Oriental helmet, he looked like nothing so much as a sight-seeing Londoner come to see the savages in their home ground.

But there was nothing effete under that hat. And there was nothing soft about the man who wore it. George Crook, a brigadier general, was back in Arizona for the first time in seven years. Standing there in the open square, he took in the Spartan buildings, like giant shoe boxes laid end to end and fitted with rows of gleaming windows. Beyond to the east, the peaks of the White Mountains glowed bloodred in the light of a rising sun. Far to the north the ragged edge of the Mogollon Rim staggered toward California like a file of drunken sailors.

"Seven years," he whispered. "Seven long years."

"You say something, General?"

Turning to the shorter man behind and to his left, still in the saddle, he shook his head. "No, John. Nothing."

The shorter man, his dark hair brushed back off his

ears under a slouch hat, swung down from his horse.
Captain John Bourke, too, had been here before.

"Nothing's changed, it looks like."

Crook tilted his head back, almost as if he were
watching the massive cumulus rolling and tumbling
high overhead. "I hope you're wrong, Captain."

Bourke smiled. "Me too."

Neither man was in uniform, which probably ac-
counted for the lack of attention paid to their arrival.
That was all right. Crook wanted to get a look at
things without the spit and polish that he knew was
used, more often than not, to conceal flaws in a
ragged surface.

"Almost looks like they aren't expecting you, General."

"Oh, they're expecting me, John. You can bet on
that. They're expecting me. They may not be happy
about it, but they'll keep that to themselves. For a little while, at least."

"You glad to be back?"

"You know better than that, John. When I left, I had
hoped there'd be no need ever again for someone like
me to be here." He shook his head, then heaved a
sigh.

"What do you want to do first?"

"I may as well tell Colonel Hacker I'm here. Then
we'll see. . . ."

They walked toward the huge building that domi-
nated Fort Apache, its two stories making it the one
and only such building in the facility. It had just been
built when he was here last. It looked as if it had
borne the intervening years well, but then Fort
Apache had not seen much conflict. There were no
walls of mud or stone, no palisades of spiked logs.

They weren't necessary. The Apaches didn't fight that way, and although there had been isolated shooting at the post, there had never been a full-scale assault on it.

Crook walked across the parade ground, conscious of the tug of reins in his left hand, conscious, too, of the crunch of his boots on the dry earth and the rising heat that would reach well over ninety by noon. Even at that, there was something to be thankful for. San Carlos, not that far to the south, would probably reach one hundred and ten degrees. Here, a little higher in the mountains, it would be bearable, compared with the barren wasteland the army men had dubbed Hell's Forty Acres.

A drowsy sentry outside the office of the commanding officer watched them approach, but made no sign of recognition. For a moment Crook was taken off balance, but realized he had ignored the seven years. With the annual desertion rate hovering around thirty percent, it was highly unlikely the man on the door would have been in service during his last tour.

As Crook stepped onto the porch the private straightened. "Can I help you, gentlemen?"

"Colonel Hacker?"

"He's still sleeping. Should be in his office at seven-thirty. You can wait inside, I guess."

"I'd like to speak to the colonel now, if I might."

The private scratched his chin. "I don't think so. Colonel won't be too happy I wake him at five-thirty in the morning."

"I'll take the responsibility, Private."

"Right. And tomorrow you're gone and the colo-

nel's still steamed. Looks like a bad bargain to me.
With all due respect."

Crook smiled. "Private, I won't be gone tomorrow,
I can assure you that."

The private looked skeptical. "Who might you be?"

"George Crook."

The sentry swallowed hard. *"General* Crook?"

Crook nodded. "And this is Captain Bourke."

The private snapped a salute, hard enough to leave
a red welt on his forehead. "Yes, sir. I'll get the colonel, sir."

"Good. May we wait inside?"

"Yes, sir. Of course." He leaned over to open the
door, then snapped back to rigidity.

"At ease, Private." Crook stepped past him and
into the dark room. As his eyes adjusted he saw
enough to know it was an office, and he noticed a
lamp on the desk. Fishing a match from his pocket,
he flicked it with a thumb as he lifted the chimney
with his free hand. The wick sputtered, then caught.
Clots of oily soot hovered on the rising air as he lowered the chimney into place. Rather than taking a seat
at the desk, he found a rickety chair across from it,
lowered himself into it, and pointed to a second chair,
not quite as decrepit as his own. "You might as well
have a seat, John."

Bourke nodded. "Do you know Colonel Hacker?"
he asked, pulling his chair closer to the desk.

Crook shook his head. "No. Never met him. I know
his reputation, but that's all. A good soldier."

"How does a good soldier make a mess like this?"

"It takes some doing, I'll grant you that. But you
know as well as I do that the War Department has
its hands full dealing with the Indian Bureau. That's

where the trouble comes from. We spend all our time undoing what the agents have done. But I won't have it, this time. This time we'll have a free hand."

"I hope so."

"We will. I've spoken to Phil Sheridan, and I have his assurances. It was a condition of my accepting this assignment."

"It's a familiar tune, General. I know all the words by heart."

"I don't blame you for being dubious, John. But I mean to do this right or not at all."

Bourke started to answer, but the private reappeared in the doorway. "Colonel Hacker will be here in five minutes, General. He asked me to apologize for the delay."

Crook nodded absently. The private stood there for a moment, until Bourke signaled that he should return to his post. Crook was restless; Bourke had been with him long enough to know the signs. The general got to his feet and walked to the door. Once more he watched the Arizona sun begin its lazy climb. Already the day showed signs of being unusually hot for September.

There was a tension in the air, some vague thing, invisible, but nevertheless pressing on the skin like fluid, surrounding the body, making it impossible not to be aware of it. Bourke felt uneasy. There had been trouble for more than a year, and rumors of more to come. Even back east, the papers were full of stories about Apache unrest. And Prescott was humming with lurid tales of Apache depredations. Now here he was, back in the beating heart of Apache territory. There were no Indians like them, and he had seen and read of none, nor of any fighting force in the world their equal.

Crook had had success, but it had been all too fragile, as subsequent events had proven. Bourke watched his commander, wondering what he was thinking and aware that as well as he knew the general, he could not guess what was going through his mind at that moment.

Crook backed away from the doorway then, and Bourke knew that Hacker had arrived. The colonel stepped onto the porch, his profile half-visible beyond the door frame, saluted Crook, then reached out to shake his hand.

The two men came back into the room, and Crook gestured to the desk, indicating that Hacker should take a seat.

The general introduced his adjutant, then resumed his seat.

"Welcome back, General," Hacker said. "I wish the circumstances could be more favorable, but . . ." He spread his hands helplessly, shaking his head.

"What exactly are the circumstances, Colonel?"

"Not good, General. Not good at all. The reservations, both here and San Carlos, are powder kegs. We have depredations all over the territory almost weekly. A few hundred renegades in the Sierra Madres cross the border at will. They're getting aid and comfort from relatives on the reservations, and even have the temerity to visit, if they think they can get away with it."

"Tell me about this Cibicu business. Were you here then?"

"Yes, sir, I was. It was bad."

"What happened? I read General Carr's report to the War Department, but I'd like to have your view."

Hacker shrugged. "If you want my opinion . . ."

"I do."

Hacker took a deep breath. "It never should have happened. Tiffany, that was the agent, panicked. He's gone now, thank the Lord. From what I hear, he's liable to be indicted. There's a grand jury looking into his term. I'll have Lieutenant Davis fill you in on that later. In any case, he shouldn't have tried to have the medicine man arrested. There was no reason for it."

"Oh, and why not?"

"Because there was no evidence the Indians were doing anything hostile. Sure, there were a lot of them, and the scouts were getting restless, surly, maybe even unmanageable, in a way. But all the more reason to be careful."

"Unmanageable how? I've never had any trouble with them."

"They kept wanting to go to the dances—that's what they were, really, dances—day and night. There was a lot of paint and fuss, but it was just dancing, mostly."

"You didn't feel like an outbreak was imminent? I'd heard there had been some talk of that possibility."

"Not imminent, no. Possible, maybe, but only if we made a mistake. And we did. As it was, most of them came back within two weeks. They thought we were there to attack them."

"And how would you have handled it, Colonel?"

"Man to man, I think a talk with the medicine man. He was said to be making all kinds of wild statements, about the dead chiefs coming back, the white man leaving in the fall, that sort of thing. But it was getting all twisted around. Nobody bothered to talk to Noch-ay-del-Klinne—that was the medicine man—to find out what he was really saying. And I don't think it had to come to bloodshed."

"And now?"

Hacker spread his hands palms down on the desk. He seemed almost to be trying to keep it from levitating. He looked toward the open door, then nodded. "Now we have a lot of restless Apaches. We have had nothing but trouble from the agents. The Apaches know there's disagreement, and I think it frightens them. They don't know who's in charge. Hell, half the time I don't know either."

"I gather you don't think General Willcox did a very good job. . . ."

"Off the record?"

Crook nodded. "Off the record, Colonel."

Hacker gnawed his lower lip for a moment. "No, I don't think he did a very good job. I don't think he understood the Apaches, I don't think he cared to understand them, and I don't think he really gave a damn what happened here, as long as his reputation didn't suffer. Now we have some of the worst of the hostiles off the reservation. There's trouble just about every week, and—" He stopped, embarrassed by his own breathless narration.

"We'll remedy that, Colonel. Mark my words, we'll remedy that."

"What do you want to do?"

"The first thing I want to do is to get the Apache point of view. I'd like to talk to any man of consequence among them—chiefs, war leaders, whatever.

Can you see to that? Some of them may remember me. Perhaps it's a place to begin."

"Yes, sir. When do you want to meet with them?"

"The sooner the better, Colonel."

Chapter 10 ===

September 1882—Dragoon Mountains

THE MINING CAMP at Hay Mountain wasn't much to
look at. Fifteen men broke their backs seven days a
week, scraping copper ore from the barren ground.
Small, mule-drawn carts ferried the ore out of the
shaft, rumbling over the rails and out into a sunlight
so bright, the mules blinked and shook their heads,
trying to shake off the glare.

The camp consisted of a barrackslike bunkhouse,
a single room to house all the men but the foreman,
Clayton Moon. Moon was lucky enough to have a
separate bunk in the small shack that functioned as
his home and his office. A corral of gnarled mesquite
branches kept the mules and the horses confined, and
that was the extent of civilization.

High on an eastern slope of the Dragoon Mountains, the mine shaft shot straight through, its gentle
angle taking the men no more than seventy feet lower
than the mouth. The work was hard, and there was
nothing in the way of amusement except whiskey.
Moon was known as an understanding man, but he
owed his allegiance first and foremost to the Arizona
Mining Corporation. The men didn't like him much,
but they didn't hate him either. They seemed to un-

derstand that he had a job to do, just like they did. Because he could read and write, he had an edge. That's just the way it was.

Moon rose before them and went to sleep long after them, sitting up with his ledgers for an hour or so, then spending another hour reading for pleasure. He had a vision of the future that was grander than anything the miners cared to think about. If it were to come to pass, as Moon never tired of reassuring them it would, they knew it would be built, at best, on their broad backs, and at worst, over their broken bones.

Tombstone was thirty miles away, and Sundays were reserved not so much for the Lord, although Moon was a churchgoing man, but for the saloons and, if they were lucky, a woman. They rode in late on Saturdays, getting there just in time to wash away a week's dust with a couple of drinks. Sundays were spent carousing and were capped with the long, hung-over ride back to Hay Mountain.

This weekend was no different. Moon was the only sober man, so as usual he took the point for the long ride home. It was late afternoon when they reached the foothills. Moon had been nervous all day, and he couldn't put his finger on the reason. He knew an inspector from the company headquarters at Flagstaff was due the following day. Production was falling a little as the vein of ore had begun to resist the picks and shovels of the men.

Moon felt like a chaperon, as if he had to ride herd on a pack of wayward boys. It was always like that, and Moon was too much a creature of habit himself to expect that it would ever change. Half a dozen of the miners were singing in three different languages. As near as he could tell, no two of them were singing the same song. But most were quiet, letting their aching heads loll on their shoulders in time to the rhythmic pounding of their horses' hooves.

The last leg of the trip took them through a four-mile canyon, steep walls rising several hundred feet on either side. In the late-afternoon sun the rock took on colors, belying the unrelieved beige of midday with smears of red and purple. The floor of the canyon was sandy, cactus of a dozen kinds studding the soil so evenly spaced they gave the appearance of having been planted by a gardener. Moon knew better. He knew the ground couldn't support any more than it had. A shallow creek twisted its way through the canyon, a few stunted cottonwoods marking its course.

Flashes of the reddish sun sparkled through the small trees, glinting off the rippling water. The voices of the men sounded better as they entered the canyon and echoed off the towering stone walls, creating a wash of unintentional harmony.

Moon always watched the rimrock on these trips, because if there was going to be trouble, it would come from the canyon rim. It had been two years since the last trouble with Apaches, and that would have made a less prudent man careless, but Clayton Moon had lived through repeated raids on a mine up north in the Superstitions, and it was an experience he hoped never to repeat.

There was no reason to suspect trouble now, not with most of the Apaches on the reservation and the army presence outnumbering the Indians still on the warpath by thirty or forty to one—more if you just counted the warriors. But Moon knew better than that. An Apache woman was just as dangerous as the men, and the boys, as soon as they could lift a gun, seemed to know how to use it.

The Dragoons were barren. High peaks, rocks by the cubic mile, and the Apaches knew every nook and every cranny. Moon watched the rim nervously, like he always did. But he knew that if the Apaches were there, he'd need more luck than he'd ever had to see them before they wanted to be seen. And by then it would be too late.

The canyon narrowed about halfway through, the quarter-mile expanse closing to less than a hundred yards in some places. It closed like a hungry mouth. Moon reined in and called a halt, but it took the straggling miners five minutes to realize it. They drooped over their horses like wilted flowers. Thirty red eyes stared at him from wobbling heads.

"Look sharp, boys," he said. "This is the worst place in the canyon dead ahead."

"Nothing to worry about, Clay," Dan Martin said. "Me and the boys are already so full of anesthetic we won't feel nothing anyhow."

"You'll feel it all right, Danny, you take an arrow. A bullet you won't feel. You won't feel nothing ever again. But look sharp, that's all I'm gonna say. Anything happens, stick together. You scatter, they'll pick you off one at a time, just like shooting turkeys."

Martin hauled himself up in the saddle with the exaggerated sobriety of a drunken man. "Gobble, gobble, gobble."

The other miners cackled, then stopped when Moon held up a hand. "Most of you boys never even seen an Apache, so I reckon it's understandable. But I have. And I hope to God I never see another one—

not breathing, anyhow. We got an hour until sundown, so let's just try and get home safe, all right?"

It was the same speech he always made. And the men ignored him, like they always did. Most of them were new in the territory. Once he got a taste of the inside of a mine, the first thing a miner did was look for other work. There was no future in mining, and it never took long for a man to realize it. And these were men who had an unbounded faith in their own futures. That was what had brought them west in the first place. It was hard to convince such a man that his connection to tomorrow was as tenuous as a strand of spider silk.

Moon shook his head. He was disgusted, but hadn't really expected not to be. It was a routine for him by now, one he indulged in because he would have felt irresponsible if he hadn't. He spurred his mount and moved through the men still wobbling in their saddles, and didn't look back. Let them follow him however they could, he thought.

He looked up at the rim, thought he saw something, and stared hard, but if there had been anything there, it was gone now. Probably just nerves, he thought.

Any attack would come from high above. The precipitous walls would not permit an attack on foot from anyplace on the ground except dead ahead. A jumble of boulders lined the base of each wall of the canyon, great slabs of reddish stone that flaked off and lay in heaps all the way through.

As they drew closer to the constriction, a place they called the Devil's Gullet, Moon looked more cautiously. He had a pair of field glasses, and reined in long enough to sweep the rimrock on both sides. The jagged edges of the canyon walls were lined with rocks, perfect cover for an ambush, but there was no sign anyone lurked among them.

He kicked his mount to get up some speed and plunged toward the gullet. He was almost through when he heard a rumble. Looking up, he saw a huge boulder already plummeting toward the ground. There was no way to tell whether it had flaked off the wall or tumbled over the rim.

The huge rock bounced off the wall once, tumbling end over end as its momentum carried it away from the sheer face of the canyon. It had dislodged several smaller rocks, and they set up a clatter as they rained down on the rocks below. Moon reined in, holding up one hand like the former cavalry sergeant he was. A grinding sound scraped behind him and he started to look when the boulder hit the ground with a thud that he could feel. The ground rumbled and he saw the second boulder teetering on the rim.

As the rock curled away from the rim he saw the outline of a man. By the long hair whipping in the wind, he knew what it was. He wheeled his mount as the first rifle cracked high above him. He saw the stunned looks on the faces of the miners. "Ride!" he shouted, charging back through them. All hell broke loose then as rifle after rifle started to fire. He saw Dan Martin looking up toward the sky, then disappear behind a cloud of red. Martin tumbled back over the ass end of his mount, and the horse bolted. Martin had one foot still in a stirrup, and his body bounced as the horse charged past Moon.

The men were fumbling to draw their own weapons as more rocks cascaded down off the rim. Some of the Apaches were firing their rifles while others were shoving massive rocks into the chasm beneath them. The rocks were dislodging others as they fell, and soon the canyon was filled with two kinds of thunder.

The ground trembled, and a bullet caught Moon's horse behind the left ear. Dead instantly, the horse stumbled, then fell, spilling Moon from the saddle.

Grappling for his Winchester, he glanced back at the miners, most of whom were trying to spur their mounts and draw their own rifles. Three riderless horses had already broken away and were charging headlong toward the Devil's Gullet. A heart-stopping shriek echoed high off the walls then, and Moon saw three Apaches on foot dart out from among the rocks and grab the bolting horses by the reins.

Apaches lined both sides of the rimrock, and there was little cover to be had except close to the base of the walls. Winchester in hand, Moon darted for the rocks, zigzagging as bullets kicked up puffs of sand all around him.

He dived in among some rocks, remembering that the ammunition for his Winchester was in his saddlebags. He had one full magazine, and then would be down to his Colt revolver. Without looking, he ran his fingers over the gunbelt. Half the loops were empty, and he cursed himself for not remembering to fill it. But it was too late for that now. Now all he could do was pray he would live long enough to keep on regretting it.

He saw Stefan Makowski, the big Hungarian, fall from his horse, leap to his feet, and grab a carbine from its boot. He held a Colt in his right hand, waving it uncertainly as he ran. Plunging toward him, Makowski fired his pistol up toward the rim without looking. The carbine looked small and frail in the big

Hungarian's massive hand. He was ten feet from the rocks when he went down. A small geyser erupted from his chest, just over the heart, and his body quivered and jumped as several more bullets found him. He lay still then, his fingers curled through the lever of his carbine. The Colt lay on his stomach, glittering like silver. There was another reflection above the pistol, where the sun glinted on the spreading bloodstain.

The firing let up a little. Pete Rogoff charged past, still in the saddle, but he didn't get far.

The horse was hit above the fetlock, snapping the bone, and the horse flailed, the broken foot flopping like a tailless kite for several steps until the horse went down. Rogoff jumped as the animal fell, his rifle held high over his head.

"Pete," Moon called, "get the saddlebags." Moon rose halfway out of his cover and pointed. The miner stopped in his tracks, looked back toward Moon's horse, and started running. He snatched at the bags as bullets slammed into Moon's dead mount. The bags came free, and Rogoff turned, running on his toes and ducking into a crouch.

He stumbled just before reaching the rocks and crawled the rest of the way.

Moon scanned the canyon rim, looking for a target, but the Apaches were already moving. They'd fire once, then disappear, only to pop up somewhere farther along the rim. It didn't look as if anyone was still on horseback. Most of the animals wandered aimlessly, darting away from the next rifle shot, then changing direction when the next cracked.

Moon looked up at the sun. It was sinking already, just a sliver of brilliant crimson peeping over the canyon rim. If they could hold out long enough, they might make it away during the night. Some of the miners were returning fire now, two huddled behind one dead horse, another in the rocks fifty yards deeper into the canyon.

As near as Moon could tell, six men, counting himself, were still alive. Six. Against how many? he wondered.

Another war cry pierced the gathering dusk. Then it grew very quiet. The two men behind the horse fired another volley, the clouds of gunsmoke drifting slowly away until they thinned and disappeared.

"What now?" Rogoff whispered.

Chapter 11 ═══════

September 1882—Dragoon Mountains

MOON KNEW the silence meant the Apaches were still there. All he could do was watch the sun and keep his fingers crossed. If they lasted until dark, there was a chance they could slip away. But how far would they get? he wondered. Without horses, and without water, they couldn't leave the canyon. If the Indians were inclined to wait them out rather than risk an assault in the dark, thirst would do them in if they stayed where they were.

He didn't know how many warriors there were, but he'd guess there must have been eighteen or twenty. The Apaches were notorious for fighting only when they had the upper hand. That could mean, in a simple ambush, when they held the high ground, regardless of the size of the opposing force. Or, as it might in this case, it could mean when they had the weight of numbers on their side.

"Awful quiet, Clay," Rogoff whispered. "Awful quiet. You think they've gone?"

"No way they've gone, Pete. They're waiting."

"Waiting for what?"

"Just waiting, is all. Let our nerves do some of the work for 'em."

"Maybe we ought to make a break for it."

"How far you think we'd get, Pete? You ready to run all the way to camp? And if you are, what do you do if they follow you? Nobody there. There ain't no help for twenty miles or more. We best sit tight for now."

"I ain't waiting for no redskin to slit my throat in my sleep."

"Won't have to. After dark, we can join up with whoever's left. There's five of us, I figure. At least there was."

"Maybe one of us could slip out and fetch the army."

"The nearest post is sixty miles away. We don't have a horse. How long you figure it would take you in this country?"

"I don't want to die here, Clay. I just don't want to sit here and wait for that to happen. We got to do something."

Moon said nothing. He understood exactly what Rogoff was talking about. It was the fear that ate away at your insides like acid, chewing its way through your gut until there was nothing left. But the Apaches knew that. They counted on it.

When the silence was too much for him, Rogoff said, "Who else is left?"

"Don't know, Pete. I didn't get a real good look. There was two men behind Chuck Halliwell's pony. And there was somebody along the wall about fifty, sixty yards. I didn't get a look at none of them."

"Maybe I can move along the wall, get whoever it is to come back here."

"I wouldn't. Chances are there's Apaches all over

the place now. You just sit and wait, you want my advice."

"I can't, damn it. I can't wait. Besides, we ain't heard nothing in fifteen, twenty minutes. Them bastards is gone. They're laughing at us for the damn fools we are."

As if to contradict him, an earsplitting shriek resounded from the rimrock. It seemed to fill the entire canyon for a moment, then died slowly away. Long after it was gone, Moon could hear its echo inside his skull. He looked at Rogoff, but knew he didn't have to say anything.

"Maybe we could call them others, at least see who they are."

"We do that, and the Apaches'll know how few of us is left. They already got the upper hand, Pete. I don't want to make it worse than it already is."

"Can't be," Rogoff said. He tried to laugh, but his voice cracked, and he coughed to cover his embarrassment.

"Don't worry about it, Pete. Everybody's scared his first time."

"Scared don't rightly cover it, Clay." This time he did laugh. "I still think I'm gonna go on down there, see can I get to whoever it is."

Moon looked at the sky. "Be dark in half an hour, Pete. Maybe you should wait."

"I wait, and whoever it is, is likely to shoot me."

"All right. We'll both go, then. How's that?"

"Now?"

Moon nodded. He opened the saddlebags and rooted around for the box of shells, stuffed half of them into his pocket, and gave the rest to Rogoff. The miner looked at the box, tilted it to spill the cartridges into his callused palm. He tucked a handful into his shirt pocket and buttoned the flap. The rest he poured directly from the box into his pants pocket.

"You ready?" Moon asked.

"Ready as I'll ever be."

Moon got into a crouch. He looked at the sky once more, hoping he wasn't making a mistake. "We'll leapfrog it," he whispered. "I'll go first. You catch me up, then move to the next cover."

Rogoff cleared his throat. "All right."

Moon wiped his palm on his jeans, then darted out from behind the rock. He ran as fast as he could, bent over like an arthritic old man. With every step, he expected to feel the bullet that would put him out of his misery, but it never came. He skidded on his knees in behind a slab of red rock canted up and over a smaller, roundish boulder.

Turning toward Rogoff, he raised his hand, and the miner dashed toward him. In the extraordinary silence every crunch of Rogoff's boots on the sand sounded like the beat of a snare drum. The miner winked as he moved past, and Moon watched him creeping along the edge of another stone slab. They looked to Moon like huge gravestones, the ruined cemetery of giants.

When Rogoff was in position, he waved a hand, and Moon darted into the open, moved on past, and found the next rock. When he was covered as well as he could be, he craned his neck to look up at the rim. In his mind's eye he could see an Apache grinning, sticking an elbow into another warrior's ribs, as if to say, "Look at the crazy white man. He thinks we don't see him."

Rogoff was waiting for the high sign, and Moon finally came out of his reverie and waved. The miner swept past him, running more easily now, less bent over than he had been. It seemed to Moon that the motion was draining the anxiety away. Doing something was better than doing nothing. At least you didn't feel so damned helpless.

Rogoff edged around a boulder and turned to look back. Moon saw the Apache then, on the other side of the rock. "Look out!" he shouted, raising his Winchester at the same instant. Everything moved so quickly then. He saw Rogoff in the act of turning, saw the Apache spring onto the boulder's flat top and launch himself into the air.

Moon fired, knowing even as he pulled the trigger that his shot was wide. He heard the whine of the ricochet, then a grunt as the Apache landed on top of Rogoff. Instinctively, Moon charged out from behind the rock. He couldn't use his gun for fear of hitting the miner. The two men were rolling over and over, like dervishes in a wrestling match as Moon reached them. He saw the knife in the warrior's hand, reached for it, and locked his hand around the Apache's wrist.

Rogoff kicked up and away, tossing the Apache onto his back. The arm in Moon's grasp came loose as he swung his carbine like a club. Landing a glancing blow on the warrior's shoulder, he pulled the carbine back and Rogoff landed knees-first on the Indian's chest. The whoosh of escaping air was accompanied by the crack of bone—probably a rib, Moon thought.

He swung the carbine again, this time breaking the Apache's nose. Even so, the warrior struggled away, rolling once, then getting to his feet. Blood streamed down his chin, catching the last rays of the dying sun. It looked like he was breathing liquid fire.

He threw his knife then, a quick, underhanded flick, and Moon winced when he heard the solid thunk of the blade and saw Rogoff clutch at his chest, just above the breastbone. The Indian darted forward, and Moon swung again, catching the brave across the face a second time.

He went down hard, Moon on top of him. The Indian was unconscious, and Moon locked his hands around the warrior's throat. He leaned forward with all his weight, squeezing for all he was worth. He felt the larynx give way, and suddenly the neck felt as if it were full of jelly.

The Indian didn't move. Unlocking his hands, Moon waited for some sign the man beneath him was playing possum, but there was nothing. The chest didn't move, there was no bubble of air through the bloody nose and mouth. Nothing.

He got to his feet and turned to see Rogoff holding the bloody knife by its handle. His eyes looked empty, as if he couldn't understand what it was he held in his hand.

"You all right, Pete?"

Rogoff shook his head. "No," he said. He threw the knife then, and slumped back against the rocks, sliding down to land hard on the seat of his pants. Rogoff's shirt was already drenched in blood. A bubble of sticky red ballooned through his lips, and he winced. Coughing, he doubled over as blood spilled over his chin. Rogoff cupped one palm to intercept the stream of bloody water, brought it to his eyes, then wiped it on his pants.

He coughed again. "You was right, Clay. Shoulda

stayed put, I reckon." He fell onto his side then and curled into a tight ball.

"Pete?"

There was no answer. Moon moved close enough to reach out and feel for a pulse. There was none.

"Damn!"

He looked up at the rim again. Like before, it was deserted. The ragged edge of the stone looked like a jawful of black teeth. The charcoal sky behind it seemed to darken as he watched. A moment later the day was dead.

Moon collapsed on the ground, sitting with his back against a rock. He felt helpless. Rogoff was dead, it was pitch-black, and he knew there was no way in hell he was going to get out of the canyon alive. It was getting chilly now, and he wondered whether it was the temperature or a failure of nerve. He wrapped his arms close around his chest, and rocked a bit, trying to calm himself down.

He heard something behind him, and stiffened. A moment later, a shriek exploded, then was choked off. He got to his feet, but in the blackness, he could see nothing. He was tempted to call out, but knew that it would just give away his position. With the sun gone, the Apaches would not come after him unless he made it easy for them.

He listened to the night. A catamount snarled high above him, but he knew he couldn't see anything and didn't even bother to look. All he wanted was to live through the night. In the morning he would try to even the score a little. He knew they'd get him in the end, but he was determined to make it an expensive proposition.

The night grew quiet again. Not even a coyote

broke the silence. He could see the stars high above him. They looked like pinpricks in a black paper held up to the sun. In the perfect stillness, he could hear his own breathing. The sound of his racing heart thumped in his ears, and he could feel it flutter against his ribs, like a live thing trying to get out of a cage.

"Please, God," he whispered. "Just let me make it through till morning."

But his prayer, like so many uttered in such circumstances, went unanswered.

Chapter 12

October 1883—Fort Apache

GEORGE CROOK SAT up all night. His tour of the reservation had been anything but encouraging. All the reforms he had instituted were gone. He had fought so hard for each of them, investing time and energy, arguing with his commanders, pleading with politicians, and now nothing remained of all that effort. It was tempting to throw in the towel. Why should he have to go through it all again?

Bourke sat with him. The captain was devoted to his commander, and he recognized the warning signs. No one could believe so strongly in something, the way Crook did in the rightness of his policies, and not come close to despair gazing on the ruins his successors had left him.

"General, I know you must be disappointed, but—"

Crook exploded. "Disappointed? My God, John, that word doesn't half do it. I can't believe my eyes. Why, tell me please, if you can, why those fools would have allowed this to happen?"

Bourke shrugged. "Not everyone is as reasonable as you want to believe, General."

"Reason is only a small part of it, John. There's justice, there's fairness, there's plain human decency, for God's sake. Don't they matter anymore?"

"For some people they never did matter, General. You know that as well as I do. But you did it before, and you can do it again."

Crook shook his head. The great wave of whiskers under his chin trembled with the movement. "I'm too damned old for this, John."

"Maybe the Apaches don't think so. Maybe they're depending on you."

"They can't depend on someone they can't trust."

"They trust you, General."

"They used to. But I made them promises, John. And none of them have been kept."

"That's not your fault."

"I don't know whether they'll care about that. You know, there are times—very few, mind you—but there are times when I wish I could find solace in a bottle. And this is one of them."

"You don't mean that."

"Don't be too sure."

"What do you want to do first, General?"

Crook ran a palm over his tired features. He toyed with his beard for a few moments, then nodded. "There's only one thing *to* do. Start from scratch. I'll have to talk to the chiefs and try to find out just how bad things are. Once I know that, I'll see what can be done, if anything at all can be. All these people want is respect, John. They've lost almost everything, not lost it really, but had it taken away from them. The least we can do is see to it that they are left with their dignity. Take that away, and we'd be kinder to kill them all."

"You want me to set it up?"

Crook nodded. "Yes, I do. And don't talk to that damned agent, either. You do it yourself. Don't let him influence you. And I want everybody, those who are angry and resentful, especially. I want them here even if they're mad as hornets. That's the only way to get the true picture. I want the truth, and I want to speak the truth to them. No promises that won't be kept. I want to hear every last complaint they've got. We'll sort it all out, and see what we can fix ourselves and what we'll need help with. But the one thing I insist on this time is total control. I've told General Sheridan that, and I've also told the secretary of the interior. I will brook no interference this time. From anyone . . ."

"A tall order, General."

Crook sighed. "I know that, John. But it's the only way."

Crook stayed in his seat, watching Bourke make ready to leave. When the captain was gone, he went to bed, but sleeping was another question. He lay there a long time, thinking back to his last tour of the Arizona Territory. He had thought then that he was onto something, that he had found a way to treat the Apaches fairly and still preserve the peace. His last year or so in Arizona had seemed to confirm that notion, but there was no way to know for certain. Only time would have proven him right or wrong. But time was an enemy now. He hadn't been here in seven years. And seven years was a long time. So much could have happened. He had his suspicions, but did not want to prejudge the matter.

By the time the first gray light of dawn started to filter into his room, he had finally managed to drift off. He would be up in three hours, he knew, but a little sleep was better than none.

When his orderly rapped cautiously on the closed door to his bedroom, the general was already awake and dressed. He didn't answer right away, thinking that maybe the extra few seconds could somehow change things, make what he had to do a little less difficult. But the second knock came, and he knew things hadn't changed.

Bourke was already seated at the breakfast table. "Morning, General."

"Captain," Crook said, pulling up a chair. "You look a little tired."

Bourke laughed. "I wonder why."

"Anything to report?"

"I've sent messengers. They left before the crack of dawn. The first meeting is scheduled for eleven o'clock. I'm sure all of the chiefs won't be there, but we can get started."

"First meeting, eh? You think more than one will be necessary, do you?"

Bourke wasn't sure whether his commander was pulling his leg, so he played it straight. "At least one more will be necessary, General, for those headmen we don't get to interview this morning."

Crook smiled. "I suppose you're right, Captain Bourke. You usually are."

During breakfast they talked about everything but the single most important problem confronting them. It wasn't until the cook had cleared the table and come back with a second pot of coffee that Crook got around to the inevitable. "We have to make sure we don't go off half-cocked this morning, John."

"Sir?"

"These Indians have had a bellyful of unkept promises. I won't make one I can't keep. That just might not do the trick. But I won't lie to them."

"I think they know that, General."

"I hope you're right, John." Crook sipped his coffee slowly to make sure it wasn't too hot and, when it met his exacting standards, took a long pull on the cup. Setting it down carefully, he said, "I want you there with plenty of ink and paper, John."

"Whatever for?"

"We're going to make a record of this."

"Do you think that's wise?"

Crook glanced up sharply, and Bourke nodded. "You know what I mean, General. If there's a record, they might not be willing to talk so freely."

"If they understand it's to make certain their words are preserved, their complaints registered in some permanent form, I think they might talk not only freely, but to the point. At least that's what I hope will happen." He finished his coffee and stood up. "I've got a few things to do before they get here. You'll excuse me, John."

Bourke stood and snapped a smart salute. Crook grinned. "Rather formal, aren't we, Captain?"

"It seemed appropriate." Bourke laughed. "I'll be back at ten-thirty, with plenty of writing materials." He left then, closing the door quietly behind him. Crook watched him go, wondering what he would have done without him. Bourke was more intelligent than most officers he'd encountered in his long career, and seemed peculiarly appropriate for his current duties. He had the ability to abstract himself from any situation and examine conflicting ideas from every angle. He was a scientist, really, not a military officer, despite the uniform. He had somehow missed his calling and ended up at the doorway to hell.

There wasn't a dishonest bone in his body, and more than honesty, Bourke had a sense of fairness about him, one that brought the captain more than his fair share of attacks in the newspapers.

The so-called journalists who persisted in attacking the army in general, and Crook and his staff in particular, from their safe havens in San Francisco and San Diego, did little but inflame the white citizens of the territory. Not that they needed much to inflame them. Tiffany and his ilk were good at only one thing, and that was dousing a fire with kerosene. The brighter the flame, the heavier their pockets.

The businessmen in Tucson in particular, but all over the territory, clamped their voracious jaws to the side of the army mules and sucked every drop of blood. It seemed as if they would not know how to turn an honest dollar if their lives depended on it. Keep the army in Arizona, and keep selling supplies at triple the reasonable cost. That was how they made their fortunes. And the Apaches knew it as well as Crook himself.

How to stop it was not nearly as clear as identifying the problem in the first place. But he was going to try. The new agent, P. P. Wilcox, seemed like a good start. With Tiffany out of the way, although not rotting in jail where he ought to be, some immediate relief ought to be possible.

There was so much paper to be sifted that it was time for the meeting before Crook realized it. His orderly came in to advise him that some Apaches were asking for "Nantan Lupan," whoever that was.

"That's me, Corporal. It means 'Tan Wolf' in Apache. They gave me that name because of the clothes I wear. I think they have a sneaking admiration for an army officer who doesn't bother with his uniform unless he has to. Show them in."

"Are you sure, sir?"

Crook nodded vigorously. "Damned sure, Corporal. Hop to it, would you?"

"Yes, sir." He watched the orderly go out and spotted Bourke behind the corporal's shoulder. The captain entered with the first band of chiefs and took a seat in one corner.

Crook recognized several of the Apaches from his previous tour. They seemed glad to see him and shook his hand warmly, asked after his family, and he did the same.

Foremost among them was Alchise, a man whom Crook had come to admire greatly. He felt that the old chief epitomized the best of Apache traits and provided all the evidence any reasonable man might need that decency and integrity and intelligence were not confined to the white race alone.

More Apaches drifted in, some in small groups, others individually. It was nearly 11:30 by the time greetings had been exchanged all around and they were ready to begin.

"I know you are curious about this meeting, and I want to get right to the point." Crook, used to waiting for translation, cocked an ear toward Severiano, who, although Mexican, had been raised by the Apaches and had added English to his linguistic arsenal during years spent as a scout. "I know things here are not to your liking, and I want to know how they can be made better. But before we begin, I want you to know that Captain Bourke"—he pointed with a nod of his head, Apache style, toward the studiously transcribing captain—"will preserve all of our words on paper, both yours and mine. That way there will never be any doubt about what was said here. This will help us both to see to it that things are made better where they can be. Is that fair?"

The Apaches muttered among themselves, then seemed to nominate Alchise to speak for them all.

"That is fair, Nantan Lupan," he said.

"Good; now, why don't you tell me what your problems are?"

Alchise grunted. "It will take a long time, but we can begin at least. When you were here before, things were good. There were no Apaches out, and there was no fighting between Americans and Apaches. The officers you had here were all good officers, but when you left us, that all changed. Why did you go? We don't understand. Things were good then, and if you had stayed, they would still be good."

Crook smiled. "I am a soldier. I must do what my superiors tell me to do."

Alchise nodded gravely. "Not all soldiers are good soldiers. Major Randall was a good soldier and a good man. So was Colonel Green. But when they went away, those who took their places were not so good. One would tell us to do something and we would do it, then another would tell us to do the opposite. If we did that thing, the first officer was angry. If we did not, the second officer was angry. We didn't know what to do, ever."

"That will all change now," Crook assured them. "You will always know what I want you to do. And there is a new agent, who seems like a good man, too."

Alchise smiled, but there was no enjoyment in it. It looked like the expression of a man trying to smile to keep from crying. "We plant corn," he said. "The corn sprouts and grows and is green for a while. Then it turns yellow and dies. It is the same with agents. They start out good, but they then wither. Always the same."

"I believe this man is different."

"We will see," Alchise said. "Only after time will we know."

Crook nodded. The talk went on for nearly three hours. Alchise, and later Pedro, who had always been friendly to the whites, described Apache grievances in meticulous detail. The list was long, and it was appalling. They talked of how agents sold food intended for the Indians to mining camps, and put the money in their own pockets. They talked of being given land and planting crops, only to have the land taken away before the harvest.

They talked of miners taking their land, and of how Tiffany came to the chiefs one day with a piece of paper and a bag of Mexican pesos. He told them they had to sign the paper and take the pesos in exchange for their land, or men would come and shoot them all. They told Crook of how they were forced to give up their homes and move to San Carlos, where it was too hot, and where there were too many flies, as well as bad water and bad air. They got fevers, and the children were often sick. They wanted to know why they could not live in the mountains, as they used to do.

Crook kept them at it, prodding Alchise, Pedro, and

Uklenni, the principal leaders, with questions that showed not only that he was listening to them, but that he wanted to know everything. It was an exhausting experience.

"We are glad you have come back, and we hope that you never leave us again. We want to be good and to do what we are supposed to do. You have always told us the truth, and we appreciate that. If you stay with us, there will be no more trouble," Alchise said. "Nantan Lupan, you know that I fought with your soldiers against the Apache-Yumas and even against my own people. I did this because I trusted you and believed what you said. I have never been sorry for that."

Crook was nearly overcome. There was no way he could articulate the turbulent emotions swirling inside him. He respected these people, and found them less savage by far than many so-called civilized whites he had had to deal with over the years, men who were little more than parasites at best, and murderous scoundrels at worst.

"I appreciate your trust in me, and I want to tell you now that I will do my best to be worthy of it. We will make things better. This much I can tell you now. To begin with, you will no longer have to live at San Carlos. You can take your families and live anywhere on the reservation. We will use the old way, the medals with numbers, not so that we can protect you, but so you can show where you are at all times. If a white man says Alchise and Uklenni and so and so killed my ranch foreman and stole my cattle, the medals will help you show that you were here, and nowhere near the ranch.

"But this means that you will have to be responsi-

ble for your people. We will have the Indian police
again so that Apaches, not white men, will see to it
that Apaches behave as they ought to. There is much
to do, and we will have to talk again. And you will
have to tell others to come to the next talk so that
I can hear what everyone has to say. I cannot promise
that things will be exactly as you wish, but I can, and
do, promise that no one will steal food from the
mouths of your children if I can prevent it."

The Apaches were silent for a long time. Crook, his
emotions drained by the unremitting and unflinching
testimony, could say no more. One by one the
Apaches filed out. Alchise was the last to leave. He
stepped close again, grasped the general's hand, and
nodded. But he said nothing.

There was no need for words.

Chapter 13 ═══════════

March 1883—Casas Grandes, Mexico

THEY WERE SAFE in the mountains now. The Sierra Madres towered around them for miles in every direction. In their secluded valleys, there was game and water, relief from the searing heat, and protection from the Mexican army. But they were prisoners of their own safety. And they were too used to the white man's weapons. They needed ammunition.

Juh and Geronimo called a council to discuss ways of obtaining new weapons and ammunition for the ones they already had.

Juh started. "We know we are secure here," he began. "You all know that. But you also know that the day may come when we are not so secure. The Americans cannot come after us because the Mexicans won't allow it. And the Mexicans"—he paused for effect, and was not disappointed, as laughter rippled around the fire—"the Mexicans do not have the courage to come after us."

A loud chorus of amused assent lightened the moment. But Juh was not interested in entertaining the warriors. They had a problem, and he wanted them all to be clear about it. "But that could change. Before, the Mexicans have agreed to let the American soldiers come across the border. This could happen again. And if it does, we are not ready to fight them."

"They have never come into the mountains after us," Chatto said.

"Not yet."

"They never will. We will always be safe here."

Juh smiled. "Chatto forgets that Nantan Lupan is coming back. He is not like the other soldiers. He might come."

"He couldn't find us."

"Not alone, he couldn't. But he is not alone. He has used Apaches against Apaches before. He will do it again. Even now there are rumors that he is trying to get the Mexicans to give permission for his soldiers to enter the mountains. And there will be Apaches to lead him here."

Geronimo grunted. "Nantan Lupan is just one man. He is not afraid of Apaches, but his soldiers are. They will never follow him here. But Juh is right. We need to be sure we can fight if the Americans do come."

Chatto got to his feet. "Is Geronimo afraid of the Tan Wolf? Does he tremble when he sees the whiskers?" They all laughed, including Geronimo.

Then his broad features turned to stone. "No, I am not afraid. But we are few and they are many. They have the big guns that throw the exploding balls great distances. If we expect to defend ourselves, we will need much ammunition. We cannot make our own, and the White Eyes have more than they need."

Chatto sat down again. He had been put in his place without being directly challenged, and everyone at the council knew it. "What would you have us do, then? Should we go back to the reservation?"

Juh shook his head. "No. We can live here in the

mountains, but we will have to trade with the Mexicans. We will have to get ammunition from them."

"That won't be easy," Chatto insisted.

Chihuahua, who was sitting next to him, stood then. "We can go north and get all the ammunition we want. It is better if we do that. The Mexicans are afraid of us, but they won't give us what we want because they are afraid. Besides, the American guns are better. Better we should get new rifles and bullets for them. We can't do that here."

"The weapons we already have are old. Many of them were taken from Mexican soldiers. I think we should do both," Geronimo said. "First we get bullets for the guns we have. We can do that here. Then, with enough ammunition, we can go north and get more and better weapons."

"It is easy for you to say so," Chihuahua pointed out. "You already have an American soldier's gun. Some of us do not have such good weapons."

Juh, conscious that a split could develop all too easily in the fragile coalition, said, "We can do both at the same time. Some of us can try to deal with the Mexicans. Others can go north and see what they can find of use. As always, we will share what we get."

"I'm going back north," Chihuahua said. His jaw snapped, leaving no doubt that he had spoken his last word on the matter.

"I will go with him," Chatto said.

"I'll leave in the morning," Chihuahua announced. "Anyone who wants to go will be welcome."

Juh stood then, for the first time. He was one of the most fearless of the warriors, and his association with Cochise gave him additional influence. He was comfortable with his power to lead the warriors and felt no need to flaunt his courage. "Geronimo and I will stay. We will protect the women and children so you don't have to worry about them. And we will get what we can from the Mexicans."

"Be careful," Chatto said. "Don't trust them."

Juh smiled. "Would I trust a scorpion?"

The council broke up quickly, as if the men were anxious to avoid the problems Juh and Geronimo had raised. Doing something, anything at all, was better than sitting in their wickiups and staring at the walls. They were anxious to reclaim some control over their lives, and it was best not to look too closely at what they proposed to do. Already they were few, and getting fewer. The best men took the most chances in battle, and often got themselves wounded or even killed. Slowly but surely the White Eyes were grinding them to dust. They all knew it, and it was only the stubborn courage of a few, men like Juh and Geronimo, that kept them going. But even such warriors were weary of the constant warfare. There wasn't a man in the band who, secretly, perhaps locked away in some fifth chamber of his heart, didn't harbor the wish that peace could be made. And kept. But not one of them wanted total capitulation. It had to be peace with dignity, or it was not a peace worth having. Better to die to the last man than to become no better than slaves.

Juh and Geronimo spent the night arguing how to approach the Mexicans without taking an unnecessary risk. They wanted to be left alone, but they needed access to a Mexican town in order to get supplies they needed. Geronimo argued for simply taking them, but Juh was less vehement, suggesting that it might be possible to find some way to live peaceably, side by side with the Mexicans.

"You can't forgive the Mexicans for Alope, for your mother and children," Juh argued. "It colors everything you see."

"Should I forgive them?" Geronimo asked.

"You are not the only man to lose family."

"I know that. But I might be the only man who doesn't forget. We cannot trust the Mexicans. We cannot trust the Americans."

"You always said you could trust Nantan Lupan. He is back now."

"But he went away once before. Then it was no longer up to him what happened to the Apaches. Who is to say the same thing will not happen a second time? They send him to San Carlos because we are out. If we surrender and go back to the reservation, it will be the same thing all over again. Some White Eyes will find the yellow metal they love so much, and we will have to move. If we succeed in growing melons and corn, they will see that the bad land they gave us is good for something and they will want it back. If Crook is there, he will stop it. But if he goes away again, there will be no one to stop it from happening."

"There are other good soldiers. The man with the long nose, Gatewood, Crawford. Britton Davis. We can trust them."

"What should we do then, ask them for bullets for our guns?"

"No. But we can tell them that we will stay in Mexico. If they believe us, they will leave us alone. Then all we have to do is worry about the Mexicans. If we can make peace with them, then they, too, will leave us alone."

Geronimo stepped out of the wickiup and called Juh to follow him. Waving a hand across the horizon, where stars glittered like so many hard, cold fires against the moonless black, he said, "All this used to be ours. Then the Spanish came. Since then, it has always been war. We don't have books, like the White Eyes, but that doesn't mean we don't remember what it was like before they came."

"But there was war then, too. War with the Maricopas, war with the Pimas, war with the Tarahumaro."

"But we always won."

"Not always, Goyahkla. You know the stories as well as I do, about how we lived in the north, where there was no desert, and where great animals provided everything we needed. They say a man in one day could kill enough food for a month. But then the others came, and we had to move south, always more and more of them."

"We could go back now. We could go back north, past the Navajo, into the tall mountains."

Juh shook his head. "No. We can't go back. The White Eyes are everywhere. It would be the same thing, no matter where we went. Except here."

"And here we live like squirrels, stealing mesquite beans to stay alive. We have no land. We have no home."

Juh waved his own arm. Even in the dark, it was possible to see the bulk of the Sierra Madres, an obsidian mass against the coal-black sweep of the sky. *"This* is home now. It is the only home we shall have. We will have to learn to accept that. Or go back to the reservation."

"So we will try then. Tomorrow we will send a woman to the Mexicans. There are Apaches living there, in the place they call Big Houses. We will tell them we want to be at peace, and see what they say."

Juh grunted. "I think it is the best way. And if I am wrong, then we can stay in the mountains and hunt with bows the way the old ones did."

Geronimo smiled a bitter smile. "Yes . . . that's what we'll do . . . hunt with bows. Until there are no more Apaches left."

Geronimo walked out into the darkness. It seemed to him that the world had been dark for a long time. The sun might try to smother him with its oppressive fire, heating the air around him until it hurt to breathe, but there were still so many things that no one saw. His power told him things that no one else wanted to hear spoken. They followed him because they believed in him, just like they had believed in Victorio and Mangas Coloradas and Cochise, but they were so few now.

It seemed almost pitiful how they roamed from place to place, always with the threat of soldiers hanging behind them as real as the cloud of dust kicked up by their horses. But the power wasn't enough anymore. Too many were tired. Some, like Nana and Loco, were old. It wasn't their fault. Geronimo knew that they had suffered as much as he had, but the others had been defeated. They had lost the will to fight. All except a handful. Juh had not lost it, but Juh wanted to hide from the world. He wasn't afraid, he just didn't think it was worth it to fight anymore. Even though he would never say it, Juh believed they had already lost the war.

Geronimo walked down a small hill and up a taller

one across a shallow valley. From its peak he could see the fires, now as small as the stars in the sky, the light pale, washed out, like Loco's spirit. There was nothing to see, and he turned his back on the *rancheria* to look up at the sky. With nothing to interfere he could see the stars much more clearly now. He wondered where they went during the day. He knew they were there, because he had seen them from the bottom of deep canyons, not stars he recognized, but there all the same.

He sat on the hill, his back to the *rancheria,* and prayed. The sun would be up soon, and he would pray to Ussen, facing the east when the sun rose, his arms extended to the sky. If Ussen were listening, maybe he would tell him what to do. But it had been a long time since Ussen had told him anything useful. It sometimes seemed as if even Ussen had given up, lost something, the will to fight. Or perhaps he simply refused to help those who no longer had the will to help themselves.

By the time the sky had started to gray, he knew what he would do. He knew what they all should do, but he knew, too, that it was a desperate gamble, one that would almost certainly explode in their faces like a bad gun, hurting the man who held it instead of his enemy.

When the sun started to bulge above the eastern peaks, its bloody red color seeping across the edge of the world and turning the mountains from black to purple, he got to his feet. Facing the swelling mound of bloody fire, he prayed, his voice rising almost in desperation. He chanted aloud, listening to his words dwindle into tiny echoes then die way. His voice rose almost to fury, and he felt ashamed, as if he were defying Ussen instead of asking his help.

But it made no difference. When he was done praying, had asked this one last time for the help without which he could not hope to succeed, he knew the prayer was wasted. When he stopped chanting and his last words drifted away like so much milkweed down on a stiff breeze, there was nothing but silence to take their place.

Shaking his head, possibly in disappointment and almost certainly tinged with anger he could not control and could not ignore, he turned away from the sun and walked back down the hill. When he reached the fringes of the *ranchería,* some of the women were already tending the fires. Some of the older children were playing, shooting small arrows with their tiny, blunt-tipped bows, stalking one another. Their play used to be meaningful, a prelude to the intense training they would receive when they were old enough to learn the ways of the warrior, the craft of the hunter. Now it looked like a mockery, one last remnant of a history that he knew was coming to an end, just as the people who had made that history were coming to an end. If they went back to the reservation, they were no longer free. And no longer Apaches. They would be tame, like the Navajo, little better than the animals the sheep-eaters raised on the edges of the deserts to the north.

Juh was waiting for him. He nodded, and Juh walked out to meet him. "We should send a woman," Juh said. "There are Apaches there, living with the Mexicans in the place of the Big Houses. She can see what they tell her, maybe talk to the *alcalde* of the town. If it is safe, she will tell us, and we can go down to trade."

Geronimo nodded. "They will tell her what we want to hear. You know that."

"Maybe so. But maybe it is what they want to believe."

"Mexicans and Apaches never want to believe the same things," Geronimo said. "Red Sleeves knew that. So did you, once."

Juh shook his head. Instead of answering, he ran a thick-fingered hand through his black hair, tinged just noticeably with silver now. *He is getting old, too,* Geronimo thought. *We all are.*

The woman waited just out of earshot. Chatto and his people, and Chihuahua and his, were making ready to leave. Both men climbed into their saddles and waved to Geronimo. Geronimo waved back, then, as they started to move out, he turned away. It seemed to him that maybe this was the beginning of the end of things, maybe of everything. He wondered whether he would see Chatto again, or Chihuahua, or Nana.

"All right," Geronimo said. "Send her."

She was gone overnight, and when she returned, she brought good news. The Mexicans wanted the past to be past, she said. They were tired of fighting. *They want to live side by side with us, without fighting.*

Juh had questioned her, and Geronimo sat silently, taking it all in, but not believing it.

"Even the Apaches there said the same," the woman went on. "The alcalde is coming to meet us."

"You didn't tell him where we are?" Geronimo's voice was sharp.

The woman turned her head, almost as if she had been struck, the words were so brittle and hard. "No," she said. "They will come to a place on the creek down on the edge of the town. We can meet them there."

"I will go," Juh said.

"It's a trap," Geronimo warned.

"Maybe. Maybe it is. If no one goes, we will never know."

"Then I will go with you," Geronimo answered. He called half a dozen warriors. The men gathered in a small circle around him while he was still seated. They listened to the woman, their feet shifting nervously on the sandy ground, and when she was done, Juh stood up. "We should go soon," he said.

"Now," Geronimo said. "If it is a trap, the sooner we know, the better."

The ride was not that long. In three hours they could already see the small dust cloud thrown up by the horses of the alcalde and his escort.

"Not many," Juh said.

"Not yet," Geronimo said. "But it is early yet."

The meeting went well. The alcalde of Casas Grandes assured them he and his people would be happy to live peaceably with the Apaches. He invited them to a celebration, one, he said, to signify that the past was dead, that history was finished, and that a new history was about to begin. "Come," he said, "see our town. Celebrate the new peace with us."

"When?" Juh asked.

"Two days. We are already making preparations. There will be no trouble. The old days are behind us now. Apaches and Mexicans can be friends, can help each other, the way God intended all men to live, together without war."

"We will come," Juh told him.

The alcalde smiled. The men with him were nervous. Their eyes kept darting around from one Apache face to the next. They lingered longer on Geronimo than on any other. He stared back impassively, his face a puzzling, immobile mask. They seemed to sense his resistance, but said nothing directly to him. When they rode away, they didn't look back, as if afraid their faces would show something they wanted to keep hidden.

"You see," Juh said. "It can be."

"We will see," Geronimo said. "We will see."

They rode back to the *ranchería* in silence.

Chapter 14 ═══════════

March 1883—Casas Grandes, Mexico

THE APACHES were wary. Approaching Casas Grandes, they split into several small groups. Drifting into the town in threes and fours, each group watched the reception of its predecessors with a jaundiced eye. The town was bedecked as if for a festival. Banners and piñatas twirled in the warm breeze. Groups of townspeople stood in the main square, watching the Apaches cautiously and talking among themselves.

Juh was one of the first to arrive. He dismounted, and was surprised to see a little Mexican boy tiptoe toward him, one tiny hand outstretched for the reins. He squatted down to encourage the boy, who leaned forward from the waist to avoid getting too close. Juh reached out, let the tiny fingers circle the reins, then snatched at the boy and picked him up.

The boy's mother screamed, but Juh tousled the youngster's hair and hefted him to his shoulder, swinging the boy around and planting him securely across his broad back. Getting down into a crouch, he mimed the canter of a frisky horse, and soon the boy was squealing with delight, kicking his feet as if they sported spurs.

"Where's your mama?" Juh asked in his excellent Spanish.

The boy leaned over to point toward a slender young woman who stood to the front of a small knot of townspeople, one fist clenched against her lips. Juh cantered toward her, and the woman tried to smile, but it was more than she could manage. The thought of her child on the back of this fearsome savage was more than her nerves could bear.

The boy's father stepped forward, and Juh straightened, extending a hand. The man, three or four inches smaller than the Apache, his hands callused from fourteen-hour days behind the hoe, smiled. It was more genuine, but no less nervous than his wife's attempt. He shook Juh's hand and reached out to take the boy, but the youngster wanted his ride to continue and would only agree to get down after Juh galloped in a small circle around the nervously giggling Mexicans.

When the boy was back on the ground, the ice seemed suddenly to melt, and the people pressed forward. More Apaches were drifting in, and the townspeople started to surround them, extending their hands and chattering giddily. Juh turned to watch as Geronimo rode into town. He could hear the awed hissing of the Mexicans, who recognized the stone-faced war chief. "Geronimo . . . Geronimo . . . that's him. That's Geronimo. Yes, it is!"

Geronimo dismounted, but wouldn't let the young man who came to him have the reins. Instead, he walked toward the church across the plaza, tugging the horse behind him.

Tables ringed the square, and people had begun to load them with food. Geronimo noticed the bottles of

aguardiente and mescal. He knew the warriors
would soon break them open and start a bout of
heavy drinking. It was one of the things they most enjoyed about Mexican hospitality, which had been an
on-again, off-again proposition for years. It had not
been unusual for isolated towns, desperate for relief
from Apache depredations to afford hospitality to the
Apaches in exchange for being left unmolested.
There was a time when Apaches from the entire state
of Sonora would raid only in Chihuahua, and vice
versa. Goods stolen in Sonora would be taken to Chihuahua to be traded for supplies.

Despite the attempts of the feeble Mexican central
government to enforce its ban against trading with
the Indians, the people themselves did what they had
to to stay alive, and if that meant trading with the
hostiles, then so be it. But that had been ten years
ago. Things had not been so easy in recent years. The
Mexican army was getting more aggressive, and
some of its officers seemed to have a personal stake
in exterminating the Apaches. The new aggressive-
ness had led to the ill-conceived bounty on scalps,
a policy which failed to consider the fact that one
lock of black hair was like another, and that most
Mexicans themselves had black hair.

This looked like one more attempt to get the
Apaches to lower their guard. Geronimo tied his
horse to a hitching post and walked to the nearest
table. Snatching a bottle of mescal, he ignored the attempts at conversation and walked back to the steps,
where he sat with his back against the wall and a
Colt pistol in his lap.

Drinking the mescal slowly, he considered Juh,
who seemed to have let his guard down almost com-

pletely. It must be that Juh wants peace at any cost, he thought, otherwise so skilled a leader would not be so eager to expose his followers to the uncertain hospitality of the hated Mexicans.

The day wore on with much eating and drinking. There was some trading, but for the moment the Apaches had little of value to trade. Credit was not in the cards, and Geronimo knew there would have to be raids soon in order to capitalize on the new truce.

The sun was low in the sky now, and many of the warriors were roaring drunk. Apaches and Mexicans both were drinking. A group of Mexicans with drums, guitars, and trumpets had taken up a post across the square from Geronimo. They were banging away at the drums and guitars while the trumpeters, themselves too drunk to maintain their embouchures, blared and blurted sporadically, surrounding a tune rather than playing it.

Despite the general uproar, Geronimo maintained his solitary vigil, ignoring every attempt to get him to join the festivities. From time to time he would heft his Colt, as if to make certain it still sat in his lap. Twice Juh had urged him to relax and join the fun. And both times Geronimo had spurned him, saying someone had to stay alert to watch for the treachery that was certain to come.

A dozen warriors, handpicked by Geronimo, mingled in the crowd, but drank nothing but water on express orders from their leader, and on pain of death. By sundown the fiesta showed no signs of breaking up. The music had straggled to a halt, replaced now by Apache drums and the wild dancing that almost

always followed hard on the heels of unrestricted access to *aguardiente.*

Geronimo had long since polished off his own bottle of mescal, but he had drunk it slowly, and it had
not impaired his senses to any significant degree. Letting the bottle roll away from him and clatter down
the steps, he got to his feet and began to circulate.
If anything had been planned, it would happen after
dark, when the Apaches were too drunk to notice
until it was too late. One by one he warned his warriors to stay alert, pulling each one close to smell his
breath to make certain he had not been drinking.

The men respected him, and they knew his suspicion would benefit them all, but they still resented
staying sober when the others were long since insen-
sible. With a nod or a pointed stab of his chin, Geronimo would counsel them to stay on their guard, then
drift through the singing and dancing throng until he
found another, then another of the sober sentries.

It was near midnight before the combination of
drinking and dancing had sufficiently exhausted the
Apaches and Mexicans both. Slowly the celebrants
began to drift away, the Mexicans to their homes,
their wobbly progress marked by the squalls of children and the drag of drunken feet across the sandy
earth. The Apaches drifted a few hundred yards beyond the edge of Casas Grandes and built temporary
camps, little more than small fires surrounded by
horse blankets, on which those able to arrange themselves were already fast asleep. Others, less in control of their faculties, lay on the bare ground, their
drunken snores ripping at the dark fabric of the night
like so many saws.

Geronimo rode nearly three miles before reaching

the small spring surrounded by a clump of gnarled mesquite trees where he had pitched his camp, and where his family had spent the day. He lay down and listened, unable to sleep until nearly dawn. Now and then a drunken cry would pierce the stillness, and he would sit up, expecting gunshots to follow. But the cry would die away and the silence would return. Twice he thought about waking his wife, but decided he would rather be alone with his suspicions.

He was awakened by the sun on his face and found himself staring up at an already blue sky. He could hear the growl of trumpets again, and stopped only to rinse his mouth and wipe away some of the dust of the day before. Chee-hash-kish, his wife, asked if he wanted something to eat, but he shook his head, warned her to stay at the camp, then sprang into the saddle to head back toward Casas Grandes. As an afterthought he reached into a rawhide sack slung across the back of his Mexican saddle and pulled out a second Colt revolver. Pressing it into her hands, he said, "If any Mexicans come here, shoot."

Riding back toward the town, he was beginning to wonder if maybe he was too suspicious. Nothing had happened. Juh seemed unconcerned, and the Mexicans couldn't have been more hospitable. His natural reserve was what kept him alive. He knew that. But he knew, too, that there were many among the band who wanted things to be more peaceful. They longed to stay in one place for more than three or four days, to plant a few crops, to watch their children grow up with some sense of stability.

He wanted that, too, far more than the others knew. But he had seen too much that he could not forget. Victorio had been lulled by a flag of truce, and it had cost him many lives. Mangas Coloradas had also taken the fluttering bait of the white flag, and had been publicly humiliated once and, even after having been fooled by the White Eyes, had once again respected a truce and been murdered for his troubles. He hated the Mexicans for what they had done to his family. He was right to hate them, but maybe he hated them too much. Maybe he could hate them and still walk the same ground, as long as he was careful.

By the time he reached the town, Apaches and Mexicans were already beginning to mill around in the streets. The food was plentiful once again. And once again Geronimo noted the bottles of mescal and *aguardiente*. It was almost too good to be true. Or was it? Was this really what peace with the White Eyes could be like?

He looked for Juh, but couldn't locate him. He found Daklugie, Juh's son, sitting under a table, a bowl of rice and black beans for breakfast balanced on his knees. Geronimo dropped to a squat. "Where is your father?" he asked.

"Sleeping, Uncle," the boy told him. He pointed back to the edge of the town, and Geronimo followed the point. All he could see were dust-colored mounds, Apaches still sleeping off the excesses of the day before.

Nodding his head, Geronimo straightened. He saw a small group of Mexicans, including the alcalde, standing to one side of another table. They were talking among themselves, apparently wrapped up in their conversation, but their eyes did not follow the words. They were watching the Apaches, not warily, as they had the day before, but with a different kind of concentration. He didn't know what it meant, but he didn't like it.

For a moment he considered walking over to join them. His Spanish was good enough to carry on a conversation, but he decided it would be better just to watch them during the day, to see if the huddle continued.

Walking back toward the edge of Casas Grandes, he stepped carefully among the sprawled bodies, looking for Juh. Nearly two hundred Apaches, mostly men, were still sleeping. The children, who of course had not been drinking, sat quietly, within reach of their parents. The women, who drank less and enjoyed it less, were mostly awake, but still lying on their blankets, exhausted from the day's dancing and, Geronimo thought, the past years of constant flight. One by one he examined the sleeping men. Finally he spotted Jacali, his niece and one of Juh's daughters, sitting with her back to the town.

He sat next to her without speaking. She was aware of him, but did not turn to look at him.

"Juh is very tired," Geronimo said.

"We are all very tired," Jacali said. "It would be better if we were not here."

"Is that what your father thinks?"

She shrugged. "Who knows what Juh thinks?"

Geronimo considered the response for several seconds before saying, "You do. You know better than he does what he is thinking most of the time. Does he still think this is a wise idea?"

"I'm not sure," Juh grunted. Geronimo turned then to see his fellow chief sitting up, rubbing his eyes to sweep away the clouds of sleep. His face looked drawn, thinner than Geronimo remembered. It seemed he was looking at Juh for the first time in years. Maybe it was age catching up with him, Geronimo thought.

"The Mexicans are talking among themselves."

Juh shrugged. "That's what people do. Even Mexicans. Look at our people. They are talking among themselves. Does that mean they are plotting something against the town?"

"No. But the Mexicans are different."

"I still think we should wait and see. They seem to welcome us. No one has mentioned the old days, except to say how glad he is that those days are gone. Dead and buried, they say."

"I think it is the Apaches they wish to see dead and buried."

"We are enough to defend ourselves. It is not as if we are helpless. You worry too much. And you don't like Mexicans. You don't trust them."

"No good comes of trusting Mexicans. No good comes of trusting anyone but ourselves. We are the only ones who don't wish to see the Apaches exterminated."

"Relax just a little bit, brother. Have some food, drink a little mescal. Celebrate. We have found a place where no one will bother us again. I think we should still be watchful, but it will work out. You will see."

"Watch the alcalde today."

"Why?"

"I don't want to tell you. Just watch him. We will talk later, and you tell me what you have seen. Then I will tell you what I have seen, and what I think it means."

Juh nodded. "If you say so." Stretching his powerful arms over his head, he yawned, then got to his feet.

Jacali said, "Father, you are stealing my uncle's name. It is he who yawns, not you." She laughed, and Geronimo smiled in spite of himself. He hadn't heard her laugh in so long that its music came as a shock.

One by one the sleeping warriors revived. Most were ready for another day of gorging themselves and emptying a bottle or two. It was the mescal and the *aguardiente* that troubled Geronimo most.

"Juh," he said, "when do you remember the White Eyes being so generous with their whiskey, except for money?"

Juh shook his head, but said nothing. He was watching Geronimo closely now, as if the words had triggered something in the back of his mind, something he hadn't known was there, but that had been trying to break through to the light.

Geronimo continued. "Always the White Eyes say that Apaches can't drink, they don't know how to control themselves. On the reservation they tell us we can't even make *tizwin*. It is all right to grow corn to eat, but not to make drink of it."

"What are you getting at, Geronimo?"

"Why are the Mexicans not afraid to give us mescal? Why do they encourage us to drink *aguardiente*?"

"It is the way the White Eyes celebrate, that's all." But Juh sounded tentative, as if he didn't quite believe his own explanation. Rather than wait for more of Geronimo's suspicion, he got to his feet. "I need something to eat," he said. "Come with me."

Geronimo shook his head. "No. Today I will watch. I will drink nothing and I will eat nothing. Today I will watch, and I will see things you don't wish to see. We'll talk tonight."

He walked back toward the town, where the celebration of the day before had already risen from its own ashes. The Apache warriors were drinking again, with more abandon than they had shown the day before. There seemed to be less mingling this time, though, and Geronimo wondered whether it was his own jaundiced view of the Mexicans that made it seem so. He looked for the alcalde, but he was nowhere in evidence. Some of the men he had seen speaking with him were scattered around the square. They were not drinking, although they held glasses in their hands. He wondered whether they had drunk yesterday, but could not be sure. So many of the Mexicans looked alike, it was difficult to tell one from another.

As on the day before, he walked to the broad steps of the church and sat beside them, his back against the adobe wall. Again he held his Colt pistol in his lap, but this time he had no bottle. He was determined to stay as clearheaded as he could. Some of the Mexicans eyed him cautiously. Now, it seemed, things had been turned on their head somehow. Instead of being afraid of a drunken Apache, the Mexicans seemed to feel threatened by one who did not drink. The observation only confirmed his suspicion that something was being planned.

He saw Ko-tay-nah, one of the "tame" Apaches who lived near the village. Beckoning with a crooked finger, he got up as Ko-tay-nah shambled toward him, looking back over his shoulder like a child sneaking away from camp.

Geronimo shook the man's hand, then resumed his

seat. He patted the ground beside him, but Ko-tay-nah was not eager to sit.

"I know who you are," he said.

"Good for you. And do you also know why I am here?"

"No, I don't."

"Very good. Because I don't either."

"What do you want from me?"

"You have lived here among these Mexicans for many years, am I right?"

Ko-tay-nah nodded. "Yes . . ."

"Do you trust them?"

"Of course. Why shouldn't I? For more than ten years I have lived here, and there has been no trouble. I farm, like they do. I raise my crops and trade them for the things I need. No one bothers me or my family."

"How many Apaches like you are there here in the place of the Big Houses?"

"A hundred, maybe a little more."

"And how many Mexicans?"

"Thirty times that, even forty times. I don't know exactly, why?"

"Do you think they would like you as well if there were nearly as many Apaches as there were of them?"

"I never thought about it."

"Think about it now. . . ."

Geronimo stared at him, trying to read the thoughts drifting across his face like the shadows of high clouds. Finally Ko-tay-nah shook his head. "No, I don't think they would like us as well."

Geronimo shook his head. "No, they wouldn't."

"Is that all?"

Geronimo nodded. He watched the tame Indian drift back to the crowd now looking over his shoulder at his interrogator, his face strangely inflexible, as if he were trying very hard to show no feelings.

The celebration wore on in the late afternoon. As the bottles were emptied more appeared, and still more to replace those as they were emptied, too. By sundown most of the warriors were rip-roaring drunk, as they had been the day before. The same few men who had been ordered to stay sober were again watching.

Just after sundown Geronimo saw the alcalde again, for the first time since that morning. Once more he skulked on the edge of the crowd of celebrants, talking to some men who were watching the milling Indians as they listened to him. Still, Geronimo could make nothing of the conference.

When the musicians started their racket again, Geronimo got up and walked away from the church. Without calling attention to himself, he drifted through the crowd, reached the far edge of the square, and eased away from it. Watching from the greater distance, he found it harder to point to anything amiss. But something was wrong. He just couldn't put his finger on it.

He stayed in the shadows then, deciding not to rejoin the fiesta. He would sleep again at the spring, as he had the previous night. It was better to stay away. Even if he was wrong, he was in no mood to celebrate. There was nothing *to* celebrate. Let the others have their fun, if that's what they wanted.

Chee-hash-kish was already asleep, the Colt by her outstretched hand. He curled up in his blanket and fell asleep quickly. In the distance the blare of the

music and the thunder of pounding feet could still be
faintly heard, but he was tired, and he pushed it out
of his mind.

He felt a hand on his shoulder and sat up abruptly.
"Geronimo," Chee-hash-kish said. "Wake up. I heard
something."

He was wide-awake then. He could hear it for himself even as he started to ask. Screams, yelling. Something was happening. He scrambled to his feet and
ran for his horse. He was in the saddle and kicking
his horse's flanks in one fluid motion. Charging across
the dusty flat, he could hear the screams growing
louder. There were shouts now, and gunshots, but not
many.

As he neared Casas Grandes he could see fires
burning, tall flames licking the bottom of the sky. Figures were outlined against the flames, dark shadows
like those he had seen once in a vision. But this was
no vision. As he got closer he drew the Winchester
carbine from its sling on his saddle.

Apaches were milling around, most still dead
drunk, others drugged with sleep from two days of
celebrating. Mexicans were moving methodically
through the Apache campground, some armed with
clubs and knives, others with single-shot rifles.

The drunken warriors were confused, and there
were so many Mexicans. Some tried to fight back,
hand to hand, using knives and fists, as if their weapons had been taken away. And it all came clear to
him as he charged into the slaughterhouse. The Mexicans had waited until near morning. With the gray
light, and the Apaches all deeply asleep, they had
moved among the sleeping Indians and confiscated
many of their weapons.

Now they had begun the systematic murder of the Indians, trying to take the men first, leaving the less threatening women and defenseless children for later.

He looked for Juh, but didn't see him anywhere. Some of his own warriors were in a ragged line trying to drive the Mexicans back, but they were desperately outnumbered. The firing was picking up as more Apaches came awake, and more Mexicans, soldiers and civilians both, joined the assault.

Staying in the saddle, Geronimo circled the square, calling to his warriors, trying to rally them behind him. But the attack had been a complete surprise, and they were only half-conscious of what was happening. He saw the alcalde then, standing across the square, a rifle in his hands, but not engaged in the assault. Geronimo charged toward him. He knew now what the man had been talking about, plotting with the others. This was his idea.

And he would have to pay. Geronimo roared toward him, his mount's hooves pounding on the packed earth of the square. The alcalde saw him coming and raised the rifle. But Geronimo launched himself from the saddle and drove a shoulder into the alcalde before he could raise his weapon to firing position.

Both men tumbled to the ground, the Mexican, scrawny under the powerful Apache, struggling and kicking, but unable to break free. Grabbing the alcalde's head in both of his hands, Geronimo raised the head and stared into the Mexican's eyes. The man's eyes grew huge, as if they were trying to escape from their sockets, then Geronimo gave a sharp jerk, and he heard the snap of the neckbones and the man lay

still. But Geronimo was unable to let go. Enraged by
the treachery, feeling as foolish as he accused others
of being, he continued to tug on the dead man's head,
twisting it from side to side as if he wanted to tear
it from the body. Pounding it now on the hard earth,
he smashed it with his fist again and again, feeling
the face cave in. His knuckles hurt, and his hand went
numb and still he pounded, as if he were crushing
grain.

Then his rage spent, and nothing but contempt left
of his hatred, he slammed the head into the ground
once more, as if he could throw it from him and bury
it all in a single motion, and stood up.

The Apaches were running now in every direction.
Geronimo could see the bodies of the dead. Most
looked small and feeble—women, probably, and children.

The Mexicans were chasing after the escapees, but
without much heart. Some of the warriors had roused
themselves sufficiently to organize a rearguard action, holding off their attackers while the remaining
women and children ran for their lives.

Climbing back into the saddle, Geronimo charged
across the square. He fired his rifle again and again,
seeing two men fall, and cursing the gun when it ran
out of bullets. Swinging it like a club, he charged
through the startled Mexican line from the rear,
grunting with satisfaction when the heavy stock of
the Winchester crushed a skull, then swept across his
own body and cracked into the face of a Mexican soldier who was trying to raise a pistol.

He was through the line, his back to the Mexicans,
and it seemed then as if everything froze in a single
moment. The firing stopped. The Apaches watched

him charge toward them, and when he cut through their line, they resumed firing.

He wheeled his horse then, skidded to a halt, and shouted to his men. There was still no sign of Juh. But there was no time to worry about that now. Now there was time only for flight.

He yelled to his warriors to run, then wheeled his horse and galloped toward the spring. He wanted to get Chee-hash-kish back to the stronghold. He knew that Juh and the others would regroup and work their way into the mountains. Now each man had to protect his own family.

A thin tendril of smoke wound up into the brightening sky as he neared the spring. He shouted for Chee-hash-kish to pack her things, but there was no answer.

He called once more, and when there was still no response, he dismounted to sprint toward the campsite, his Winchester ready at his waist. The fire was still there. So were the blankets. The Colt lay between them, its muzzle clogged with dirt where it had fallen barrel downward to the ground. There was no sign of Chee-hash-kish.

Bending to retrieve the pistol, he saw the boot prints. And he knew what had happened. Looking carefully at the blankets, he saw no sign of blood and was thankful for that. He had to leave now, before they found him, too.

But he would come back.

Chapter 15 ═══════════

March 1883—Lordsburg, New Mexico

FROM THE HILLTOP the ranch below looked almost like a toy. Chihuahua watched the main house through binoculars. It was a big spread, and he wanted to know what sort of opposition to expect before making his move. Beyond the large barn, its sides dull red in the gray morning light, a weathered bunkhouse made the third side of a triangle.

Looking back over his shoulder, he waved a hand. One of the men on the slope below sprinted toward him, staying in a crouch to keep his head below the ridge line. Francisco was young, but he had already demonstrated his courage on this raid across the Mexican border.

"Go to the bunkhouse," Chihuahua said. "See how many men are inside."

Francisco nodded. He started to crawl backward, but Chihuahua, his blue eyes almost the same color as the slowly brightening sky, grabbed him by the shoulder. "Don't start anything. We need to get more ammunition, not waste what we have. If there are only five or six men, signal, and we will come down. If there are more than that, come back, and we'll decide what to do."

The young warrior nodded again. He was gone almost immediately. Chihuahua watched him slip and slide down the scree-covered hillside until he reached the bottom, then creep back to the hilltop. The valley behind him swept to the north. Francisco would need several minutes to reach the end of it, then several more to work his way back into the second valley. There wasn't much cover, except for a few scattered cottonwoods along the bank of a sluggish creek winding across the valley floor behind the bunkhouse.

Even in the weak early light, Chihuahua could see the green skin of algae on the slow-moving water. It wasn't like the swift and cold streams of the mountains, but in the bottomlands any water at all was a blessing. It was always easy to find where the White Eyes had settled, because they almost never built too far from the water.

Turning again, he saw Francisco loping easily, his short, powerful legs pumping in a smooth, steady stride. He watched until Francisco disappeared behind a wall of broken rock. It was nearly ten minutes before he saw him again. Keeping low, Francisco was using the rolling contours of the uneven valley floor to stay out of sight of the house, because there was no other cover.

Occasional flashes of Francisco's red hairband signaled his progress. He was heading for the creek, intending to follow it toward the bunkhouse. The stream bed came within fifty or sixty feet of it, and the trees, although sparse, would offer more protection than the grass-covered valley floor.

Chihuahua looked back at his small band. He had only ten men, counting himself. The women and children who had come on the raid were with the main group. It had been a successful raid, so far. Ammunition was still scarce, and they needed a lot of horses. They were riding hard, and wearing out their own animals. Food, too, was hard to come by. At this time of year the game was pitifully scarce. There hadn't been much in the way of cattle, and they were subsisting mostly on the meat of the worn-out horses.

It had been nearly two weeks since they left the main band. Chatto had wanted them to stay together, but Chihuahua wasn't impressed with Chatto's abilities. He was brave, but not especially imaginative. More concerned with succeeding old Nana, Chatto seemed to be wandering aimlessly, almost like a tumbleweed, letting the wind push him wherever it felt like. The men were grumbling all the time. Some even wanted to go back to the reservation. Only their fear of punishment was keeping them out.

Neither he nor Chatto was as fiercely opposed to the White Eyes as Juh or Geronimo, but they both knew that the White Eyes were not particularly interested in distinguishing one Apache from another. Better to stay out, try to find someplace where they would be safe, and where there would be enough food to keep them from starving, if not well fed.

Francisco was at the creek now. Chihuahua watched him darting among the brush, using the cottonwoods as his primary cover. He flitted from one tree to another, the way a bee goes from flower to flower. Francisco was within seventy-five yards of the rear wall of the bunkhouse.

This would be the most dangerous part of the scout. Chihuahua couldn't tell whether the back wall of the bunkhouse had windows or not. There were two on the front, and the back, which faced north, might not have any. But if it did, Francisco might be spotted by one of the ranch hands. Judging by the sun, he knew they were almost certain to be waking up soon, but so far there had been no sign the place was even inhabited. A moment later, a puff of gray smoke ballooned above the chimney of the main house.

Someone had built a cook fire, most likely.

Chihuahua saw the headband dart out of the brush. It flashed once or twice more, bright as the wing of a red-winged blackbird against Francisco's hair. A moment later, Francisco disappeared behind the roof of the bunkhouse. Now there was nothing to do but wait.

The smoke belched steadily now from the chimney of the main house. A bright flash of light, still tinged red as the sun began to swell above the horizon, stabbed at him, and he saw a door swing open on the main house. A man in dungarees, suspenders draped over his hips, stepped onto the porch carrying a wooden pail. The sunlight flashed again as the door swung shut behind him. He stepped off the porch and crossed the yard, stopped at a pump and set the bucket down, grabbed the pump handle, and started to work it up and down.

Water, bright as liquid silver, gushed from the pump, sloshing over the sides of the pail. Chihuahua could see the ground around the pail darken with the wasted water. That was a thing about the White Eyes he could never understand. They were able to get water from the ground so easily, they didn't seem to care whether they used it well or not.

He watched the man closely, looking for some sign that he was aware of anything out of the ordinary.

But when the pail was full to overflowing, he let go of the pump, snatched at the pail, and lugged it back toward the house, more water sloshing over the sides and leaving dark brown shadows on the packed beige dirt of the yard.

The man went inside and the door closed with a bang. Blades of light, orange now as the sun climbed higher, slashed out of the cottonwood trees. Francisco was signaling. Only a few men in the bunkhouse, then. Chihuahua scrambled away from the ridge and instructed his warriors. He divided them in two, sending four men after Francisco. He kept the other five with him. As soon as the others were ready his men would sweep over the hill. Surprise should work to their advantage.

He watched the handful of men trot off, circling the far end of the hill the same way Francisco had done, then sent the others up toward the hilltop. He stayed below for a few minutes, until he could no longer see the flankers, then sprinted up the hill and dropped to the ground. Using his binoculars again, he swept the front of the bunkhouse, saw no sign of movement, then turned them on the main house again.

Still no indication of exactly how many defenders there might be, but so far they hadn't been seen, and that was all that really mattered. A place like this should yield quite a bit of ammunition. And the horses in the corral, nearly two dozen of them, would be welcome, too.

He could see the warriors darting along the creek bank now. One by one they moved ahead from cover to cover, only one exposing himself at a time. When the last man was in place, Francisco again flashed the mirror, and Chihuahua raised a hand. He took one last look at the house. When the hand fell, his men scrambled up and over the ridge line. They moved quickly and silently. There was no need of a war cry. All Chihuahua could hear was the hiss of leather soles on the sand and scree on the downslope.

Francisco's men moved out of the brush along the creek. So far neither band had been seen. Chihuahua led the way to the bunkhouse door, throwing it open and barging inside. In the dim light of a lantern it took his eyes a moment to adjust. He saw several men, too many to take in at once, but not too many to handle.

He fired the first shot, aiming at a fat man sitting on a bunk in his underwear. The ranch hands started to shout, and they scrambled for their weapons, but they never had a chance. One explosion of gunfire, its thunder deafening inside the low-ceilinged bunkhouse, killed all but one man, who dived through a rear window. Several guns cracked almost in unison out back, and Chihuahua knew Francisco's men had killed the last of the ranch hands. The warriors tore the place apart, scooping boxes of ammunition from some rough wooden shelves, then slitting the mattresses and tossing them aside, looking for anything else they could use. Two new Winchesters sat in a corner of the bunkhouse, and Chihuahua grabbed them and handed them through the window to Francisco.

Now it was time for the house.

The Apaches rushed out of the bunkhouse. Chihuahua paused just long enough to shatter the lamp on the floor. The kerosene spread across the wooden floor, its edges smoking and the flames seeming to dance an inch or two above the slick surface. He ducked out, the tang of kerosene still in his nostrils.

Francisco and his men swept around the corner and Chihuahua led the charge toward the main house. He saw a rifle poking through the front door and shouted to his warriors to be careful. So far there seemed to be only one gun in the house. The first defensive shot sailed high, the bullet whistling over Chihuahua's head.

A window to the left of the door shattered and a second gun barrel poked through, chipped the rest of the glass out of the window frame, and then hovered in the opening. Just beyond it, in the shadowy interior, the outline of a woman, head and shoulders barely visible, floated behind the rifle barrel.

The Apaches spread out and surrounded the house. Detailing Francisco to take the front, Chihuahua raced to the rear. The windows at the back of the house were all intact so far. Chihuahua charged toward the building, his eyes darting from window to window. As he drew closer a window shattered, and he heard the whine of a slug just over his head. He looked at the shattered glass, but saw no one. Moving to the right, he could see the woman again. She must have seen him and fired through the window without leaving her post at the front of the house.

So, there were only two people inside, he thought. This would be easy. He thought for a moment about torching the house, but if he wanted whatever ammunition might be inside, he'd have to hold off. Dropping to the ground, he slithered toward the house the remaining thirty-five feet or so. Turning to his warriors, he called two forward, instructing one to take either end of the house.

When the two men were in position, he jumped up, pressed his back against the wall just left of the shattered window. He could hear sporadic gunfire from the front, as if his men were trading shots with the defenders without trying to press their attack.

He leaned over, stole a look into the house. He could see the woman, still at her place by the front window. Ducking back, he moved away from the house just enough to let him raise and aim his rifle without obstruction. The woman saw him then and fired, her shot tearing a hunk of the window frame loose and ripping more glass free.

It was a near miss, but he held his ground, drawing a bead as the woman struggled to lever another round home. He could see her only dimly over his rifle sights, squeezed the trigger, and heard the startled rush of breath from her lungs as his bullet slammed into her chest. She fell back against the window behind her, and her head seemed to explode. A split second later, he heard two or three shots fired almost simultaneously by Francisco and his men.

"Emma," someone yelled, obviously the man he'd seen at the pump, probably the woman's husband. "Emmmmmaaa!" The sound rose higher in pitch, ending with a strangled moan. Furious fire erupted then, all from inside the house, as the man fired blindly, emptying his rifle without bothering to pick his targets.

The rifle was empty now, and Chihuahua charged toward the window, shielding his face with one arm as he crashed through it, landing on his shoulder and rolling. Loud gunfire then as the rancher opened up with his pistol.

Chihuahua was trying to get his gun up when he saw one of his warriors through the window behind the rancher. A single shot caught the man in the back,

and he staggered, turning to see who had shot him.
He was hit again, fell to his knees, and still tried to
bring his pistol to bear. A third bullet hit him high on
the shoulder. Chihuahua heard the crack of bone as
the bullet plowed through. The rancher dropped his
gun and fell over on his side without uttering a sound.

The Apaches poured in then, using windows and
both doors. Chihuahua stood over the rancher,
pushed him gently with one foot. The rancher rolled
onto his back, his eyes flat and unblinking. He was
old, maybe fifty. Chihuahua shook his head. This was
the part he hated most. Killing was not something he
shrank from, but it was not something he relished either. The man on the floor, his white hair splattered
with blood, his blue eyes already beginning to cloud
over, might have been a decent man. The chances
were he had never harmed anyone in his life, not
even an Apache. But war was war, and when your
enemies didn't worry about such things, you couldn't
afford to either, not if you wanted to win, or at least
keep from losing.

They searched the house quickly. One of the warriors tugged a rug aside and grunted when he saw the
oblong hatch cover. There was probably some sort
of hiding place below, but everything had happened
so fast, the rancher and his wife had not had a chance
to reach it.

Chihuahua removed the hatch, staying away from
the opening, in case anyone were below. He'd known
men who had been too eager and gotten a bullet in
the brain for their troubles. It wasn't going to happen
to him or his, if he could help it. He knew ranchers
and farmers often kept extra bullets under their
houses, both for the defense of whoever might be

forced to take shelter there and as a place for simple storage.

The hole was pitch-black. Before he would send anyone down, he wanted to make certain it was safe. He went to the fireplace and used a shovel and a poker to haul a medium-size log out of the flames. Carrying it to the hatch, he tossed it down below. There was no reaction. He peered down into the opening. He could see one wall and part of a second. The chamber was small. Circling the hatch, he checked a third wall, this one lined with shelves of raw timber. The fourth wall, like the third, was shelved. The chamber was deserted.

One brave dropped into the small room and searched the shelves by firelight. He shouted, then tossed two rifles, both fairly new Winchesters, up through the hatch. He followed the guns with a dozen boxes of shells. There was a pistol, too, a Colt .44 that took the same ammunition as the rifles.

The warrior hauled himself out of the hatch. The rest of the men had started to drift outside. They seemed almost listless, drained somehow, as if they, too, regretted what they had had to do for some reason they would not be able to explain if asked. Chihuahua knew the feeling only too well.

He was the last one out. There was a lantern on the mantel over the fireplace, and he screwed its reservoir free, spilled its contents on the floor, and then yanked another log out of the fire. Backing out, he couldn't get the sharp tang of the kerosene out of his nostrils. It stayed with him, adding to the lingering stench from the bunkhouse lantern.

Outside again, he saw that the bunkhouse was already half-consumed by flames, and thick black smoke was rising straight up in the windless morning air.

Racing back to their horses, not one of them looked back. It was as if the house and its owners had never been there and didn't matter at all. The truth was, they no longer did.

They were near the border now between the New Mexico and Arizona Territories. Mexico was to their backs. It was tempting to turn and run for the international border. They could hide in the Chiricahua Mountains for a day or two, rest and plan their trip back. But some of the braves wanted to push on to the northeast. San Carlos was only two or three days' travel, and if they could slip in unnoticed, maybe they could put the past behind them. But Chihuahua knew better.

Dodging past the west side of Stein's Peak, they were heading toward the Southern Pacific tracks. Chihuahua knew the railroad would be patrolled. The White Eyes were prisoners of their inventions. They built things that had to be watched, and it made them vulnerable. The talking wire was like that, and so was the railroad.

Ojo Caliente was to the northeast, and some of the warriors wanted to return there. It was where they had been born, and where they felt at home. But the reservation at Ojo Caliente had been closed for many years. The white soldiers knew of the attachment some Apaches felt for the land there, and there would be cavalry. There were only three choices, and Chihuahua spelled them out, knowing even as he did that his men already knew what they were. They could hook up with Chatto now, they could run for Mexico, or they could push the raid a little further north and east, crossing into New Mexico again before turning west and rejoining Chatto. There was no other option.

They were crossing the San Simon valley, not really pushing themselves, because they were too tired. They had been running hard for two weeks, never staying in one place for more than three or fours hours. Most of the braves hadn't slept the night through since they'd crossed the Mexican border.

Fort Bowie was close, too close for them to stop, even for the night. In the Apache way they voted. The men were free to do what they wanted, and a chief would have followers only so long as he continued to demonstrate that he was worth following. Chihuahua listened to the debate, declined to speak when asked his preference, and chose instead to watch the sky. Mountains sprang up on all sides, the flat, barren wasteland suddenly jagged on every horizon. The voices of the warriors droned on and on, Chihuahua losing himself in the sky and hearing the words only the way a dozing man would hear the babble of a slow-moving creek.

When the vote was concluded, Tzo-ay had decided to return to the reservation while the others agreed to continue the raid, before joining up with Chatto in the Dragoons near Cochise's old stronghold. Chihuahua had listened to the vote without changing his expression. Now that it had been concluded, he simply nodded. "All right," he said. "Two days more, then we find Chatto."

The men mumbled among themselves again. He wondered whether they were disappointed or relieved at the thought of two more days. If he had listened, he would know, but maybe it was better he hadn't. Tzo-ay climbed onto his horse, took a second mount with him, and pushed out across the flat bottomland. The others watched until he had dwindled to a speck, then finally vanished the way a spark disappears when it climbs too high in the air above a dying fire.

With Tzo-ay out of sight, they remounted and headed northeast, crossing back into New Mexico Territory. An old road ran parallel to the railroad, using the same draws and notches to slip between the mountains. Chihuahua sent two men ahead to reach the railroad and see whether any soldiers were waiting for them.

In two hours the men were back. There was no sign of soldiers, so Chihuahua pushed harder, hoping to reach the railroad just after midday. They would camp on the south side of the tracks and cross them during the night, reducing the possibility of being discovered.

Stein's Peak was to the west and south now, the railroad just a mile ahead. Chihuahua sent the same two scouts out once more and watched them dismount and climb the last rise before the railroad. The flash of a hand-held mirror told him there was still no sign of troops. This time the scouts stayed put, letting the rest of the band catch up. Chihuahua was in the lead. As he neared the spine of the hill one of the scouts backed away from the crest and sprinted downhill to meet him.

"A wagon," he said.

"Soldiers?"

"No. And no escort. Three people, one a child."

Chihuahua nodded. "All right then," he said. Turning his horse, he moved back down the hill a few yards to fill in the rest of the warriors. He watched the scouts, who stayed on the hilltop, tracking the wagon as it drew closer. Stringing his men along the side of the hill in a ragged line, he waited for the sign that the wagon was in the narrow draw on the other side, then charged up the slope, digging his heels into the sides of his exhausted mount.

He broke over the ridge and started down the far side, letting all his anxiety out in a single bloodcurdling shriek.

The man in the wagon snapped his head around so fast, Chihuahua was amazed it didn't keep on spinning till it flew off of its own accord. The rest of his warriors broke over the ridge behind him, Chihuahua leading the wedge-shaped assault. The man in the wagon handed the reins to the woman and shoved the boy down into the back as rifle fire started to crackle from the advancing Apaches.

The woman was screaming, stopping only for breath. The man knelt on the wagon seat and swung a rifle around. He fired one shot, nearly lost his balance, then levered another round into the Winchester carbine's chamber. But the wagon was rocking and bouncing, and the man was unable to aim the rifle. He fired rapidly now, hoping that a stray bullet might knock one of the Apaches out of the saddle.

Chihuahua could hear the man in the wagon as he kept shouting to the woman to drive the horses still harder. She lashed with the reins, the two-horse team bobbing and bouncing as it struggled. The wagon wheels weren't spinning smoothly, and the drag of the reluctant wheels was slowing the horses.

The man's rifle was empty, and he was trying to reload as Chihuahua reached the bottom of the slope.

He was still a hundred and fifty yards behind the
wagon when the man finished reloading. He climbed
into the wagon bed, shouting again to the woman to
push the team. He tried to brace the rifle against the
side of the wagon, but it was pitching so wildly, it
was of no use in steadying his aim.

On hands and knees, the man climbed over a pair
of trunks, shoving the small boy down out of sight
again. The Apaches were having no better luck with
their marksmanship, because all but two of their
mounts were moving downhill. The man climbed
over the tailgate of the wagon then, and dropped to
the ground. The fall stunned him for a moment, but
he recovered quickly and got to his knees. He drew
a bead and snapped off a quick shot. The horse to
Chihuahua's left stumbled, then snapped its right
front leg, pitching its rider forward, where he landed
on his back and rolled as the horse struggled to regain
its stride despite the injury. But the leg was too frail,
and the horse went down. Chihuahua bore down on
the man, who fired once more, then again. The whis-
tle of the bullets sounded close, and Chihuahua
pulled a Colt from his belt, firing rapidly as he
charged headlong toward the kneeling man.

The furious gunfire took its toll then, the man falling over on his side as Chihuahua thundered past. For
a split second the Apache saw the man looking up
at him, his eyes wide, but his face remarkably calm
under a shock of white hair. His coat was covered
with pale dust and he raised the rifle once more, one
hand clapped over a bright stain on his pale gray
vest.

The wagon was skidding now, and the horses were
struggling to keep it moving. The woman had stopped

screaming, either because she was too intent on trying to drive the team or because her throat would no
longer make a sound.

The boy in the back of the wagon lay on his stomach, his arms curled over his head as Chihuahua
drew closer.

The team shied as a warrior drew even on the right,
and the woman reached for the whip and slashed out
with it, but her aim was off, and the lash fell short
of her target. Moving toward the slope on the far side
of the draw, the horses were out of control now. The
woman couldn't stop them if she wanted to. As the
wagon started to tilt, Chihuahua saw what was coming. Higher and higher rose the right side of the
wagon, then gravity took over and it fell on its side.
A rooster tail of choking beige dust curled into the
air as the woman fell from the seat and the wagon's
contents scattered. The small boy tumbled out of the
wagon bed, landed on one of the trunks, then rolled
off.

Another gunshot caught the woman in the back as
she tried to scramble to her feet, croaking for the boy
to come to her. On all fours, she tried to claw her way
toward the boy until another bullet slammed into her
side and her hands went out from under her. She lay
there, her arms still scratching at the dirt but no
longer able to move her. "Charlie," she moaned.
"Charlie." Another shot shattered her spine, and she
lay still.

Chihuahua jumped from the saddle and handed the
reins to another warrior. He saw two of his warriors
straddling the body of the man and raced toward
them.

He saw the arc of a knife and shouted, "No!"

The knife stopped in mid-flight, its wielder's stunned face peering over one shoulder.

"No," Chihuahua said again. "He was a brave man. He tried to save his family. He deserves our respect."

The warrior glowered, but shoved his knife back into its sheath. He looked at Chihuahua a long time, looked down at the dead man, and spat, then walked away, his shoulders hunched, the tight muscles spasming in rage. But he did not turn back.

Chihuahua turned back to the wagon. The boy was unconscious, lying on his back. Chihuahua bent and hoisted the child to his feet. Holding the boy, who appeared to be about five or six years old, he walked close to the woman and knelt down. Holding the boy to his chest, he reached out to feel for a pulse, knowing there would be none under his thumb.

"What about the boy?" Francisco asked.

"We'll take him with us," Chihuahua said.

Chapter 16

April 1883—Fort Apache

GEORGE CROOK SAT behind his desk, one hand raking the biblical whiskers struggling to hang on to their color and losing. There were days when it seemed all he could manage to do was to collect rumors, sort them out, and send telegrams, telegrams to Sheridan in St. Louis, telegrams to Washington to the Indian Bureau, telegrams to San Francisco to General Sherman at the army's western headquarters.

He was sitting on a powder keg, and it seemed as if no one knew or cared. He got up from behind the desk and walked to the front door. Stepping outside, he glanced at the eastern sky, where the sun was just beginning to rise. It bled color all along the horizon, turning the heavens pale gray overhead and staining the edge of the eastern mountains a brilliant scarlet. As he watched it turned orange. He could see half the sun's globe now, already beginning to shrink to its midday size. It looked almost as if it were bleeding to death, losing size as it lost color.

Fort Apache was deathly still. The square of single-story buildings looked almost like toys in the early dawn, like something a child might build out of sticks and sand. He stepped out from under the ramada and walked to the center of the parade ground.

Looking around, he couldn't help but feel as if the camp were a monument to a misguided career. Thirty years of service, and here he was at the bottom of hell. By midday the sun would be hammering the roofs, making the ground shimmer, squeezing his eyes to slits if he wanted to see anything at all. There were times, more and more often of late, when he didn't really want to.

He reached into his duck jacket and pulled out a tobacco pouch. Rolling a cigarette with the same meticulous attention he devoted to everything he did, he made a tight cylinder, tapped both ends on the heel of his left hand, and stuck the cigarette between his thin lips.

Striking a match on the heel of one boot, he took the first puff, holding the smoke longer than usual to get the extra rush of nicotine the first of the day seemed to demand. He felt as if he had to get away, to leave it all behind. He fancied he could hear a frail little voice whispering to him, telling him to let someone else have the headaches. It was almost time, anyway, time to go home, to rest for a while.

He walked across the parade ground to the corral. The mules and horses, quartered separately to keep them from squabbling, shuffled nervously as he approached. Two hostlers were forking hay over the split-rail fence, and the animals ignored them, either uninterested or unaware that the morning's ration was being served.

He wondered where Davis was, thought about going to his quarters to rouse him. He felt close to some of his men, Bourke, Crawford, Davis, Gatewood, and to some of the Apaches, too. His had been a strange life, he thought, spent in a stranger business. He was good at it, better than anyone else, in all probability, but he found little satisfaction in the fact.

He walked beyond the confines of the parade ground and climbed up the low hill to the west. His boots crunched on the gravelly earth, hissed in mounds of sand until he reached the top of the dome-like rise. It wasn't much of a promontory, but it gave him an unobstructed view of the mountains on every side. To the north, off toward Turkey Creek, hundreds of Apaches slept in their wickiups, each a short-fused stick of dynamite ready to go off at a single spark.

Crook felt responsible for them, almost as if he had somehow robbed them of something that could not be replaced. Looking at the northern mountains, drenched in pines, the fast rivers full of silver water and glistening trout, he thought it almost paradise. Too good, some complained, for a bunch of damn savages. But it was, after all, Apache land, for hundreds of years before Cortés. How could they be blamed for wanting to hang on to it?

He thought about the rumor from the south, about a bunch of vigilantes, calling themselves the Tombstone Rangers. He knew about such men, knew that what motivated them was as much greed as it was vengeance, the latter just a gauzy veil, barely concealing the former. There was gold and copper and coal in the mountains. There was timber, and there was fertile land for farming, rich grasslands for grazing cattle. That much of it belonged to the Apaches did not sit well with men who made their fortunes at the expense of others. For such men the Apaches were an unwelcome obstacle. Rather than accepting peaceful surrender, they wanted extermination. Hunt them down to the last woman and toddler, bash out their brains, and bring home their hair to prove it.

Crook thought back to the days before the Civil War, when the Mexicans had been so desperate for relief, they had offered bounties, two hundred dollars American, for every Apache scalp. The bounty hunting still went on. He knew that, knew that some of the rancho owners in Sonora and Chihuahua paid out of their own pockets. And most of the scalp hunters were Americans, the kind of men who had ridden with Quantrill, gotten a taste for blood, and were helpless to slake that thirst, no matter how they tried.

The Tombstone Rangers weren't like that, but the net result was the same. Bloodshed, cruel and unnecessary. And the general suspected that more than a few of the Rangers were men who profited from the constant depredations of the Apache, men who sold beef and hay to the army, who subcontracted for guns and ammunition. The more trouble the better, as far as such men were concerned. If the army went home, profits went down, business went belly up like so many poisoned fish. Better to slip the Apaches a few guns here, a few bottles of whiskey there.

A handful of warriors would bolt, run for the Mexican mountains, and the army would stay another year, another wave of bloated contracts and fat profits. Bourke was down at San Carlos, trying to skin this particular rumor, but Crook was afraid there was meat and bone to this one. It had been too persistent for too long to be just another ghost story. The indictment of Tiffany was more than smoke.

Crook had spies, nearly a dozen, scattered among the bands. Davis ran them, and he ran them well. It was a dangerous business, not for Davis, but for the spies themselves. If they were discovered, if one of the more violent warriors, Chatto or Nana maybe, or Geronimo himself, were to get wind of it, the spy wouldn't last a day. Complex as Apache psychology was, the one thing an Apache didn't do was betray his kinsmen. Motive didn't matter. The best of intentions would not save such a traitor.

And the bloodshed would not stop there. There were too many unreconstructed hostiles, men who would take such treachery as confirmation that the White Eyes could not be trusted. It was already half-believed as it was. The general knew he had a very shallow reservoir of goodwill, one based as much on fear as on trust. The Apache knew him to be a man of his word. Geronimo himself had said as much. It was that word that had brought the hostiles in, but Crook wondered whether they were in to stay, and for how long.

Bourke was due back before noon. Maybe he should just go back to his office and wait for the captain to report in. Or maybe he should mount a detachment and get it moving, try to head off the trouble before it got fairly brewing. Tombstone was a long ride, and if there was anything at all to the troublesome rumors, having men on the move might save precious time, perhaps even make the difference between a nuisance and a bloodbath.

He sucked the cigarette down to its last strands of tobacco, the paper annoyingly moist and sticking to his lip, before flicking it away and watching the ember flare for a moment then die away. He didn't approve of smoking, and said as much at every opportunity. But it helped, sometimes. And it was his little secret. Only Bourke knew about it. Not even Mrs. Crook was aware, although she suspected something, and had the decency not to ask.

The sun was all the way over the edge of the world now, and the warm orange light had given way to a pale yellow, rapidly whitening and promising to make the coming day hellishly uncomfortable. He was still not used to the dramatic difference between day and night temperatures out here. He was more accustomed to the brutal siege of winter on the plains, where the temperature never rose above freezing for days at a time, and where the broiling summer days bled one into another with barely a ten-degree drop in the thermometer for a week at a time. It was far hotter in Arizona Territory, but he preferred it, almost the way Beelzebub must prefer his current address over a more celestial climate, not so much by choice, but by bowing to reality. He was reminded of the old joke about an opportunist, defined as one who, when finding himself in hot water, decides to take a bath. His adaptation to the southwest had been like that, perhaps more than he cared to admit.

He loved the austere beauty of the desert, didn't even mind the hundreds of miles he had ridden on muleback, chasing Victorio and Geronimo, Loco and Nana from one end of the uncivilized world to the other, as it sometimes seemed.

He dropped to the ground and watched the sun climb a little higher. He wondered what the great chiefs of an earlier time must have been like, Cochise and Mangas Coloradas in their prime. Bourke had been spending every free minute studying the Apache culture, such as it was, and to the extent his informants were willing to divulge it. But Johnny was more a scientist than a soldier. His own interest was more detached, less passionate, but in some ways deeper. He had made his living waging war, and every engagement convinced him more firmly than the last that knowing your enemy was half the battle and, if you were studious enough and a decent enough man, might save you a few along the way.

He had no patience for the more virulent Indian haters in the military, although his own experience had shown the army men to be more compassionate and more understanding of the red man than any politician or bureaucrat. There were do-gooders in the capital, of course. They were like a pestilence, and caused as much good as they prevented harm, but there were some vicious men as well, men who understood little about the Indian and wanted to know nothing at all. Just solve the problem, they said. As if you could solve so complex and expansive a problem by throwing money or cannonballs at it.

Crook sat down and watched the camp come alive. It was a slow process. A trooper would appear in a doorway, check the sky, then head across the open square to the mess hall. An Apache scout would drift in from outside somewhere, stop at the corral, and leave his horse. Another trooper. Another scout. The monotony of daily life was being acted out in dozens of tiny movements. Viewed from his vantage point, it was as random as watching ants scurry around an anthill. There was a purpose to it, but only an eye as practiced as the general's would pick it out.

He was tempted to roll another smoke, but remembered that his wife kept hinting that she knew he was cheating on his promise not to smoke. It was his only vice, and he thought he had a right to it, but Mrs. Crook would not be persuaded by so specious a logic as that.

Crook got to his feet and started back down the hill. His legs ached a little. They always did this early. He was getting old, and thirty years on the frontier were not helping matters. He fancied for a moment that if he listened closely, he would hear the squeak of bone on bone at hip and knee. But he had never tried, more out of fear than anything else.

By the time he reached the packed earth in front of his headquarters, Fort Apache was alive. The sun was already heating up the parade ground. As he reached for the door a centipede half a foot long scurried out from under it, raced across one boot, and evaded the vicious stamp of the other.

Inside, he went to his desk almost reluctantly. Paperwork was not his favorite thing. But it had to be done. Deep in his gut, he had the feeling he was going to be busy this afternoon. It would be better if his desk were clear, because there was a chance he might not get back to it anytime soon.

He set to work with a vengenance, scribbling page after page of reports. Everybody wanted to be informed, but nobody wanted to do anything with the information. He sometimes wondered why he bothered to be so meticulous in his reporting. It seemed almost as if the very accuracy of his reports bred a kind of paralysis, as if politicians, whether in or out of uniform, functioned better in that gray area between ignorance and knowledge, where instincts and a sense of the way things *should* be were all they had to go on. Facts were like stone walls. A bureaucrat came flush up against one and stopped in his tracks, as if it were something he'd never seen before.

Crook believed that it was that one single fact more than any other that had prolonged the Apache agony. And he blamed himself in a way a less conscientious man would not. He pushed the thought aside, and let the scratching of his pen lull him into a monotonous half sleep, where the ink flowed, the facts accumulated, and the world stopped spinning for a while as he tried to pin it down long enough to itemize its shortcomings.

When he finally scrawled his signature for the last time, Captain John Bourke stood in the doorway, a frown pinching his ordinarily open features.

"General," he said, "I'm afraid we have a problem."

Chapter 17

April 1883—Fort Apache

CROOK LAY DOWN his pen and then, thinking better of it, picked it up and stuck it into the inkpot. He fidgeted with the last few sheets of paper on the desk and, when they were straight, finally looked at Bourke. "Well . . . ?"

It wasn't exactly a question, more a vague wonderment, which hung in the air between the two men like some rare butterfly. Bourke took off his gloves and walked over to the front of the general's desk. With both gloves gripped tightly in one fist, he tapped the front edge of the huge oak slab. "Possibly one hundred men. They are well armed, but badly organized. They seem to fuel themselves with alcohol, and they are making their way toward San Carlos by fits and starts."

"These would be the Tombstone Rangers, I assume?"

"That's what they call themselves, yes. It's less a posse and more a passel of drunken vigilantes."

"But you think there's the potential for trouble, John?"

"I know there is, General. These men are whipping themselves into a frenzy. Every rumor finds a home with them, gets magnified, distorted, then cut loose to float among them, comes back transformed once more. All they can think about is Apaches, and all they can talk about is what they're going to do once they find one."

"Is there a leader, anybody we can talk to or, better yet, threaten? I'd like to find some way to head this off before anybody gets hurt."

"There are more than a few bad apples in this barrel, General. One of them you will remember well, I think. A man named Glen Sutton."

"Sutton, the scalp hunter, from Sonora?"

"That's the one."

"What in heaven's name is he doing with them?"

"I gather he's been brought in as a kind of consultant, an expert, if you will. He claims to know Apache habits inside and out. They think he's no less wonderful than manna from heaven. To hear the Rangers talk, Sutton can walk on water, and follow an Apache even while blindfolded in the dark of night."

"Presumably at new moon," Crook suggested.

Bourke laughed. "Precisely."

"What do you suggest?"

"I suggest we send a troop to head them off, turn them back if possible, and arrest them if not."

Crook leaned back in his chair. He was silent for a long time. Used to these long, reflective silences, Bourke took the opportunity to drag a chair over and set it in front of the desk. He sat down, the gloves still coiled in his fist. Absently tapping his thigh with the leather, he listened to the steady rap the way one would listen to a clock he couldn't see.

When he broke the silence, Bourke was instantly at attention. "We have no grounds to arrest them,"

Crook said. "Unless and until they break the law, we just have to permit them to continue."

It was obvious Crook wasn't happy with his hands tied. "Perhaps . . ." He let the word trail off, then started over. "Maybe we can do something, though, as long as . . ."

"General?"

"Do you think they'll fight?"

Bourke thought it over for a long time. Finally he let his breath out in a long thin sigh. "I don't know. I want to say no, but I suppose it really depends on circumstances. I do know that at the first sign of an Apache, they will either explode or turn tail. If they turn tail, it will be over immediately, with no harm done. If they explode, Arizona might be turned upside down before it is over. I don't want to think about the cost, in lives and in dollars."

Crook nodded. "There is one thing we can do. I don't know whether it will work or not. But I do know we cannot sit by and let those damned fools ruin everything we've worked so hard to build. Here's what I want you to do."

An hour later, Bourke was on his way. Behind him rode two dozen Apache scouts. None of them, not even Bourke himself, wore a single trace of his military connection. Out ahead, two of the best trackers still under color were pushing hard, trying to get as far south of San Carlos as they could before nightfall.

As a bonus, he had a recent defector, an Apache warrior named Tzo-ay, who had surrendered himself to Britton Davis. Tzo-ay—immediately rechristened "Peaches" by Davis, because of his rosy complexion, so different from the ordinary Apache duskiness—

told Davis he had been riding with Chatto and Chihuahua, had been to the hideout of Geronimo and Juh deep in the Sierra Madres, and then volunteered to be of help in any way he could, even, if General Crook wished, offering to guide troops back to the stronghold in the heart of the Mexican mountains.

It would take Bourke one, maybe two days to get within range of the Tombstone Rangers. The farther away from the agencies they were when that happened, the better for everybody. Crook had been adamant about that.

The captain was more than a little dubious, but his commitment to preserving order was no less fierce than his commander's and if anything, he was more attached to the Apaches, his early, scientific detachment having dissolved away under the corrosive influence of day-to-day reality, and been replaced, much as had the wooden hearts of the trees of the petrified forest, with something much harder. It looked almost the same, but it was tougher, more stable, more durable. It was more than respect, it was a kind of admiration for a people who had fought so long and so hard, against overwhelming odds, simply for the right to continue to live as they had always lived.

They left Fort Apache behind, cut down along the Black River, then passed by the outer fringes of the San Carlos Agency. Bourke wanted to keep as far away from the settlements of the reservation Apaches as he could. Two dozen men would not easily be overlooked. He couldn't explain what he was doing, and speculation would be even worse. If they were spotted, they might very well precipitate the very thing they were so desperate to prevent—a general outbreak of some of the most volatile warriors.

By late afternoon Bourke had made the decision to push on through the night, and rest during daylight hours. It would reduce the risk of discovery. Their pace would be considerably hampered by the darkness, but it was a sacrifice well worth making.

They were east of San Carlos, keeping to the Gila River basin. By zigzagging, they'd be able to avoid the rough country of the Pinaleno and Santa Catalina mountains, heading east between the two ranges, which funneled traffic down toward Tombstone and, beyond it, the Mexican border. It was nearly a hundred and forty miles from San Carlos to Tombstone as the crow flies. But life on the ground was considerably less direct than that. Just counting the twists and turns of the valleys would add another fifty miles or so, and if you took time for trigonometry, to figure the upslope and downslope, you might add another fifty or sixty to that.

During daylight hours, riding hard, they could do it in a day and a half. But they couldn't afford to push the mounts that hard, and Bourke knew he had to rely on the scouts to scare up the Rangers, cut their trail somewhere northeast of the Santa Catalinas. If he missed them, they had a straight shot to the reservation.

A bunch of drunken miners, no matter how fired up, didn't scare him. But Glen Sutton was another matter entirely. The man made his living by selling human scalps. He stood to gain quite a bit if the territory were to break into open warfare again. And he had nothing to lose. If Sutton had been able to work the men up beyond the point of reason, there was no telling what might happen.

Bourke had chosen Peaches as his principal scout. The young Apache missed nothing, and understood everything. With him along, there was a chance disaster could be avoided. As the sun set the scouts spread out to cover as much of the dry wash of the San Pedro as they could. They had cut back to the west again, in the flat wasteland between the Galiuro and Rincon ranges.

There was not much moon to speak of, and only the sharpest eye could pick up a sign in the near darkness. Bourke felt tense, not nervous exactly, but hypersensitive. Every nerve seemed to be on fire, ready to spark at the first input. He was conscious of his breathing, too rapid and too shallow for comfort, and he forced himself to slow down, to breathe more deeply. He felt the tension begin to drain out of him as his muscles relaxed a little. He was still alert, but it didn't feel as if a sudden movement would snap something inside him like a cheap gumband.

At sunrise they found a spring a half mile east of the San Pedro. Bourke called a halt, and they made a quick camp. The scouts were divided on whether to stay put or push on, but Bourke wanted them fresh, knew they would have to be able to think clearly and make split-second decisions once they found the Rangers. That meant rest, at least for him. He had known Apache warriors to go seventy-two hours without sleep, much of it in the saddle. But that was desperation. This was reality. Whatever they did, or failed to do, in the next two days, might very well change the course of history for reds and whites alike. John Bourke was not about to make such a decision while his eyes were propped open with toothpicks.

By sundown the men were rested, and even Bourke was itching to get back on the trail. There had been no sign from Peaches, and that wasn't encouraging. The moon was waxing, so they'd have a little more light this night. Little enough to look forward to, but you found reason for optimism where you could.

It was nearly four A.M. before Peaches rode up, his horse lathered, and his eyes bleary from lack of sleep.

"You found them?" Bourke asked, barely able to conceal his excitement.

The scout nodded. "Fifteen maybe sixteen miles."

"Camped?" Bourke asked.

"*Sí,* camped. In a small canyon."

"How many?"

"Eighty-nine."

"Is Glen Sutton one of them still?"

Peaches made a face. "Yes, he's still with them."

"Good. We'll focus on him. He's the lightning rod. If he goes, they all go. We'll just make sure he goes."

"Goes where?"

"To hell or to home, the choice is his, so long as he turns tail."

"When do you want to go?"

"As soon as you fill all the men in."

"I thought you would want to see for yourself first, before we make a plan."

Bourke shook his head. "I want to come to this one fresh. I want to improvise. I think that would be best. There's no way to figure everything that might happen, anyway. We'll just lean on them, the sooner the better, and follow their lead. Just make sure everyone understands, no shooting first. But if we're fired upon, every man should decide for himself whether to shoot back. And make sure they all know what Sutton looks like. If they have to shoot somebody, let it be him. Understand?"

Peaches studied the captain for a long time, then smiled. "I understand."

Bourke dismounted and walked off to one side while Peaches briefed his fellow scouts. Rather than watching them, as he usually did, in some almost ritualized attempt to read their minds, this time he chose to turn his back. This was, after all, a white man's thing. The Apaches were only incidental to it, and he hoped he didn't let his loathing for Sutton color everything he was about to do. He wanted to believe there was little chance of that, but he knew himself too well.

By the time Peaches had finished, it was nearly 4:30. It would take them an hour to reach the Ranger camp. It would be nearly sunup by then, the timing almost perfect.

Peaches approached, his mount following him, its reins dragging the ground. "Are you ready, Captain?" he asked.

Bourke smiled. "Are you?"

The scout nodded.

"Then I am."

"Be careful, Captain. These are strange men. They seem loco, almost."

Bourke clapped him on the shoulder. "I'll be fine. We all will. This is one we have to win; no mistakes, and no one gets hurt. All right?"

The scout looked away for a long moment. "All right," he said.

The hour's ride seemed to take forever. The scouts

were careful to make as little noise as possible, muffling the metal links of their bridles with strips of cloth and communicating only by hand signals. It was nearing six when Peaches raised a hand to signal that they were close enough to move in on foot.

Bourke listened for a moment before dismounting. He could hear a noise that sounded almost otherworldly. Dismounting, he held the reins in his hand, and it took him a few moments to realize it was singing. Drunken and tuneless, but definitely singing. He smiled. If the Rangers were in their cups, this might be quick and painless.

Peaches led the way, Bourke and the rest of the scouts fanning out behind him in a wide arc. They were heavily armed, and Bourke prayed it would not be necessary to use their weapons. There was little doubt that Sutton would be difficult to reason with, but if they were lucky, it would be over before Sutton had a chance to rally the miners behind him. And they were due for a little luck.

Peaches waved them down, and Bourke wormed his way forward, skirting a clump of mesquite and lying on his stomach beside the Apache. The scout pointed, and Bourke peered through the lifting darkness. A handful of campfires in various stages of extinction glowed dully. The singing, still loud and raucous, seemed even less coherent up close.

Bourke was getting to his feet when he heard a sudden exclamation. One of the miners had wandered away from the camp, probably to relieve himself. He stood there, backlit by the dying fires, peering into the darkness, his trousers still around his knees and held loosely in one fist. "Who's there?" he shouted, letting his pants go and bending over to grab his pistol from the ground beside him.

Before anyone could move, he started firing. Bourke and Peaches fired their own weapons into the air, and Peaches gave a bloodcurdling yell. The other scouts picked it up almost in unison, and Bourke felt the hair stand up on the back of his neck. Gunfire exploded from all over the camp, and men sprinted, stumbled, and staggered for their horses.

The gunfire was wild, and the bullets sailed harmlessly overhead, the miners firing more in terror than anger. To spur them on, the scouts fired randomly, aiming high, but not so high the terrified Rangers couldn't hear the whine of bullets just above their hats.

Ten minutes later, all that remained of the Tombstone Rangers was a half-dozen mounds of dying embers. In the first light of dawn Bourke found one miner dead, the only casualty on either side. From the look of it he had probably been hit by one of his own men, clearly an accident, since none of the Rangers seemed to be in any condition to hit anything by choice.

Looking off to the south, where a harmless cloud of dust marked the flight of the vigilante band, Bourke hoped the engagement hadn't exhausted his luck.

Chapter 18

April 1883—Willcox, Arizona Territory

THE TRAINS SEEMED to come one after another. The Southern Pacific station at Willcox was the closest rail depot to the Mexican border. General Crook had been planning for three weeks, and now he was ready to move. Supplies were pouring in from everywhere—forage for the horses and mules, ammunition for the scouts and the regular troopers, cattle cars crammed with beef on the hoof, pack mules, mounts, and crates of the hundred things an army on the move might need and couldn't afford to be without.

Tzo-ay, aka Peaches, was confident he could lead Crook back to the Apache stronghold in the Sierra Madre Mountains. But finding the hostiles was a few notches down on the general's priority list. He still did not know whether he would be permitted to cross the border. The existing treaty with Mexico allowed hot pursuit only. It was vague in defining the term, and left much to the imagination. But Washington had been adamant. Sheridan's last telegram had said simply, *Abide by the letter of the treaty's terms.*

Not exactly encouraging. Crook had tried to get a broader interpretation, first from his immediate commanding officer, then from the secretary of war. But no one wanted to shake the tree. Crook had just returned from a meeting with General Luis Torres, the governor of Sonora province. The two men had taken it upon themselves to interpret the treaty more loosely. Torres had asked only for some time to get his own troops into position to assist in the expedition, should that be necessary. Crook had agreed, hoping it would not be necessary and, more important, that it would not prove to be a hindrance.

He had made his final deployment decisions and was confident that this time nothing would prevent him from bringing hostilities to a close. He watched one more trainload of forage being stacked on wagons and hauled out of the depot. He let the gauzy curtain drop and stood with his back to the window, the bright sunlight behind him making him look to the others like a statue carved out of obsidian.

"Major Biddle," he began, "you're comfortable with the deployment?"

Biddle cleared his throat. He was not used to discussing strategy in the presence of an Apache. He glanced at Tzo-ay, who had agreed to act as a guide into the Sierra Madres, then at Mickey Free, the one-eyed translator who might as well have been Apache himself, so familiar was he with Apache culture. Crook saw the look, understood it, and set the major's mind at ease.

"Tzo-ay is indispensable to this operation, Major. There are no secrets from him. And Mickey is essential to communication."

Biddle nodded. "I'm comfortable, General. I still think you ought to consider taking more of my regulars with you."

"Out of the question. We need to move quickly. As

far as I am concerned, I would prefer to take no white troops at all, but I think that might upset the Mexicans."

"I think we have enough men to cover the border. There hasn't been anything significant since the McComas affair."

Crook moved away from the window. The change in light softened his appearance somewhat. He looked at Tzo-ay for a moment, then at Captain Bourke, the other man in the room. "That was a terrible business. I still hope we can find the boy, but . . ."

"I wouldn't count on it. He's probably dead already."

"Tzo-ay says no. He says the boy was taken back to Mexico. The Apaches often treat captured children very well, raising them as their own, as you well know. My fear is that an attack on the Apaches might expose the boy to harm."

"When do you leave, General?" Biddle asked. It was apparent he disagreed with Crook on the likely fate of little Charlie McComas, and was nervous about discussing it.

"As soon as we're done here, Major."

"Good luck, General."

Crook turned toward the window again. "I think we'll need more than luck, Major. Divine intervention might be more like it."

"I can't help you there, General."

Crook laughed, his deep baritone surprisingly mellow. "No, I don't suppose either of us has much pull with the Almighty, Jim."

Biddle rose, clearly anxious to leave. "I'd better see to my troops, General."

Crook nodded. "Fine, that will be all then, Major. I'll stay in touch by courier."

"Be careful, General."

Biddle excused himself. When he was gone, Crook turned to the Apache scout and the interpreter. "Have all the scouts been outfitted?"

Mickey Free answered. "Yes, sir, General Crook."

"Let's go then." He led the way to the door, the crisp duck pants whispering as he walked. He stopped at the door just long enough to grab his canvas-covered helmet and held the door for Bourke and the others. Out in the hallway he closed the door, let his hand linger on the knob, like a man wondering whether he had forgotten something, then shrugged.

Bourke led the way out into the brilliant sunlight. They walked toward the rail depot, moved through the teeming traffic, wagons piled high with bales of hay, and crossed the tracks. The scout troop and pack train were all ready to go. A buzz rippled through the assembled company. Crook had put together a hundred Apache scouts, and the pack train consisted of about thirty packers. There were more than two hundred mules, carrying supplies for three months. He hoped it wouldn't take that long, but once he got into the desert wastes of Sonora, food would be impossible to come by. He hated the cumbersome trains, but he used them more brilliantly than anyone in the army, and had reduced the process to a fine art, logical in its order and economical in its disposition.

An Irish private named McConnell saluted smartly, then clicked his heels, holding the reins of Crook's mule, Apache. The general took the reins, swung into the saddle, and nudged his mount with spurless heels. The mule started to move, and Bourke swung into his own saddle, commanded the column to mount, then to move out.

The first day was always the worst. Staring south, the sun burning into his eyes, Crook shook his head. What lay ahead was a stretch of the most barren and inhospitable terrain on the continent. He glanced back at the column, wondering why it was even necessary to go one more time into the Mexican wilderness. He thought about all of the lessons he had been taught by the Apaches, all the sacrifices made by so many, white and Indian alike, to guarantee a peaceful solution, and it had all come to nothing.

Five days' march brought them to San Bernardino Springs, close to the border. The springs had once watered thousands of cattle, and now the cattle were all gone. The constant warfare had depleted the ranks of the settlers and frightened away the ranchers. The Apaches had stolen thousands of head of cattle, and now the springs sat amid the lush, park-like greenery like so many blue eyes blinded by the sun and staring at a sky they mirrored but could not see.

Crook kept to himself during the five days, except for infrequent saddle-borne conferences with Bourke and Tzo-ay and Mickey Free. He seemed distracted to Bourke, and often let his attention drift elsewhere, the conference dwindling away as Crook turned his mind to something he preferred not to share, even with Bourke.

Once at the springs, he was joined by Captain Emmett Crawford, commanding another troop of Apache scouts. He now had fifty white soldiers, nearly two hundred Apache scouts, and five trains of pack mules. Among his column were the best

scouts and interpreters the territory had to offer—Al
Sieber and Sam Bowman, Mickey Free and Severiano and Archie McIntosh. If the expedition came to
naught, it would not be for lack of competence. They
were ready now, as ready as they would ever be.

Crook spent the first day establishing lines of communication with the Mexican generals. He sent a
telegram to each, advising him that the expedition
was about to cross the border. He sent telegrams to
Biddle and to Sherman and to Sheridan. Late in the
afternoon Sherman wired back, reminding him that
he was not to cross the border except in strict con-
formity with the terms of the treaty. Crook responded
with an acknowledgment before turning in for the
night.

The following morning they crossed the border.

The main column made better time than the heavily loaded pack trains. Crook decided not to push too
hard, because he wanted to keep the supplies close.
Each mule carried nearly two hundred rounds of ammunition and rations for at least sixty days. He could
ill afford to have the supplies fall into the hands of
the Apaches. And he was reluctant to have his scouts
separated from the means of sustenance and self-
defense.

The scouts were familiar with the terrain and
eased the burden somewhat by supplying their own
food. They knew every plant that managed to thrive
in the rocky draws and winding canyons. Following
the San Bernardino branch of the Bavispe River, they
were keeping pretty much to the easiest route, knowing that the Apaches would be able to find them easily and follow them without being seen. But Peaches
was convinced Geronimo would keep his people in

the mountains south of Casas Grandes, still several
days' travel.

Bourke occupied himself during the tedious eve-
nings talking with the scouts and making notes on the
plants and wildlife. The scouts were so comfortable
in the inhospitable terrain, they lived almost as they
would if there were no white man within a thousand
miles. Bourke was fascinated by the seemingly endless ability of the Indians to utilize everything around
them, even the apparently forbidding and invulnera-
ble Spanish bayonet plants, the roots of which the
scouts used to clean their hair, working a mixture of
the root pulp and water into an efficient and fragrant
lather.

Some even found the leisure to build *ta-a-chi* huts
of willow boughs thatched into small huts and covered with blankets. The Apaches dug a hole in the
center of the hut floor, filled it with heated rocks, and
constantly drenched them with water to provide a re-
laxing steam bath. Bourke tried one, squirming in
among dozens of scouts, then plunging into the swift,
cold current of the Bavispe to complete the invigorat-
ing ritual.

Everything seemed to have its use. The century
plant and mesquite, even the inner bark of the pine,
provided food. The scouts found the hives of ground
bees and pirated the honey, hunted deer in the rocky
draws and flushed game birds from the thick cane-
brakes along the riverbank. Even the cane was whit-
tled into flutes, and the scouts filled the night air with
their exotic melodies.

Flowers were everywhere, only the variety of colors matching their profusion. Hummingbirds of blue
and gold rose in clouds, giving the thick brakes a

tropical flavor. Nearing the first sizable town still inhabited, they found themselves in a depressing col-
lection of hovels called Bavispe. The people, once
they overcame their fear of the Apache scouts,
greeted them warmly and offered them the modest
hospitality their meager subsistence allowed them.
All the adobe buildings, even the church, showed
signs of age and decay.

Bourke thought they looked like a convention of
scarecrows, perched on the rotting roofs of their pa-
thetic huts. The trail led through a procession of similar hamlets, Bacerac and Huachinera smaller, even
more desolate, the towns growing more primitive as
they pushed on into the mountains.

Signs of Apache passage were now more prevalent
than the hummingbirds. Carcasses of horses and cattle, mules and deer, littered the precipitous walls
dropping away from the trail. The signs of butchery
gave mute testimony to the fact that the animals had
served their purpose and been reduced to steaks and
jerked meat. The canyons grew deeper, more desolate, and the mountains higher, their edges sharper,
a drawerful of God's cutlery, honed to butcher the
sky.

But the aridity of northern Sonora began to lose
ground. The peaks were thickly forested with pine
now, and the lower slopes covered in scrub oak. Wil-
lows, cottonwoods, and junipers filled some of the
valleys, making them difficult of passage, and offering perfect cover for Apaches bent on ambush.

Trees were flagged with useless plunder. Bolts of
calico reduced to tatters, scraps of rawhide, rusting
pots and pans—the detritus of civilization left behind
by the Chiricahua, either because they couldn't carry

it any longer or had no need for it where they were
going.

Ruined buildings, far older than Cortés, older even
than the Tarahumaras and Apaches themselves, lay
in the shadows, overgrown with vines, trees sprout-
ing inside and out, roofs long gone, both timber and
thatch. Passage was growing more difficult by the
day. Footing was almost impossible, even for the
hardy little pack mules. In one day alone, five went
off the trail and tumbled down a particularly dangerous stretch. Three broke their necks outright and the
other two had to be shot. Each such accident slowed
them a little more, as the equipment had to be re-
trieved and allocated among the surviving animals
in the train.

Every gorge, no matter how forbidding, was well
watered. Swift, cold streams, capped with white in
narrow passages, swarmed over boulders and
foamed around curves in the winding canyons. The
deeper into the mountains they went, the more insis-
tent Crook became that scouting parties search every
direction. He had not come this far to lose what he
had come to believe was his last, best chance to put
a permanent end to the Apache wars.

Trees had to be felled to let the heavily freighted
mules maneuver the narrow trails. A thousand feet
below, the Bavispe foamed toward the north. A thousand feet above them, impossible peaks, any one of
them a potential lookout for the fleeing Chiricahuas,
stretched toward the increasingly remote heavens.
They were close to the headwaters of the Bavispe
now, and Tzo-ay said they were getting close to the
ranchería where he had been camped. They had yet

to see a living Indian, but the weight of evidence that they were there was impossible to ignore.

Lieutenant Gatewood took a detachment of scouts and, along with Al Sieber, Sam Bowman, and Mickey Free, stabbed out ahead of the main column. Crook wanted the earliest word possible. Gatewood was ordered to track, but not to engage the hostiles, unless the weight of numbers was securely in his favor and rifle fire would not spook the remainder of the hostile band.

Through it all, Crook kept his own counsel. Even Bourke was unable to read his commander's mind. It seemed to the captain that Crook was almost meditative in his solitude. Except for the issue of direct orders, he said little. His face showed the strain, his cheeks thinning with wear and tear, the aging apparent even under the deepening tan.

The temperature was adding its own uncertainty to plague the expedition. During the day the thermometer climbed well into the eighties, and the nights were bitter cold, water freezing in pails and not thawing until the sun was well up in the sky. In addition to the litter they found caches now—food, cloth, tanned hides, everything necessary to sustain life. It seemed as if the Apaches were unaware that they had been tracked so deeply into the mountains. They would not have been so cavalier about their stores unless they were confident no one would find them.

And then, sweeping away below them so unexpectedly it seemed like a mirage, there it was—a broad, grassy swale, watered by a swift, broad stream of cold, clear water, surrounded on all sides by thick groves of trees. Three dozen wickiups, tucked in among the trees around the edge of the open meadow, were all that remained of Chihuahua's *ranchería*.

Crook took Bourke and Tzo-ay aside then. The Apache explained that this is where he had been living, and where Chihuahua and Chatto and Bonito had been living with their bands when he had slipped away and headed north.

Crook drew up his assault plans quickly. In conference with Gatewood, Crawford, and the other officers, he made it clear he wanted no women or children harmed. Everyone, even the hostile bucks, was to be given the chance to surrender. But if they met resistance, they were to be forceful.

The rain was over almost before it began. Apaches swarmed like drunken bees, but there was little gunfire. Most of the inhabitants were women and children. The few warriors, just enough to offer protection, put up little resistance, and that half-hearted. Most simply fled into the trees. But five women were taken prisoner.

One of them asked to see General Crook, and he complied. With Mickey Free translating, she told the general that most of the men were off on raids in Chihuahua and Sonora. She said that Chihuahua himself wanted to surrender, and so did many of the others.

"Geronimo?" Crook asked.

She shook her head. "I don't know. He doesn't believe the White Eyes will deal fairly with the Apache. But I think even he and Juh would surrender if they could be made to believe that they would not be harmed."

"Would you go to him? Tell him, and Juh, that they will not be harmed?"

She nodded. "And there are captives," she said, "mostly Mexicans. Geronimo has sent to the Mexicans, telling them he will surrender his hostages if the Mexicans will free the Apache slaves they have taken."

"Are there many captives?" Crook asked.

She shook her head. "Not so many. Ten or twelve, maybe. And the little boy, Charlie."

Crook looked at Bourke then, his face suddenly animated. "Charlie McComas," he whispered. "He's alive. . . ."

"I will bring him back if I can," she said.

Crook ordered rations for her, enough for three days. He talked to her for nearly an hour, telling her that no harm would come to any Apache who surrendered. They would be dealt with firmly, he said, and all of them would be allowed to come back to the reservation to live. "But you should tell them, too," he warned, "that they should know they cannot hide any longer. We have found them here, and the Mexicans are coming, too. Even if they choose not to surrender, they will not be left alone any longer. Not even here."

She nodded. "I understand," she said.

"You tell Geronimo that. Make sure he knows."

The woman left an hour later. The sun was starting to set, and Crook stood there watching her until she disappeared into a pine grove. Even then, flashes of color, bruised by the gathering darkness, bled through the trees for several minutes, her dress catching the last few blades of light before the sun slipped down behind the peaks.

Crook stayed up for a long time. Bourke sat with

him, but the general was subdued. "Anything wrong?" Bourke asked.

Crook sighed. "Suppose they don't believe her? What do we do then, John?"

"They'll believe her."

"But suppose they don't? Suppose they ignore everything their eyes tell them, everything they have learned from history, everything that common sense and whatever God they believe in tells them is true?"

"You sound almost as if you think they are a doomed race, as if they'll disappear like the lost tribes of Israel, or something."

"Won't they, John? Isn't that what will happen, no matter whether they surrender or not? They will vanish. If they come in, they'll be absorbed, so much water in a sponge. If they stay here, we'll have to hunt them down. Even if we don't, the Mexicans will. They *are* doomed, John, and there's nothing they or we can do about it."

"You sound almost regretful, General."

Crook didn't answer for a long time. When he finally broke the protracted silence, his voice was distant. "I suppose I am. They are so glorious a people in so many ways. They never asked for us to come here. Like the Sioux, John, they had a way of life. Who in God's name are we to tell them they have to change?"

He stood up then. Bourke tried to frame a response, but there was none that would suffice. And there was none he believed. It started to rain then, suddenly, and the wind picked up. Bourke thought there ought to be some grand flourish to the arriving storm, a clap of thunder, a slash of lightning, something biblical in its power, but there was nothing but the hiss of cold rain.

Crook walked off into the darkness toward his tent. Bourke watched the flap open briefly, the pale orange light of a lantern spill through the opening and glisten on the damp grass for a few seconds. When the light went out, he walked to his own tent and lay down.

It rained all that night, and all the next day. Despite the weather Apaches had started to drift into the bivouac in twos and threes—all ages, men and women, children barely old enough to walk on their own. By that evening the total was nearly two hundred. Crook made sure each new arrival was welcomed. Food and shelter were offered. Even the scouts, subdued either by the weather or the elegiac somberness radiated by the general himself, built wickiups in the rain, in expectation of additional arrivals.

Chihuahua came late that day. Stately, even magnificent, his long hair drenched with the continual downpour, he sat on the floor of Crook's tent. He spoke candidly, watching the general's face as Severiano interpreted phrase by phrase. He told of the hardships on the reservation, and how he wanted to be peaceful, learn to farm, and live at peace. He talked also of how he feared for the safety of his people.

"You have nothing to fear," Crook told him. "I promise you. No one will harm you or your people. I will see to it."

"Then I would like to go back out into the mountains and gather my people. I will send them back, and when I have gathered them all, we will go with you to San Carlos."

Crook listened, and when Chihuahua was done,

the general asked, "And Geronimo . . . will he surrender?"

Chihuahua shrugged. "I don't know. He has tried before, but always the treaties are broken. The promises are made on Tuesday and forgotten on Wednesday. . . ."

"Not this time," Crook said, staring at the chief. "Not this time."

Chihuahua nodded. "I will tell him. He knows Nantan Lupan does not lie. But he knows that you went away before, and everything you did for our people was undone by those who came after you."

"You tell him to come in. You tell him we should talk. And tell him, too, that we are not afraid of him."

"I know that," Chihuahua said.

"You tell him," Crook said again. "You tell him that if he does not surrender, he and his warriors will be hunted like wolves."

The two men listened to the rain hissing on the canvas walls.

Chapter 19 ═══════

May 1883—Sierra Madre Mountains, Mexico

THE RAIN CONTINUED to drench the mountains. Organizing the camp to absorb the flood of Chiricahuas became a full-time job. Crook spent much of his time talking to Chihuahua, who had already made three trips back, each time bringing several members of his band. The chief said he had spoken to Geronimo, and to Juh. Juh's band had dwindled away to a mere handful, he said. Geronimo had more warriors, but they were all tired of the warpath. They wanted to come in, but they were afraid. Loco and Nana felt the same way. So did Chatto and Nachite.

"I understand their fear," Crook said. "But I can't promise any more than I have already promised. I don't want to make a promise I can't keep, and I have already gone as far as I can go."

Chihuahua nodded slowly. "I know that, Nantan Lupan. They know that, too. But it is not an easy thing to put yourself in the hands of your enemy."

"If they surrender, we will not be enemies any longer. That's all I can say. They have to be made to understand that."

Shortly after noon of the third day, the rain finally broke. It dwindled away to a fine, sifting mist that continued for an hour or so, and then the clouds broke and the sun came out. Crook and Chihuahua left the tent, eager as children to see a new pony. Both men walked out into the center of the broad bowl of meadow and watched the clouds swirl and shrink and the blades of sunlight broaden until they were too bright to look at any longer.

"We don't appreciate the sun until it isn't there," Chihuahua said.

When Severiano translated it, Crook broke into a grin. He held his hands up toward the sun and tilted his head back to let it bathe his face. With his eyes closed, he stared through his blood-reddened lids for several seconds. "Glorious," he said, "just glorious."

He started to laugh then. He heard Chihuahua say something to Severiano, and cocked an eye toward the interpreter.

"He wants to know what is funny," Severiano said.

"Nothing. Tell him nothing is funny. It's just that it seemed for a while as if the sun would never shine again. Now that it has come back, I realize how much I missed it."

He heard Severiano's translation and lowered his face again. Chihuahua was smiling at him, then broke into a broad grin. The chief's bright blue eyes sparkled with amusement. Crook wanted to analyze the moment, then shook his head, knowing that analysis would only change the thing he sought to understand. Better to just let it be, just let it happen.

The sky was almost unbroken now, the last few dark rags slowly dissolving off toward the horizon, as if some unseen stagehand were raising the curtain for the last act. The greenery seemed almost alive with sunlight, where the drops of water trapped it and broke it into millions of rainbows swirling in the blades of grass.

"I will tell them again," Chihuahua said. "But even if they do not come in, I want to go to San Carlos and live in peace. My people also wish to go."

"And you shall," Crook said, and smiled. "I promise you."

He turned then to watch Chihuahua walk toward the new wickiups where his band had concentrated. The chief went inside, and Crook went back to his tent.

The general was exhausted. He lay on his field cot, trying to gather his energy. Sleep was out of the question. He felt as if he were close to something now, something he couldn't put his finger on, and something he couldn't see, but it kept buzzing around him, just out of reach and out of sight, like a hungry mosquito in a nighttime tent.

Someone scratched a finger on the canvas flap, and the sunlight was so piercing that Crook could see a faint shadow on the canvas, etched clearly enough that he could recognize the silhouette of Captain Bourke.

"What is it, John?"

"General, I think you ought to come out here."

Crook twisted his head, listening to the creak of his neck bones, the pop of tension forcibly released. He sat up, let his feet hit the ground, and rested his face in his hands. "I'll be right out, John."

Taking a deep breath, he got up slowly and walked to the flap, pushed it aside, and stepped out into the brilliant sunshine. "What's wrong?"

"I'm not sure anything's wrong, General, but I thought you'd want to see this." Bourke pointed toward a high, almost sheer cliff, nearly a mile away. Crook winced as he looked up, then, shielding his eyes with his hands, scrutinized the wall.

"On the rim," Bourke coached.

Shifting his gaze higher, he traced the ragged lip of the mountain wall. He was nearly halfway across when he saw what Bourke wanted him to see. There, in stark outline against the sun-bleached blue of the sky, two men, Apaches beyond question, stood very near the lip of the rock face.

"They wanted to be seen, there's no doubt about that," Crook said.

"What do you think it means?"

Crook shook his head. "I wish I knew, John. But I'll tell you what it doesn't mean. They don't intend to attack us, that much you can count on. If they wanted to attack, we would never know they were there until the first shot had been fired."

As the general watched, another figure appeared, then two more. They continued to materialize out of thin air in pairs and threes until the count reached nearly thirty. Crook raised a hand and waved vigorously, but the silent Apaches made no response.

Crook ducked back into his tent and reappeared with a pair of binoculars. He started from the left, sweeping the glasses slowly along the rim until he'd seen them all. "I can't see clearly, John, but if I had to bet, I'd swear one of those rascals is Geronimo himself."

"Are you sure?"

Crook shook his head. "No, but pretty damn near."

Crook seldom swore, and Bourke realized the general was far more certain than he was letting on.

"What do you want to do about it?"

"I don't think we ought to do anything. If we move too quickly, they might spook. They're there for some reason. In their own good time I'm sure they'll show us what it is."

Word of the apparition spread quickly through the camp. The scouts drifted out into the open and stood in groups of half a dozen. Their excited chatter buzzed incessantly as they took turns pointing and guessing what the warriors wanted.

The women and children came into the open now, too, the latter running and playing for the first time since their arrival. The mood of the camp had changed abruptly, more suddenly even than when the storm had broken. Crook waved again, and again got no response.

"Maybe we should gather the officers and get Sieber and McIntosh in here. Maybe they can tell us something."

"No," Crook said, shaking his head. "I don't want them to get the wrong idea. If we break our routine, they might. I don't want them to think we're in the least nervous. Get Gatewood and Sieber. Tell them to spread the word that we continue as we have been."

Bourke looked doubtful. The general was about to explain his reasoning when a shout went up from the far edge of the meadow. Crook started walking in that direction, Bourke at his elbow. The crowd of women and scouts began to part, and suddenly, like Moses crossing the Red Sea, Chihuahua strode through the milling throng.

He spotted Crook and changed direction. The general moved more quickly, meeting Chihuahua almost in the center of the grassy bowl.

With a broad smile Chihuahua reached out to take Crook's hand. Crook signaled for Mickey Free, who was standing on the edge of the crowd, a curious look on his face. Mickey sprinted over.

"You saw?" Chihuahua asked. He started to point, then thought better of it.

"I saw," Crook said. "What does it mean?"

"It means they want to surrender, but they are worried."

"Will they come down?"

Chihuahua switched to Spanish. *"Quien sabe?"* he said.

"We'll wait then," Crook said. "But we can't wait too long. We're running short of rations. And it's a long way back."

"We can help," Chihuahua said. "There is much mescal we can gather. There are deer, turkeys, rabbits, pinole."

"Fish?" Bourke suggested.

Chihuahua wrinkled his nose. "No fish . . . Apaches don't eat fish. Nothing that lives in water. But there is plenty of food."

"We'll wait as long as we can." Turning to Bourke, the general said, "John, work with the chief, please. Organize foraging and hunting parties."

"The women will jerk the meat," Chihuahua said. He started to turn, then stopped. Tilting his head, he looked at Crook closely. "Geronimo wants to know why you have not taken our guns away."

It was Crook's turn to smile. "You tell him it is because we are not afraid. And tell him, too, that if the Mexicans find us, you will need them."

When the sun set, the Apaches were still there on the high wall, motionless as statues. The novelty had

worn off, and Bourke and Chihuahua had given so
many orders, there was little time for the curious,
white and Apache alike, to stand and gawk. Bourke
wondered whether that might not have been part of
Crook's reasoning, since too much idle curiosity
might lead to a slip. They were so close now, and the
thought of it all coming apart was like a Damoclean
sword hanging by the slenderest of threads.

The mood of the camp was almost jubilant. Huge
bonfires burned in several places, and the constant
thunder of drums made sleep impossible. Crook
watched the dancing with a certain detachment. He
knew that peace, while possible, was anything but
secure. The scouts mingled freely with the warriors,
some of whom were still drifting in. The mutual suspicion that often marred relations between the hostiles
and the scouts seemed to have been put aside, at
least for the moment. Every new arrival was greeted
with a cheer, as if some long-lost brother had returned from the dead.

As the celebration continued through the night
Crook retired to his tent, but made no attempt to
sleep. Instead, he lay on his cot, a Bible open beside
him. From time to time he would flip through the well-
thumbed pages, read a few lines, then set the Good
Book down again to meditate on what he had just
read.

At four o'clock Bourke poked his head into the tent.
The captain had been scribbling in his journal for
several hours, sitting on the edge of a circle of jubilant dancers. Several of the warriors stopped to
watch him, and each time the captain would ask a
few questions, Severiano interpreting for him when

the warrior's Spanish was less than fluent and he had no English.

The natural reserve of the Apaches about their culture and their religion seemed to have been shelved for the time being. It put Bourke in mind of the Lupercal or the Saturnalia, those Roman feasts when all rules were temporarily suspended. The warriors answered freely and with more than a little pride. It seemed almost as if they suspected Bourke could somehow manage to save a way of life that was besieged on every side. Bourke himself wondered how much longer the way of life he was anatomizing, at such length and from such short range, would manage to survive. Even some of the warriors seemed to sense the peril, their answers often given in somber tones more appropriate to a eulogy.

Now, his fingers cramped and nearly numb, he had to put aside his pen. Crook waved him in, and Bourke collapsed with a sigh into a canvas-backed folding camp chair.

"It'll be light soon," Bourke said.

Crook nodded. "Yes. But then what?"

"You think Geronimo'll come in, General?"

"I hope to God he does. What do you think?"

Bourke didn't answer, and Crook leaned toward him. The captain was asleep. Crook got up from his cot, snatched a blanket from its foot, and draped it over his adjutant. Sitting back down on the cot, he watched Bourke with a mixture of fondness and envy. He wished he could sleep himself, but there was a knot in his gut the size of an apple. He folded his hands across his stomach and pressed them hard against its wall, massaging it with his fingertips. He leaned back and closed his eyes.

Staring at the canvas ceiling of the tent, he watched the daylight slowly rise behind it. The drumming continued, as it had all night long. It was so much a part of the fabric of the camp's life now that he had forgotten it. When the light grew so bright that he knew the sun must have risen above the eastern mountains, Crook got up and walked outside.

He didn't need binoculars to see that the rim of the mountain wall had been deserted. It could mean only two things, one of which he couldn't bear to consider. The other, the one he hoped and prayed would be the case, was that Chihuahua was right, that Geronimo would come in at least to talk. If the war chief had decided that it was better to die fighting in the mountains, the entire expedition would have been a waste. No matter how many of the Chiricahuas surrendered, if one man of stature remained on the warpath, others would follow sooner or later. Crook's only hope of keeping the control he needed was in ensuring that there would be no depredations on U.S. soil. If he couldn't deliver on that promise, then abuses might eventually drive others to flee San Carlos and head back into the mountains. There would be an endless cycle of violence.

Standing there, the unused glasses held in his hand as if he had been struck suddenly motionless, Crook watched the rimrock. The camp was quiet. If he didn't know better, he'd think it had been deserted. Only the tight little coils of smoke spiraling through the smoke holes in the wickiups suggested otherwise.

He saw the man then, across the camp, on the edge of the stand of pines. The trees stabbed up, their green almost gray against the lighter rock. The solitary Indian, his red headband holding thick black locks in place, was watching him. "Geronimo . . ." Crook whispered. He wondered if it could be. It was tempting to use the glasses, but he decided against it, knowing the Apaches were proud of their eyesight and not wishing to appear too dependent on the binoculars.

The man started to move then, his powerful legs looking almost frail under the massive torso. Broad shoulders sporting two cartridge belts, *bandido* style, the warrior walked toward him in a smooth, almost fluid movement.

As the warrior drew closer all doubt was dispelled. It was Geronimo. Bourke stood behind him, his breath short, shallow, raspy as a distant saw in the forest. "It's he, isn't it, General?" Bourke whispered.

"None other, John. This is it. We make it work now, or it's back to square one."

Geronimo closed the gap. Crook could see heads peeking out of the nearer wickiups. All of them had their entrances facing east, toward the rising sun, and faces peered out of the shadows, the Apaches staying back from the entrances, but able to see Crook and Bourke and, as he covered the last hundred yards, Geronimo himself.

The great war chief lengthened his stride the last twenty yards, stopping directly in front of the general. He put out a hand and took Crook's firmly in his grasp. He shook the hand several times.

Realizing there was no interpreter present, Geronimo spoke in Spanish, which Bourke spoke well and in which Crook was conversant, although not fluent.

"Buenos días, Nantan Lupan."

"Buenos días, Geronimo."

The Apache nodded his head, then grunted. "I was

a long way from here, a hundred miles or more. I have come a long way to see you."

Crook nodded. "Come inside," he said.

Geronimo shook his head. "No. Not yet. I wish to negotiate with you."

Crook shook his head again. "No negotiation," he said. "You must surrender. It cannot be any other way."

Geronimo tilted his head back. His face seemed to be struggling to rearrange its parts, as if he could barely restrain his anger. "I have much to do. Even now I am talking to the Mexicans. We hold some of their people and we wish to exchange them for some of our own people. My own wife is a captive of the Mexicans. I cannot surrender."

"You must."

"I will think about it." He turned then and walked away, not bothering to look back.

"I'll be waiting for you," Crook called. He watched the Apache cross the open ground, pass among the wickiups, then vanish into the pines.

"What do you think, General?" Bourke's voice was still low, as if he feared he would be overheard.

Crook turned to look at him for the first time. "I think we have to be firm. If he senses the least weakness, we'll lose him. He has to be convinced that he can't win, and that we will stay here until he knows it's all over."

"I'm not sure we can win, if it comes to that, General. We're outnumbered. I think the scouts will stay loyal, but . . ."

"I'm not sure, either, John. They hold the high ground. And we don't even know how many warriors he has. Chihuahua's people want to surrender, but if it comes to a shooting war, they'll have to choose sides. I wouldn't want to guess which way they'll go."

Crook went back inside. He was painfully aware of the tenuous nature of the peace he had managed to shape. But Geronimo was a lit fuse. If the angry Apaches rallied around him, it was possible no one would get out of the mountains alive. The scouts were formidable soldiers, but if they remained neutral or chose to side with their own people, nothing could save the expedition.

Sitting on the camp cot, Crook reached for his log, an inkpot, and a pen. He hated to write a report when things were so much up in the air, but he thought that attempting to describe the predicament might give him some insight. Maybe he was too close to things. Sitting back and reflecting on it, trying to shape it for the page, might let him see things from another angle.

He used some loose sheets of paper to begin a draft. The scratching of the nib on the paper filled the tent. Words filled the sheets of paper, and he found himself striking nearly half of what he had written. Twice he started over, balling the paper and tossing the rejected drafts into a corner, where they accumulated like drifting snow.

He had still not found a way to begin when Chihuahua and Bourke stepped into the tent.

Crook was startled and looked up with some embarrassment. "I didn't hear you coming," he said.

"Geronimo's back," Bourke told him.

"Does he want to surrender?" He directed the question at his adjutant, but watched Chihuahua's face.

Bourke shrugged. "I don't know. Maybe."

Crook put the ledger and inkpot aside, grateful for the interruption. He went outside, followed by the other two men. Geronimo was standing with his back to the tent, about fifty yards away.

"Get Mickey Free," Crook snapped.

Bourke went in search of the interpreter, and Crook moved forward, his stride reflecting a boldness he did not feel.

Geronimo turned when Crook was ten feet away. Once more he shook the general's hand. *"Buenos días,"* the Apache said.

"Buenos días." Crook waited for Geronimo to make the first move. He wanted the Apache to feel the pressure, to know that the decision lay in his own hands, no matter which way he went.

Crook saw Free and Bourke racing across the meadow, their legs kicking high to get through the tall grass. When the interpreter arrived, Geronimo looked at him with contempt, but said nothing.

Crook nodded to Mickey. "Tell him we are ready to talk whenever he is."

The interpreter relayed the message, then translated Geronimo's response. "I am ready to talk."

"Good," Crook said.

Geronimo stared at Crook, never letting his eyes wander, even for an instant. It seemed to the general that the war chief didn't even blink, even though he knew that wasn't possible. "In Arizona the Americans say many bad things about us. They want to arrest us, they want to hang us. I cannot bring my people back if they are going to be arrested."

"They won't be harmed. If you surrender to us, I will personally guarantee that no charges will be brought. Nothing like that will happen. You can go to the reservation and learn the new ways. You can learn to raise crops and cattle. You can make a living without having to raid."

"Suppose Nantan Lupan goes away again. What happens to the Apache then?"

"Nothing. I will see to it. The Great Father in Washington wants the war to end. He does not want to punish anyone. He understands that there was wrong on both sides. All he wants is for the killing to end and his Apache brothers to learn new ways."

"We have tried the new ways before. But always the agents steal from us. They sell our food to white men and say we received it. They make us move our homes. They make us stay at San Carlos, where the air is bad and our children get sick and die."

"You won't have to stay at San Carlos. I have already allowed other Apaches to live where they want on the reservation. And I have made it clear that no white men will be allowed to come in and cut the forest or dig in the ground. It is your land. As long as you stay on it, as long as you want it, no one will take it away from you. You can keep your weapons. You can hunt game to help feed yourselves. The new agent is a good man. He is not like Tiffany. He does not steal from the Apaches. You can ask the others. Ask the scouts. You know they will tell you the truth, because they are not afraid of you. I am not afraid of you either. I respect you and want only a good life for you and your people. But if you do not surrender, you will be hunted like wolves until the last Apache is gone. I don't want that to happen. It is up to you."

Geronimo thought long and hard. Crook knew he had offered a proud man a difficult choice. He didn't know what Geronimo would do, any more than he knew what he would do if he found himself confronted with the same choice.

"I will ask questions," Geronimo said. "I will talk to the scouts and then I will talk to my people."

"Time is running out, Geronimo. The Mexicans are getting closer. Soon we will have enough food for the trip north. All of Chihuahua's people will be in in a day or so. If you have not made up your mind by tomorrow morning, we will leave without you."

Geronimo nodded. "I understand," he said, then turned and walked away.

The general went back into his tent, snatched a camp stool, and carted it outside. Crook moved into the shade of a tall willow, accompanied by Mickey Free. He set the stool against the tree and sat down. Mickey Free sat beside him, his legs folded under him. Crook could see Geronimo moving among the wickiups, talking to some of the warriors. For nearly an hour the war chief moved among the Apaches, scouts, and warriors alike. It was the longest hour of Crook's life. Then he watched as Geronimo moved through the wickiups and into the trees beyond them.

Old Nana showed up a half hour later, with fewer than a dozen warriors. The ancient chief, suffering from rheumatism but still managing to lead his warriors with more courage than much younger men, expressed his desire to surrender. Crook accepted readily, knowing that every chief who came in would make Geronimo's situation look more futile.

Loco came in a short while later and, as Crook expected, expressed his own desire to live in peace with the whites. He had more warriors than Nana, more than anyone but Geronimo and possibly Ka-ya-ten-nae, a young malcontent who had slowly been building a following among the firebrands, but Crook wasn't sure the latter was willing to surrender. He had made an appearance at the camp, but slipped away before anyone could find out what he was thinking. Alone of all the principal warriors, Ka-ya-ten-nae had never been on the reservation. It was possible he would throw in with Geronimo, and that might be enough to tip the scales away from peace, depending on how many followers Ka-ya-ten-nae had.

Two hours later, accompanied by Nachite, Chatto, and Mangus, and lurking in the background like a hungry wolf pacing just beyond the reach of a campfire, Geronimo was back.

He walked straight to Crook, still sitting on the stool under the shade of a willow, and took the general's hand once more. "I surrender to you," he said. "But you must wait one week so that I can get all my people in. And we want to finish the business with the Mexicans, giving their people back and getting our people."

"I can't do that, Geronimo. The Mexicans won't permit it, and my own superiors will be angry with me as it is. We must leave tomorrow."

"Will you let us come behind you? We can get our people together and we will catch up to you before you reach the border."

Crook thought it over. Letting Geronimo know that he was trusted might not be a bad idea. But if Geronimo took the permission as a sign of weakness, it might undo everything that had been achieved. "What about Juh?" he asked.

"Juh will not come. But he has only three or four warriors. They want to stay here in the mountains."

"We can work something out then," Crook said.

Geronimo nodded, then stepped forward and embraced the startled general. "I want to be good. I will try to be good. I will be good. I surrender to you."

Crook, not knowing what else to do, returned the embrace. Geronimo then held him at arm's length. Peering deep into the general's eyes, he asked, "Can you give us some writing that will say we have surrendered? That way the Mexicans and the White Eyes in Arizona will know we are not on the warpath."

"You mean safe-conduct passes?" Mickey Free translated, and Geronimo nodded his head vigorously.

"Yes, passes . . ."

"No, I can't do that. They won't mean anything in Mexico anyway, and we will meet you at the border if you haven't caught up to us by then."

Geronimo looked crestfallen, but kept his hands on Crook's shoulders. "As you say," he said.

Crook stared past the chief for a long moment. Kaya-ten-nae was staring back at him, his face as void of emotion as any the general had ever seen.

Chapter 20

THE COLUMN THREW up a cloud of dust that hung in the air for hours behind it, spreading out like a pall of beige smoke. Hundreds of men, women, and children, the latter on mules and horseback, the old and the infirm, too, drooping in their saddles. So far there had been no sign of Geronimo and his followers. Crook was getting worried, but he tried not to let it show.

As the caravan crossed into Arizona Territory it was greeted by another detachment of scouts under the command of Britton Davis, and two cavalry troops under the command of Major Biddle. The major looked relieved to see his commanding officer. Crook greeted him with a firm grip of his sun-darkened hand, the skin like old parchment from the harsh Mexican sun.

"We were getting concerned, General," Biddle said. "The newspapers have—"

"Don't tell me about the damned newspapers, Major. Those vultures are almost as bad as the drunken miners who read them."

"But they're saying you were wiped out—worse than Custer, they say."

224

"So much for the accuracy of their reporting, Major." Turning in the saddle, he swept a hand across the horizon. "Let's get these people home, shall we?"

Biddle nodded. "You probably want to rest overnight. We can leave in the morning."

"That'll be fine."

Looking past the general at the vanguard of the column, Biddle asked, "Geronimo there?"

Crook shook his head. "No, Major, he's not."

"But you did find him . . . ?"

"Oh yes, I found him, all right. He'll be along later."

Biddle looked confused. "Later?"

Crook was on the verge of losing his patience. His own ambivalence about the decision to trust the volatile chief was gnawing at him from the inside. Biddle's persistence was scraping away from the outside. Finally, the boiler worn to the thinness of an onion skin, the pressure exploded. "Jesus Christ, Major! Don't you know what later means? Is that too abstruse a term for you?"

Biddle leaned back in the saddle, stunned by the uncharacteristic severity of Crook's response. "I just meant . . ."

"I know what you meant, damnit! He'll be along later. I'll explain when we get to San Carlos. Let's move out!"

"I take it you changed your mind about laying over?"

Crook sighed. "Yes, Major Biddle, I changed my mind. I'm sorry, it's been a long campaign. I'm afraid I'm just a little touchy."

"Yes, sir." Biddle saluted, then wheeled his mount. He took command of his cavalry units, then ordered

Davis to wait for the column and bring up the rear.
In fifteen minutes they were on the move, a giant,
dusty snake suddenly twice its former size.

Despite the rumors and the angry agitation of the
newspapers, the rest of the march was uneventful.
Talk was cheap and whiskey only slightly more expensive, but for once the volatile mix failed to reach
the point of combustion. Here and there along the
way, small groups of settlers, miners, small ranch
owners, and the rest of Arizona Territory's motley
citizenry turned out to watch the column pass. But
nothing more violent than the shake of a clenched fist
impeded their progress. By the end of June they were
back at the agency in San Carlos.

There was a good deal to do, getting the Chiricahuas settled on the reservation again, but in the back
of Crook's mind was the promise of Geronimo. As the
new arrivals settled in, established their camps, and
were assigned numbers for rationing and roll taking,
the absence of the most pivotal of all Apache chiefs
hung in the air like an invisible cloud.

Crook was aware of a simmering discontent. The
Apache tribes did not get along with one another particularly well, despite marriage customs that sent a
man to live with his wife's people. It was a rule that
made for confusion, since most warriors had more
than one wife, not always from the same tribe. The
Warm Springs Apaches were generally inclined,
probably due to Loco's influence, toward peace. The
Tonto and White Mountain groups less so, and most
of the smaller tribes were strung out across a broad
spectrum, with the Chiricahua, the most warlike, at
the opposite end from the Warm Springs.

With the infusion of the Chiricahua, the temperature of the great caldron of San Carlos climbed several degrees. They were not popular with the other Apaches, some of whom remembered the old days of wars fought and families lost, while others blamed the Chiricahua for the restraints imposed on every Apache. Added to the intertribal animosity was the long-standing resentment of abuses suffered by all Apaches at the hands of the seemingly endless parade of malefactors who sported the title "Agent," often for only a few months at a time before lining their pockets and riding off into the sunset.

There were some exceptions. Vincent Collyer had been exemplary during his tenure near the end of Crook's first tour. But those who came after Collyer had undone his work and abused their position to such a degree that Crook was convinced the thievery had led to the repeated breakouts of the late seventies.

Others had been honest, but bullheaded, like John Clum, whose insistence that all Apaches be concentrated in one place had caused the removal of the Warm Springs band from Ojo Caliente and the Chiricahua from their separate reserve in the Chiricahua Mountains. Clum was arrogant, if well-meaning, and his arrogance had caused nothing but trouble. But Tiffany was the worst by a country mile, and Crook waited anxiously to see what would be done by the grand jury currently looking into abuses under Tiffany's administration of San Carlos. The general didn't expect much, because one fox seldom indicted another for raiding the henhouse, but hope was reputed to spring eternal. Maybe it would send up a few shoots this time.

Crook knew it was pointless to hope for civilian redress of Apache grievances. Better to set things right himself, if he could, and he had gotten all the backing he needed from General Sherman and from Secretary Lincoln. But he couldn't do it all by himself. He needed men he could trust and, more important, men he knew the Apaches could trust. That was almost as difficult a search as that of Diogenes, groping through the murk with his solitary lamp.

September 1883—San Carlos Agency

George Crook put down his pen. The young lieutenant stood nervously, his feet scraping the floor. Crook looked at him. "Lieutenant," he said, "I think you and I should have a talk."

"Yes, sir. What about?"

"I understand you're concerned about a few things here. About the way the Apaches are being dealt with. Is that right?"

Lieutenant Britton Davis nodded. "That's right, General."

"Have a seat, Lieutenant. You seem nervous."

"I suppose I am. A little . . ." He scraped a rough-hewn chair across the wooden floor and sat down.

"Why don't you tell me what's on your mind? We probably should have had this talk before, but there has been so much to do, and either one or the other of us has been away. Sometimes both of us. But I've been favorably impressed with what I've seen. You've handled the scouts well, and the Indians seem to respect you."

Davis shrugged. "I try to be fair."

"I know you do, Lieutenant. So tell me what's on your mind."

Davis twisted his head, trying to relax the knot across the back of his broad shoulders. He was used to important men. His father had been governor of Texas, and high-level meetings with bigwigs were nothing new. But he had never been on the spot before. All his experience had been as an observer. And General George Crook was not just a run-of-the-mill army officer. Davis took a deep breath. "To begin with, General, I think the Apaches have been getting short weight. I've been watching the ration distribution when I could, and I have the feeling that something's wrong, but—"

"Are you referring to Mr. Wilcox or to his predecessor, a man who shall remain nameless, lest I lose my temper?"

"Well, it started under Tiff—under the last agent. I don't think Mr. Wilcox is responsible, but I have the feeling the scales are off, not by accident, and not just a little. Especially the scale used for the beef rations."

"What do you propose to do about that, Lieutenant?"

Davis cleared his throat. "Well, General, I guess we could get some weights and calibrate the scales, but out here . . ."

"I think that can be handled, Lieutenant. Use my name. If you have any trouble, let me know. The quartermaster at Prescott might have what you need. You have my permission for a temporary requisition."

"Yes, sir."

"And let me know what you find, Lieutenant."

"Yes, sir, I will."

"What else, Mr. Davis?"

"I think maybe it would be useful if we had some form of intelligence from the Indians. They're scattered all over the place, and it's hard to know what's going on."

"You disapprove of my decision to let them live away from the agency?"

"No, sir, I . . . that is, I think that's fine. But since the worst of the hostiles have come in—except for Geronimo—Chatto, Chihuahua, even that old man, Nana, who must be damn near seventy—"

"Actually, he's closer to ninety, Lieutenant."

"Jesus!"

"And as recently as this past summer he was riding ninety to a hundred miles a day, raiding with Geronimo all over Sonora and Chihuahua."

"That I knew, General, but—"

"But I'll tell you what I think should be done, Lieutenant," Crook interrupted. "I agree we need some sort of intelligence service—spies, if you will—enlisted from among the Apaches, men and women both, people who can be trusted."

"It'll be hard, General. I think it would be dangerous work. The Apaches aren't likely to be too happy with their own people reporting on them. They're tough on the scouts sometimes. This? I don't know. . . ."

"Well, I think we should try. But I think I need a special kind of officer to handle it. What do you think?"

"It would have to be someone the Apaches trust. Someone they know they can rely on to protect them."

"I agree. And I think you should start right after you tend to the problem of the scale."

Davis gulped. "Me, sir?"

"You, sir."

"But . . ."

Crook smiled and shook his head. "You're perfect for it, Lieutenant. I have a few ideas, but I think it should be your baby. And you might consider talking to some of the leaders among the hostiles as possible additions to your scouts. Chatto, maybe Chihuahua."

"There is another man, General, a young warrior named Ka-ya-ten-nae."

Crook nodded. "I know him. What about him?"

Davis ran a hand across his lips while he tried to frame his reply. "I think he's . . . well, let's just say I think he could be trouble. He's surly as hell, and I think he has the potential to be a real troublemaker. He's never been on the reservation before, and I don't think he likes it."

"Why not turn that to your advantage, Mr. Davis?"

"Sir?"

"Make him a scout. Make him a sergeant, if you want. At least get him on your side. And give him an outlet for his energy. One thing we tend to overlook in dealing with the Apaches, Lieutenant, is that these men are used to going where they want to go and doing what they want to do. They have pride. Their dignity is immense, but it suffers here on the reservation. They feel as if they've been emasculated. It's not unlike my own situation. Often I know what ought to be done, but I have orders to the contrary, from some bureaucrat in Washington who has never been west of the Ohio. He tells me what I should do, and because he has the authority, I have to do it. I hate it, I resent it, and I get annoyed, even angry. That's what life is like for many of these warriors. Some of them adapt, like Loco has. Some have more trouble, like Chihuahua, and some, like Geronimo, are so full of resentment, they may *never* adapt. Maybe Ka-ya-ten-nae is like that. Maybe you can save him from himself, give him something to do so he feels useful, like his life has some purpose."

"I'll try, General, but it might be too little, too late."

"We'll cross that bridge when we come to it, Lieutenant. I also have some other changes I want to make. I think it would be beneficial if we had a tribal court, let the Apaches sit in judgment on the conduct of their people, instead of having some White Eyes judge decide what's acceptable conduct and what isn't. We can't expect these people to understand and accept our laws overnight, but we can help them to understand how it ought to be. If we give them the responsibility, I think they'll learn to handle it."

"You're asking a lot, General. It just might be too much for . . ." He hesitated.

"Savages, Lieutenant?"

"No, sir. I wasn't going to say that. I've seen some savages here, General, but they've had white skins, not red. I'm not sure of the words, but the idea is right here." He rapped his forehead sharply. The sound of knuckles on the skull bone was like the thump of a ripe melon. "I guess what I mean is the Apaches are not sophisticated in our ways. It will take some time."

"You're right, but the time is now. The longer we wait, the longer it will take to make them learn. I think something like a council of chiefs will do very nicely in that area. I think Loco would be amenable, and Chihuahua, maybe even old Nana. But there are plenty of candidates. Think about it, and we'll talk again. The sooner the better. With Geronimo still out, I'm afraid another breakout is possible at any moment. If we can show the Apaches we respect them, they just might resist the urge to run off again."

"Yes, sir."

"In the meantime, Mr. Davis, you get those weights over here from Prescott. And I want to know what you find."

"Yes, sir. I'll keep you posted."

"One more thing, Lieutenant . . ."

"Sir?"

"I think it would be useful if you moved your quarters to Turkey Creek."

Davis swallowed hard. "With the Chiricahuas, General?"

"With the Chiricahuas, Lieutenant."

"When, sir?"

"Now."

"Yes, sir."

"That'll be all, Lieutenant."

Davis saluted, did a crisp about-face, and walked out into the bright sunshine. Something significant had just happened, but he wasn't quite sure he understood what it was. One conclusion was unavoidable, however. Crook had just handed him the opportunity to test his own judgment. He hoped he was up to it.

The fabric of Apache–white relations was a complicated tapestry, a web of Gordian knots. But no Alexander was on the horizon . . . unless it was Crook himself. It would be an interesting few months, and that was for certain. Davis felt excited—and frightened. On the way over to the telegraph shack he kept turning the situation this way and that, a jeweler appraising a raw gem, trying to see where the flaws were.

By the time he entered the shack, he tried to push

it all aside and concentrate on the business at hand. One day at a time, he thought, that was the only way to get through it all. He walked to the telegrapher's desk, waited for the corporal at the key to finish transcribing a telegram, then asked for some blank paper and a pencil.

After scribbling his message to the quartermaster at Fort Whipple in Prescott, he shoved it across the desk and waited for the key man to read it "Clear?" he asked.

The corporal nodded. "Yes, sir."

"I'll wait for a reply." He sat down on a rickety bench in one corner, watched the dexterous fingers of the key man rap out the message then lean back, pencil in hand, ready to record the response. It wasn't long in coming. He read it with satisfaction, not unmixed with a certain amount of trepidation. But it was good news. The weights would be there in two days.

Back outside, he saw a small group of warriors standing by themselves. They watched him as he approached, then moved past within a few feet. His Apache was anything but perfect, so he greeted them in Spanish. Ka-ya-ten-nae was one. The young warrior, who was believed by some to be a chief—although no one was quite certain, except the Apaches, and they weren't talking—scowled at him.

"I'd like to talk to you," Davis told him.

Ka-ya-ten-nae nodded. "What have I done?" he asked, his Spanish better than Davis's own.

"Nothing. I just wanted to talk to you about possibly becoming a scout."

The warrior wrinkled his nose, then looked at the sole of his moccasin. His meaning was clear, but

Davis ignored it. "Seriously, come by my tent. I'm moving over to Turkey Creek. We should talk about it."

Ka-ya-ten-nae shrugged. "Maybe so," he said. "Maybe no."

"It's a standing offer." Davis nodded to the others, who had said nothing, even to one another, during the exchange. As he walked away he heard them whispering among themselves, using their own language. The few scraps he caught didn't match up well with his Apache vocabulary. It might as well have been Chinese they were speaking.

And he wondered if it might not have been better for him to be in faraway China.

Chapter 21

March 1884—The Border

BRITTON DAVIS WAS pacing the soles right off his boots. The endless waiting rubbed him raw. Months on the border, watching every damned cloud of dust, scrambling every time a solitary figure fractured the clean, unbroken line of the southern horizon, only to have some dust-grimed prospector or Bible-thumping itinerant preacher straggle in, gulp water as if it were the last well in the world, then drift on, his back a little less bowed.

The awful monotony wrapped him in its crushing embrace so tight it made it hard for him to breathe. And still Geronimo hadn't come in. There had been others, a few Chiricahuas here, a brace of Warm Springs there. Minuscule drops in a monumental bucket. And the Apaches on the reservation two hundred miles to his back sat, bubbling like some witches' caldron.

Exposing the doctored scales had bought him some goodwill, but it had also served as a focus for resentment, almost as if it were an emblem of everything the whites had done wrong. The daily tensions of Turkey Creek had made him edgy, and General Crook, typically, had understood, and agreed to post

him south for a while. Lingering doubts about
whether Geronimo intended to come in had made
Crook edgy, too. The stragglers claimed he was on
his way, but they had been drifting across the border
since September, and seven months later, no one had
seen him yet.

On the plus side, there had been no confirmed reports of depredations in the territory or in New Mexico. The newspapers continued their attack on the
military in general and on Crook in particular. One
report that gained wide currency, even to the point
of being espoused in Washington by a congressman,
had it that Geronimo had accepted Crook's surrender, instead of the other way around. So persistent
was the rumor that the secretary of war had been
forced to issue a terse and unequivocal disclaimer.
But even that hadn't quieted the bigger mouths in the
territory.

So the posting to Fort Huachuca was a kind of relief, but it also left Davis with too much time on his
hands—time to think, time to worry. A doubt lurked
scorpionlike under every rock, coiled like a side-
winder in the shade of every cactus. He'd heard that
Johnny Blake, a year ahead of him at the Point and
now attached to a Sixth Cavalry unit in the Department of Arizona, was stationed within a day's ride.
Davis had sent word by telegram, inviting Blake to
come down for a couple of days. There'd been no
reply yet, but he kept his fingers crossed.

This morning, the oppressive heat already beginning to dissolve the southern mountains into a purple
haze, Davis saddled his pony. He wanted to get out,
away from everyone, even if it meant roasting his
brains in the sun.

He rode aimlessly, trailing across the flats, so barren he might have been the first man ever to set foot on them. On every side towering mesas surged up off the billiard-table surface, their craggy strata etched on each face by erosion. The great volcanic extrusions looked misplaced, as if whoever had made the desert had forgotten them or, not knowing what to do with them at all, had chosen the most lifeless and remote place to discard them.

Davis could see all the way to the Mexican border and beyond into the Sonoran desert. He watched the sun climb, and by the time it was directly overhead, he was parched and hungry. Angling southwest, toward the nearest mesa, he planned to sit in the shade of a rock and have lunch. His mouth was too dry for the thought of food to be appealing, but he had to do something to keep his strength up and quiet the gnawing doubt in his gut.

As he shifted direction he saw it sweeping toward him, shielded from him until that moment by the mesa. A cone of dust, so tall it was almost biblical in its imposing dimensions. Something—someone— was heading his way, and by the look of the cloud, it must be a large group.

Kicking his mount, he charged toward the cloud, even while he realized he should be heading back to Fort Huachuca. The tall plume undulated in the heat, its top smearing in the winds high above the plain. Davis suddenly wished he hadn't seen it. Skidding to a halt, he stood in the stirrups, snatching at the field glasses draped over his saddle horn.

At the base of the column of dust, a dark mass seemed to writhe and boil, but he was unable to make out what it was. All he could tell was that it was large. He turned then, draped the glasses around his neck, and jerked the reins hard. If it was Geronimo, and it almost had to be, he wanted to be able to speak to the war chief. He had to get back to Huachuca and get Sam Bowman or Mickey Free, somebody who could speak Apache. There was no room for misunderstanding—not now, not when things were so close to being finalized.

As he rode he kept looking back. For a while the mesa hid the dust cloud, but on the western edge of the rock, its edge sharply defined in the brilliant light, he could see a smear of beige blotting out the bright blue white of the sky. It felt as if a great weight had been lifted from him. He could breathe again for the first time in weeks. He wanted to shout, but there was no one to hear him. Then, realizing it didn't matter, he let out a loud whoop, let it die, then exploded with another.

He ignored his thirst and his hunger, bending forward over his stallion's neck to cut down on the drag. The animal seemed to sense his urgency, its fluid stride seeming barely to touch the earth as it flew.

A half hour later, he galloped into Huachuca, leaped from his horse, and dashed to the administration building. Major Biddle, the commanding officer, looked up in amazement. Because he was on detached service, Davis, as usual, wasn't wearing his uniform. Biddle, spit and polish all the way, had had trouble adjusting to that and still raised an eyebrow whenever he saw Davis. But this time he was too stunned to disapprove.

"Brit, what in hell's wrong? You look like you just saw a ghost."

"Maybe I did, Major. They're coming."

"Who's coming, Lieutenant?" Biddle let his pen drop, looked at the blot of ink on the paper beneath it, then looked back at Davis.

"Geronimo, Major. He's coming."

"What? Are you sure?"

"Got to be. Looks like hundreds of people, horses, cows, I don't know what-all. But they're sure kicking up a lot of dust."

"Where?"

"Out beyond Blue Mesa. Ten, twelve miles."

"Did you actually see Geronimo?"

"No, sir, but it's him. I'm sure of it."

"I'd better wire Fort Whipple. General Crook will want to know. Unless you think I should wait until you're sure."

"Yes, sir, I think you'd better wait. Is Bowman around? Or Mickey Free?"

"I suppose so, why?"

"I want to go back, to meet him. They just crossed the border, I think."

"All right," Biddle said, getting to his feet. "You find somebody to translate and I'll wire General Crook to expect new arrivals. I just won't tell him it's Geronimo. If it is, this will be a load off his mind. Unless . . ."

"Unless what, Major?"

"Unless he's not coming to surrender."

"He has to be. He said he would. That's why he's coming. I'm sure of it."

"Take a troop with you, Lieutenant. Not enough to spook him, but enough to make sure you get back in one piece, whatever's on his mind."

Davis spun on his heel, forgetting his salute, and sprinted back out into the sunlight. He raced across the parade ground, shouting for Mickey. The rumpus drew a crowd, and he was surrounded almost immediately by a press of troopers and Apache scouts. He barked orders until he was out of breath, sent a private in search of someone who could serve as translator, then ran for the corral. He needed a fresh mount.

Fifteen minutes later, he was back in the saddle. He had a mixed unit, about twenty scouts and as many troopers. The private had found Mickey, who nudged his mount up alongside Davis. The lieutenant looked at him, a broad smile on his face. "You ready, Mickey?"

Mickey returned the smile, but his one good eye failed to reflect it. The interpreter nodded, and Davis barked the command to move out. An hour later, they could see the cloud again, now almost to Blue Mesa.

"Plenty of horses, looks like," Davis said.

"Plenty of Apaches, too," Mickey observed.

They pushed harder, the troops spreading out in their haste and excitement. Davis drove his fresh mount out ahead of the pack, anxious to be the first one to reach the front of the advancing horde. He tried to use his field glasses, but he was jouncing so hard in the saddle it was impossible to hold anything in focus.

Davis was convinced now that it had to be the Chiricahuas—convinced or so fervently hoping that he wouldn't allow himself to consider the possibility that it might not be Geronimo's band. And if it should be Geronimo and his people, he knew the chief would not be in the vanguard. It was the Apache way for many of the warriors to bring up the rear, where the greatest danger lay. Out front, a few scouts would be riding point, with a band of warriors behind them, then the old men, women, and children in a pack.

As they closed on the advancing column he could see a herd of cattle off to one side. It was the cattle that were responsible for much of the dust cloud. At that range it wasn't possible to tell how many, but it appeared to be two to three hundred head, at a bare minimum.

Three horsemen resolved out of the roiling mass of humanity and livestock now, nearly three miles ahead of the main body. The scouts had seen the troopers and veered toward them, lashing their mounts to close on the soldiers.

Davis drove his pony even harder, pushing the horse until it was in danger of breaking down. He held up a hand, calling for the troop to halt, then rode on alone to meet the three scouts. The last mile, he slowed his horse, allowing the advance scouts to cover most of the ground. He could make out the individual scarlet headbands now, confirming that they were Apaches. It had to be Geronimo, because only he had so many followers unaccounted for and known to be off the reservation.

He recognized one of the scouts as Ulzana, who was related to both Juh and Geronimo. The warrior raised a hand, halting the other two scouts, and he moved forward slowly, coming abreast of Davis with one hand held at shoulder height.

Davis nodded, then Ulzana reached out for a handshake.

"Geronimo?" Davis asked. Ulzana turned to look back toward the boiling smoke cloud.

"Take me to him," Davis said, his Spanish suddenly stiff in his parched mouth. Without a word Ulzana turned his horse and broke into a gallop. Davis waved for Mickey to follow him, then raced after Ulzana.

The main body was still nearly four miles away, but Davis rode hard and swung wide to the left to bypass the herd of cattle. That put the bulk of the Apaches on the far side of the herd, and Davis tried to count as he roared by, but there were too many. Hundreds, for sure.

Ulzana hung back now, and Davis reined in alongside him. The Apache pointed toward a knot of warriors at the tail of the column. Davis nodded, understanding that he would find Geronimo among them. He turned then to look for Mickey Free, and stood in the stirrups straining to see through the thick dust clogging the air.

Mickey materialized, a dark shadow against the cloud for several moments, slowly taking shape as he narrowed the distance. When the interpreter was alongside, Davis kicked his own mount to fall in step and led the way toward the small band of heavily armed warriors in the rear guard.

He saw Geronimo right away, off by himself a few yards, alternately watching his charges and scanning the rear. They were over the border, but the chief knew the border no longer meant what it used to. Crook's penetration into the mountain stronghold proved that. He spotted Davis and kicked his horse forward, coming ahead to meet the lieutenant.

When they were within shouting distance, Geronimo asked, "Where is Nantan Lupan?" His horse drifted forward slowly, stopping just two feet in front of Davis.

"Prescott," Davis said. "He sent me to meet you."

When Mickey had translated, Geronimo's already scowling face darkened further. "Why was a raw, virgin lieutenant sent to escort an Apache chief?"

"The general is busy. He has a great many responsibilities that demand his attention."

"And does not an Apache chief have as many responsibilities?"

Not knowing how to answer that one, Davis said nothing.

"Why soldiers? Geronimo has surrendered. Nantan Lupan knows that. Why soldiers?"

"There are bad white men, just like there are bad Indians. The soldiers will protect you from bad white men. The general will meet you at San Carlos. I will send word over the talking wire as soon as we get close to Fort Huachuca."

"My people are tired. We must rest a few days. A week maybe. My cattle are hungry. They need to eat and to rest."

"There's no time," Davis said. In his head he could see the threats ticking by one after another—Mexican troops, irate citizens, American cavalry, even a last-minute change of heart on the part of Geronimo himself. But he couldn't afford to push too hard. He was concerned, too, that the cattle would impose restrictions on their speed and choice of route. Without them, they could do forty or fifty miles a day, and reach San Carlos in five days. But the cattle would need water, which meant more heavily traveled routes . . . and more potential for trouble.

"One day layover," Davis said. "But not until we get to Sulphur Springs." He wanted to get north of Tombstone, and out of harm's way, before stopping.

Geronimo frowned more ominously, if that were possible. "Three days," he said. "No less."

Davis held his ground. "Two days. No more."

Geronimo smiled. "You have learned well from Nantan Lupan. He, too, is a hard bargainer."

Davis felt the tension drain out of him. He heaved a sigh. Geronimo noticed. "Did you think I would run to Mexico again?" he asked.

Davis considered his words carefully, then permitted himself a slight smile. "Geronimo is a great warrior. It is not easy to say no to such a man, even when what he wants is not in his best interest."

Geronimo, apparently satisfied, grunted. Then he kicked his pony's flanks and galloped past Davis, who wheeled his own mount and followed. All along the column, the cattle lowed and bellowed. Through the thick dust, their shapes looked like moving stones. Not until they reached the front of the herd was Davis able to see any of the Apaches. Geronimo angled to the west, cutting across in front of the herd, then headed north again, to catch up with the point of the column. Davis sat patiently while Geronimo explained that they would lay over at Sulphur Springs for two days. The chief despatched one of the warriors to ride on ahead and inform the scouts, then eased his mount to one side to let the column pass.

Davis moved in closer. "I will ride on ahead to Huachuca and make preparations. I will send word to General Crook. He will be relieved."

Geronimo turned sharply. "Did Nantan Lupan doubt my word?"

"No, but he was beginning to think you might have run into trouble. It is a long, dangerous way from the Sierra Madres to the border."

"Even with no bullets, my people kill Mexicans. As long as there were stones, there was no danger."

"General Crook will be pleased you have come."

Geronimo nodded. Before he could get himself into more trouble, Davis said good-bye. He left Mickey Free and his troops to provide an escort and rode hard to Huachuca. There was much to do, and very little time. He was wondering where Johnny Blake was and now began to think he might not get to see his old schoolmate after all.

He sent a dispatch, told Major Biddle of his plans, then rejoined the column.

By the time the Apaches moved past Tombstone, several miles to the west, the town was buzzing with the news. Fortunately, the size of Geronimo's band was great enough to deter even the most unthinking of the citizens who might otherwise take a notion to stir up trouble.

They were making only twenty miles a day. After four days they finally reached Sulphur Springs ranch. The springs were the best water for fifty miles around, and the grass, although there wasn't much in the late spring, was better than anything for a hundred miles behind or ahead.

They set about pitching a makeshift camp, many of the hostiles settling in near the ranch house, others spreading out over several acres. The livestock was set to grazing immediately after watering. The cattle, in particular, seemed to relish the grass, sparse as it was, and the dust kicked up by their grazing turned the bright sky a pale brown.

Davis was occupied directing the scouts and troopers. He had just finished disposing the scouts along the periphery, since he was still concerned about a possible attack. He was walking toward the ranch house when two men came out. They were pale as meal bugs, and he knew they must have been city men, probably from Tombstone. They introduced themselves and started asking questions about the Apaches. Their curiosity seemed boundless, and they wanted to know everything—how many hostiles, was it true Geronimo was among them, how many cattle? Davis was getting nervous, and the men, sensing it, backed off a bit, couching their continued inquiry in idle curiosity.

When he finished answering their questions, one of the men whipped open his jacket to reveal the badge of a U.S. marshal from the southern district of Arizona Territory. He then introduced his companion as the collector of customs, stationed in Nogales, the official port of entry to Arizona from Mexico.

They informed Davis that the cattle were, legally speaking, contraband, since they had been "smuggled" in from Mexico. They further informed him that Geronimo and several of the other hostiles were wanted for murder, and they produced a bill of particulars. Davis knew that Crook had promised Geronimo that all past transgressions would be waived, so long as the Apaches remained on the reservation and committed no more raids.

But they weren't yet on the reservation, and Davis was in a bind. The marshal ordered Davis to arrest Geronimo and several others named in the indictments, but Davis refused. "I can't obey your order, gentlemen. I can only do what you ask if the order comes from General Crook himself. These Apaches are under the control of the United States Army at the moment. Do you happen to have such an order from General Crook?"

The marshal shook his head. "No, sir, I don't. But I reckon I can get one, if that's what it takes." He reached into his pocket, took out a piece of paper, and used a pencil to write something on it. Then, handing the paper to Davis, he said, "This is a subpoena, sir. It authorizes me to command you, as a citizen of the United States, to assist me in making these arrests."

Davis was astounded. To have come so far, and to have endured so much, only to have trouble from so unexpected a quarter. He didn't argue, trying to decide what to do.

The marshal continued: "Tomorrow morning, I intend to issue a similar subpoena to your packers and the other white men in your command. And if you refuse, I will go to Willcox and get a posse together. In the meantime I suggest you consider staying right here."

Willcox was about fifty miles away, and not much more than a rail depot. It was doubtful it could furnish enough men to carry out the marshal's intentions. But it would only take a single word of those intentions to send the Apaches scrambling back to Mexico. And spurred on by their anger and resentment at such a betrayal, they would leave behind a trail of blood that would take weeks to soak into the parched sands. The lieutenant imagined himself as one of the first casualties.

Davis tried to dissuade him. "Look, Marshal. The scouts are mostly Chiricahuas. Many of them are relatives of Geronimo. I can't control them, if you try this. I can, however, guarantee you that none of us will live to talk about your attempt, no matter how legal it might be."

"It's my duty, Mr. Davis. And I intend to perform it."

Davis shook his head. "You're making a big mistake."

"We'll see about that." He turned then and walked back to the ranch house, the customs officer trailing behind him, apparently convinced that Davis would say nothing to the Apaches.

Davis looked around the camp. He did a quick tally and realized that the white men were outnumbered three or four to one. Even if some of the scouts refused to join the hostiles, there was a better than even chance they would sit on their hands. And even if they did, it was suicide to try to arrest any of the hostiles.

Davis walked away toward the springs and sat on a rock. He was caught between an immovable object and an irresistible force. No matter which way he went, he would be damned. Disobeying Crook's orders would get him a court-martial at best, and if he sided with the Apaches, the more vocal of Arizonans would want him strung up. He couldn't tell Geronimo what was happening, for fear the Apaches would start for the border immediately. Davis knew he was too far from the nearest military unit, and in any case, there wasn't time to send for help and have it arrive before morning.

He sat there, staring at his own face in the roiled water, watching the small swirls of trail dust from the snouts of the livestock upstream still uncoiling under the tranquil surface. Shaking his head, he looked at the sky for a moment, but there was nothing in its blank expanse to help him. He was about to get up when he heard his name called.

"Is that Brit Davis?" He turned, and the voice said, "By Jesus, 'tis himself."

Johnny Blake stood fifty feet away, arms crossed over his chest.

"Johnny," Davis shouted, getting to his feet and starting forward. "Am I glad to see you!"

Blake held up a quart of scotch whisky he had brought along. With a smile he waved the bottle high overhead. "Thirsty, Brit, me lad?"

And a germ of an idea started to take shape in Davis's mind. Blake had been a year ahead of him at West Point. Even though they held the same rank, Blake was technically his superior officer. He showed Blake around the temporary camp, all the while filling him in on the bind he found himself in and sketching his idea. Blake was dubious, but game.

They walked back to the cook fire and sat down to kick the idea around a little more. While they were talking the marshal reappeared. Davis blanched, thinking the marshal had come to subpoena Blake as well, but the smirking peace officer just wanted to talk, and gloat a little.

Seeing an opening, Davis sent word for the customs officer to join them, and Blake broke open the scotch.

Blake, prattling on and on in his thick brogue, plied them both with generous drinks, pouring triples for each man while he and Davis sipped their own weak highballs.

"Don't want to drink all that up," the marshal observed at one point. "It's too damned hard to come by out here."

"Don't you be worrying, Marshal, old Johnny

Blake's got more where this came from," Blake said. He poured another drink for the marshal and the customs man. By ten o'clock the bottle was empty, and the marshal was drooping. Davis watched them both weave their way back to the ranch house, then smiled at Blake.

"Look's like it might work," he said.

Blake cocked his head toward the ranch house. "Don't be too sure, Brit."

Davis looked over to see the customs man arranging his bedding on the front porch. Davis held his breath, pretending to sleep, but listening intently the whole time. Geronimo, unexpectedly, had agreed to the plan, seeming even to find it something of a lark.

By midnight it was as quiet as it was going to get. The scouts and the hostiles got up cautiously, moved their possessions well away from the ranch house before attempting to saddle their mounts. Davis kept watch while Blake directed the hasty retreat.

Not a dog barked. In the thick silence Davis could hear the snoring of the customs man, the raspy buzz like a ripsaw in raw timber. He walked toward the springs. Apaches, scouts, and troopers were busy pushing the herd, trying to get it moving without making any unnecessary noise. Slowly, the herd started off, its shape changing like a single organism, stretching and bending, changing direction then picking up speed.

Davis watched until it was out of sight. In the moonlight a faint haze hung in the air toward the north, then that, too, was gone.

Davis walked back to his bedroll and lay down. He was too nervous to sleep. As the sky slowly brightened he got up and made a pot of coffee on the still-glowing embers of the previous night's fire. He drank a cup black, sitting on his haunches and watching the ranch house.

The sun came up abruptly, exploding over the horizon, then contracting to a bright orange disk. He heard the door of the ranch house slam and turned to see the marshal standing on the porch, his face a mask of confusion.

Spotting Davis, he stormed off the porch. "Where the hell are they?" he shouted. "What happened?" He looked down at the still-sleeping customs man and gave him a vicious kick with one pointed toe.

Davis got to his feet, an empty cup and a coffeepot in his hand. Gesturing with the pot, he said, "Coffee, Marshal?"

The marshal spluttered, "Damn it, I told you to stay here and help me arrest those goddamned Apaches."

"I'm here, Marshal. When do you want to start?"

"What happened here? Where are they?" He stepped past Davis, staring out over the flat land beyond the springs. Davis looked in the same direction. Not even a speck of dust still hung in the air to show which direction the Chiricahuas had taken.

Davis shrugged. "Gone. But Lieutenant Blake ordered me to stay and help you, though."

The marshal took a deep breath. For a moment Davis thought he was going to take a poke at him, and steeled himself. But the marshal shook his head once, then laughed. "Son of a bitch. You foxed me, didn't you?"

Davis walked over to his horse, tightened the cinch, and swung up into the saddle. Only then did he look at the marshal. "Yes, sir," he said. "I believe

I did." He smiled. "It was damn good scotch, though, wasn't it, Marshal?"

Shaking his head, the marshal said, "Best I ever had."

He waved as Davis rode off. The lieutenant looked back over his shoulder once. The marshal, still laughing, took another kick at the customs man and went inside.

Chapter 22 ══════════

November 1884—Turkey Creek, Arizona Territory

BRITTON DAVIS FELT as if he were the last white man on earth. Fifteen miles from Fort Apache, in rolling forest where the temperature was bearable, the air clear and breathable, and the flies seemed less militant, he lived in a tent surrounded by the most notorious of the Chiricahua Apaches, with a smattering of Warm Springs Indians. Geronimo and his family had chosen to settle there. Chihuahua was there and so was Chatto. Ka-ya-ten-nae, still surly, although off and on a scout, had his wickiup in the pine forest on a ridge within a rifle shot of the lieutenant's tent.

Other Apaches, too, had chosen Turkey Creek. It was like paradise compared with the barren wasteland that was San Carlos. The Indians seemed to have adapted well. Most of the chiefs came by the tent once or twice a week, sometimes because they needed something, and sometimes, more often, because they wanted to talk. They seemed to respect Davis, and he had learned to respect them. Living with the Chiricahua on a day-to-day basis, he had managed to put aside the natural inclination of a combat veteran regarding his erstwhile adversaries.

The Chiricahua seemed to sense the change in him.

Even Geronimo paid an occasional visit, sitting outside the tent, rolling tobacco in an oak leaf and puffing between sentences. Davis was working on his Spanish and his Apache. He had mastered neither, but was able to carry on a conversation in short fragments in either language.

He had Mickey Free and Sam Bowman with him, but Bowman was half-Cherokee and Mickey was a hybrid of Mexican, Irish, and Apache, so Davis felt unique. It wasn't a sense of superiority that led him to feel that way. But the realization that he was a minority of one had driven him to explore what it meant to be a white man and, by extension, what it meant to be an Apache.

Davis didn't have the scientific curiosity of John Bourke, but the captain's occasional visits had gotten the lieutenant thinking more objectively about the people who surrounded him. It struck him as an odd irony that he was the sole representative of a conquering race, floating on a flood tide of the conquered. And it didn't seem half-bad.

Some of the Apaches were more outgoing than others. Chihuahua seldom came and Loco, who paid an occasional visit, struck him as an intelligent, essentially decent man who, in other circumstances, would have achieved another kind of prominence. The biggest surprise of all, though, was the Apache sense of humor, which ran deep and broad. Practical jokes were a daily occurrence, and barely a day went by when he didn't hear wave after wave of rich, resonant laughter come wafting through the trees, as often as not accompanied by vociferous protest from the latest victim, even a gunshot, not meant to hurt anyone but intended unequivocally to make the point that enough was enough.

But he had two problems that seemed to him insoluble. The Apache fondness for *tizwin* remained unabated despite General Crook's explicit prohibition. It was an easy matter for the more skilled brew masters, although everyone seemed to know how to make it and able to secure enough corn to concoct a batch of the vile stuff. Sometimes more than enough was made, and there would be arguments, fights, stabbings, and twice, murder.

Tracking the stash of *tizwin* down was not as easy as it should have been, because even those Apaches who disapproved of the drink, or at least of the extreme behavior it seemed to provoke, felt that a custom was a custom. Drinking *tizwin* was, even to the teetotalers, the Apache way, theirs by right. Putting a stop to it was an abridgment of cultural prerogative.

The second custom, even more troublesome and not infrequently fueled by *tizwin* drunks, was the beating of wives. Every warrior believed it his right, and even his duty, to beat a woman who displeased him. Since several of the warriors had more than one wife, some as many as four, there seemed to be no lack of occasion for the administration of a harsh and even brutal justice. Part and parcel with the beatings was its horrible, although logical extension, a custom Davis still could not understand. And as long as he lived, he would not forget his first encounter with it.

Awakened one night by a shouting match in a nearby wickiup, he sat up, reached for his Colt pistol, just to be on the safe side, and listened to the screaming. He heard other voices then, men and women alike, shouting, then someone scrambling through the brush. Pulling his boots on, he ran outside, the pistol in his hand. The noise was off to his left, and he ran into the trees. Farther away, the shouting continued, apparently two people arguing now, a man and a woman.

Davis moved cautiously among the tall pines, shoving the sparse underbrush aside with his left arm. Fifty yards into the forest, he heard the sound of whimpering somewhere ahead and slightly to the right. It seemed to be coming from one point now, as if whoever it was had fallen to the ground. He moved quickly, calling "Who's there? Who's there?" first in Spanish, then Apache, and finally in English.

Heavy steps crunched on the pine needles behind him, and he saw a shadowy form moving among the trees, then another, and finally a third, this one holding a burning brand overhead. In the wash of orange light he recognized Sam Bowman.

"Sam, over here," he shouted. Bowman held the torch a little higher and moved in his direction. When the chief of scouts joined him, they moved ahead together.

"What the hell's going on, Sam?"

"A spat," Sam said. "Seems Nochite caught his new wife with a young buck."

A whimper then caused Davis to whirl around. He had almost stepped on a young woman, lying face-down on the carpet of needles. Davis knelt, and Bowman grabbed him by the shoulder. "You may not want to see this," the scout said.

"See what, Sam? What's . . ." He stopped then as the young woman sat up. Bowman leaned closer with the torch as she turned to look at the two men. Her chin and the front of her blouse were soaked with blood. She held both hands to her face, and blood trickled through her fingers.

"Ask her if she's all right, Sam."

He tried to pry the hands away to get a look at the damage, but she resisted him. He tugged harder, and the hands came away. Davis almost gagged. Half the woman's nose was missing, and her cheeks seemed curiously flat under the bloody mess.

"Good God Almighty!" Davis mumbled. "What happened to her?"

"Nochite cut half her nose off. That's the penalty for adultery. Sometimes the cheeks get sliced, too, if the husband is careless or the woman struggles too much."

"That's positively barbaric!"

"I guess," Bowman said. "If you ain't used to it."

"This has got to stop."

"Good luck with that one, Lieutenant."

"You're not saying you approve of this, Sam? Are you?"

"Ain't up to me, Lieutenant."

"Well, it's got to stop." Davis ripped a sleeve off his long-john shirt and pressed it against the wounds. "We've got to get her to a doctor."

"No need. The women'll handle it. They're used to it."

"Not for long," Davis said. He was aware then of several figures surrounding him among the trees. Three or four of them moved closer. Bowman shifted the torch in that direction, and Davis saw several women. He nodded, and they moved in to take the disfigured young bride back to the *ranchería*. Davis stood there for a long time, watching the shadows move away.

He was alone with Bowman now. "You coming back, Lieutenant?"

"Not yet, Sam. Not just yet."

That had been his first experience, and General Crook had issued a general order the following day, reiterating the prohibition on *tizwin* drinking and adding disfigurement to the long list of forbidden customs.

It had been tempting then to see the Apaches as incorrigible savages. But after a few weeks, and a long talk with Loco, he had come to realize that customs were just that—practices that had always been, that were carried on by generation after generation who had never known another way. They would die hard, but if he hammered away at them, die they surely would.

It had happened only once since, and the offending husband had been sentenced to three months in the stockade at Fort Apache, after a trial by an Apache jury. Maybe they could change, after all.

But then there was Ka-ya-ten-nae, and this was a problem not so easily solved. The young warrior had agreed to become a scout, and he had done some good work. But he was fond of *tizwin* and jealously guarded his right to treat his wives as he saw fit. As often as not, he could be found stalking the forest by himself, sometimes his eyes red and watery, his speech slurred, and the muscles of his face slack.

He was prone to violence at such times. Three different times he had been sentenced to a day or two in the stockade. Each time he promised to mend his ways. And each time, within a week, he stumbled out of a *tizwin* cloud and confronted Davis in front of a handful of other young warriors, no less disaffected than himself, but more restrained in their demonstrations.

Davis was starting to worry that Ka-ya-ten-nae might lead a breakout. If that happened, Davis suspected some of the other warriors, especially the older chiefs like Chihuahua and Geronimo, might feel compelled to follow suit as a way of saving face. They would not want to be shown up by a younger man.

Some way would have to be found to convince Ka-ya-ten-nae to give up drinking, but it had become a symbol of defiance now, and Davis suspected the young warrior was drinking as much to spite his conquerors as he was for the sake of enjoyment.

The Apache was intelligent, a natural leader, and as brave a man as Davis had ever seen. But that combination was like carbon, sulfur, and saltpeter—all it took was a single spark to set it off. And the explosion could shatter the peace into a thousand splinters.

At least, Davis thought, there was Thanksgiving to look forward to. He was going to have a guest, for the first time in three months. A night of idle chatter in his native tongue seemed like a small thing, but it had been so long since he'd had the pleasure, he was anxious as any kid waiting for the last day of school.

Turkey Creek was not so named by chance. Davis took a rifle and went out looking for a good-size gobbler for the holiday meal. A few hundred yards from his tent, the forest sloped up sharply, giving way abruptly to a stony mesa. Between the tent and the mesa was Ka-ya-ten-nae's wickiup, on a ridge half the height of the mesa. Davis went past it, but the wickiup was quiet, as if Ka-ya-ten-nae were not there.

Crossing the ridge, he moved down into the creek bottom, following the enticing warble of what sounded like a large wild turkey. A hundred yards or so along the creek, the sound died. Davis searched for several minutes, then decided to try the mesa top. He started up the switchback and was almost at the top when he heard the same gobbler far below in the creek bottom. He debated whether to continue on up or go back after the first bird, finally deciding the one he'd been after was the one he wanted. Sliding back down the stony trail, he stepped into the creek. Moving cautiously, he went no more than fifty feet before he saw the bird.

The rifle crack sounded like thunder in the notch thick with pines on either bank. Hauling the bird back to his tent, he dressed it for the meal. His guest showed up just as the turkey was ready. The visitor, Captain Frank West, remarked on the natural beauty of the area. The two men stayed up till nearly midnight, smoking and exchanging gossip.

When West yawned for the third time in five minutes, Davis sent him off to bed. He lay down on his own bedroll and was just slipping off when he heard a rock tap the canvas of his tent roof and slide down the canted cloth. It was the signal from one of his spies. Slipping under the rear flap of the tent, Davis moved into the trees, where he found Mickey Free waiting for him, along with Nah-des-the, the lone woman agent he had managed to enlist.

"What's wrong?" Davis asked.

"Why did you turn back on the trail this afternoon?" Nah-des-the asked.

Davis explained about the turkey, then asked why she wanted to know.

"Ka-ya-ten-nae was waiting for you, with six warriors. They were full of *tizwin,*" she said. "Ka-ya-ten-nae saw you coming and thought you wanted to arrest him. They were going to shoot you and run to Mexico."

Davis looked at Mickey. "Is that right?"

The interpreter nodded. "Ka-ya-ten-nae is ready to blow up. He hates the reservation. He says it was a mistake to come in. If he can get enough men to go with him, he'll make a break for the border. As like as not, he'll try to kill you before he runs."

Davis rubbed a nervous hand across his forehead. He felt the beads of sweat, despite the chill of the late-fall night. "You're absolutely sure about this?" he asked.

Mickey Free repeated the question. The woman nodded vigorously.

"Thank you," Davis said.

He watched Mickey and the woman vanish into the trees, then slipped back to his tent. Feeling the least bit foolish, he sat on his bedroll, counting. When he reached two hundred, he left the tent a second time, this time through the front flap. Making his way to Frank West's tent, he ducked inside after taking a quick look around to make sure he wasn't being watched. Rousing West, he whispered the intelligence to him, pausing for questions. West had only one. "What do you want me to do, Brit?"

"Can you go back to Fort Apache, wire General Crook, then get four troops up here?"

"Sure thing."

"They have to be here at first light."

"All right. What are you going to do?"

"The only thing I can do. I'm going to arrest Ka-ya-ten-nae. . . ."

"Jesus H.— You sure?"

"I don't have any choice. If I let him get away with it, conspiracy to commit murder, for Christ's sake, there'll be no holding him."

"You try to arrest him, and you just might be able to do away with the conspiracy part of that."

"If I *don't* arrest him, I'll have to forget about the conspiracy. I know these people pretty well. I think I can count on my Apache scouts . . . most of them, anyhow. And most of the chiefs don't want another war. If I keep my self-control, I think I can pull it off without bloodshed. Maybe . . ."

"I'll leave right away. You sure you don't want to come with me?"

"No, I have things to do. I'm going to send for the chiefs. I want them all here."

"For God's sake, Brit, why?"

"I want them to realize I mean business. If I pull this off, I think we'll be all right. If not, we might as well find out as soon as we can. It's just a matter of time before somebody, Ka-ya-ten-nae or one of the other young bucks, goes off the deep end."

West clapped Davis on the shoulder and turned away. He was already packed, since he had been planning to leave at sunup. Five minutes later, he was saddling his horse. Five more, and he was a shadow disappearing into the trees.

Davis went to Mickey's tent and told him what he was planning to do. When he was finished, he gave Mickey a chance to argue, but the interpreter just nodded. "Send four or five runners out, Mickey,"

Davis said. "I want all the chiefs here in the morning. Tell Ka-ya-ten-nae last, at first light. I don't want him to bolt."

Mickey nodded, took a deep breath, and said, "Good luck, Lieutenant, I think you'll need it."

Davis went back to his tent. He spent the rest of the night sitting, staring at his hands in his lap. At 4:30, about an hour before sunrise, he field-stripped his Colt, cleaned and oiled it, then put fresh ammunition in the cylinder. No matter what else happened, Ka-ya-ten-nae was going to pay for his treachery. If he went peacefully, fine; if not, he would go another way.

Just before the sun came up Davis stepped outside. The morning chill had striped the forest with bands of pale fog. The wispy swatches picked up the crimson light as the sun rose, then turned white as the sun climbed above the rim of the mountains. By six they had burned off. It was a beautiful morning, and the day promised to be unseasonably warm.

Frank West was back. He had four troops of cavalry a quarter mile away. Mickey came out of the woods then and Davis gave him the high sign. Mickey moved up the ridge to Ka-ya-ten-nae's wickiup. The warrior was certain to be in a foul mood. *Tizwin* made for a nasty drunk and a positively horrendous hangover, usually a two-day run.

West moved the cavalry up, gave the command to dismount, and strung the men out in twos. He had nearly a hundred and forty troopers with him, and they were all heavily armed.

Already, word had percolated through the scattered *rancherías,* and Apaches, also armed, had begun to ring the small clearing at the center of which sat Britton Davis's tent. Already the numbers were roughly equal. Davis stood, his pistol tucked in his belt, his arms folded across his chest. He nodded to several of the Apaches he recognized. Bonito was there, and Zele, and one or two other chiefs. He looked for Chihuahua and Geronimo, but neither had shown so far. The question that taunted him was whether it was better to see them or not to see them.

The Apaches made prominent display of their weapons, holding them crooked in elbows or cradled in crossed arms. More warriors were filtering through the trees. West had his front rank kneel. The troopers leaned on their weapons while the rear rank trained their rifles in the approximate direction of the greatest concentration of Apaches. Davis noticed that many of the warriors were stripped to the waist, cartridge belts draped over their shoulders. He didn't know whether they had come intending to fight, but was certain that if a fight came, the Indians were prepared.

A broad arc of warriors swept across the front edge of the clearing, the Apaches so many teeth in the jaws of a shark, ready to swallow Davis whole. The arc parted then, almost dead center, and Davis spotted Mickey Free. Behind him, his face contorted with rage, strode Ka-ya-ten-nae. A dozen or so of the younger warriors were behind him, and they stepped through the opening, then it closed behind them. Davis nodded to Mickey, who moved to one side. Ka-ya-ten-nae continued across the clearing, a Winchester carbine dangling from his right hand.

"Why do you send for me?" he asked. "What have I done?"

Davis took a deep breath. It seemed that all the

Apaches took a step or two closer. Ka-ya-ten-nae
came closer, holding up one hand to keep his allies
back.

"You were drinking *tizwin,* in violation of regula-
tions. You also planned to shoot me yesterday, up on
the mesa."

"Who says this? Show me who says this. Point out
the Apache who told you this."

"You'll find out at San Carlos, not before. That's
the way it's done, and you know it. At your trial you
will learn who accuses you."

"Trial? What trial? Am I under arrest?"

"You are."

Ka-ya-ten-nae took several steps closer. He lifted
the muzzle of his carbine a few inches, but not far
enough to pose a threat to the lieutenant. The warrior
then spun around, sweeping his free hand around the
arc of Apaches. "Which one? Let the man who tells
you these things tell you now, in front of me."

"No, sir, I can't do that, Ka-ya-ten-nae. You'll have
to come with me."

Davis saw the warrior's thumb pull back the hammer on his Winchester. At the same moment a horde
of metallic locusts began to chatter all across the
clearing. Other, more distant clicks answered as the
troopers thumbed the hammers on their own weapons. Davis stepped closer to Ka-ya-ten-nae. "Give me
your rifle," he said.

The warrior shook his head, almost as if trying to
shake off a blow that had stunned him. "No!"

"Your weapon, Ka-ya-ten-nae."

The Apache ground his teeth. All around the edge
of the forest, the warriors shuffled closer, collapsing

in toward Ka-ya-ten-nae and Davis. The lieutenant held out his hand. "Now, please . . ."

Ka-ya-ten-nae opened his mouth. It looked for a moment as if he were ready to explode. Then, so quickly Davis wasn't sure when it started, the starch went out of the warrior. He seemed to shrivel up like a balloon losing its air. Davis reached forward and closed his hand around the carbine barrel.

"Thank you," Davis said. Ka-ya-ten-nae stared at him, his eyes glassy, the muscles of his face writhing in confusion and some unnamed distress.

Bonito stepped out of the semicircle of Apaches. "Mr. Davis," he said. "I will offer myself as a hostage if you let Ka-ya-ten-nae keep his weapon while he goes to San Carlos. This is as it should be for an Apache warrior."

Davis gnawed his lip. Another Apache stepped forward, and volunteered himself for the same purpose. Davis felt the nod of agreement coming even before he made up his mind. "All right," he said, shaking his head in the affirmative. He handed the carbine back to Ka-ya-ten-nae, who lowered the hammer and looked at Davis with a great, faraway pain deep in his eyes. They looked like twin, infathomable pools of impossibly deep sorrow. He nodded. *"Gracias, tenente . . ."*

Davis found Captain West in the corner of one eye. He waved the captain toward him. "Thanks," he said. "It's all right now. You can send the troops back to Fort Apache."

"Are you sure?"

Davis took a long look around the clearing. Some of the Apaches had already started to drift back to their *rancherías*. "I'm sure," he said.

West clapped him on the shoulder. "All right, if you're sure."

Davis thanked him again and watched West mount his troops and pull out. He turned then to look up at the sky, then to look through the pines, at the sunlight filtering down through the canopy. He was aware of a slight breeze, the sift of dead needles down through the branches. A bird darted among the trees, its shadow breaking patches of sunlight on the needled carpet. Back among the pines, he saw one man still watching. The man's face was in shade. He watched for a long time. Davis nodded to him, and the warrior returned the nod. As the Apache turned Davis caught a glimpse of his face.

It was Geronimo.

Chapter 23

May 1885—Turkey Creek, Arizona Territory

BRITTON DAVIS THOUGHT the Chiricahuas would settle
down once Ka-ya-ten-nae was removed. Davis would
then play Androcles to the Chiricahua lion. Pull the
thorn, and coexistence, at last, becomes possible.

But it didn't work out that way. Almost as soon as
Ka-ya-ten-nae had been convicted and sentenced to
five years in Alcatraz, more trouble arrived, in the
form of Huera, an Apache woman who had been sold
into slavery in Mexico. When Geronimo had released
his Mexican hostages, complicated negotiations
began between Mexico City and Washington. Huera,
one of Mangus's wives, and who was related to Chihuahua and Geronimo, was eventually located and
returned to her people. What should have been cause
for celebration, the return of a loved one to her family, instead became the straw that did in the camel.
Unfortunately for Davis, and his vision of tranquillity, Huera was an accomplished brewer of *tizwin*.

Some of the more discontented Apaches—Chihuahua, Mangus, Nachite, and Geronimo foremost
among them—liked their *tizwin*, and they didn't like
General Crook's interference in their family lives.
Chihuahua, in particular, was vehement in his pro-

tests. Geronimo, too, insisted that Crook had said
nothing about Apache customs during the negotiations for his surrender. The men wanted to drink, he
argued, pointing out that even the soldiers had their
whiskey and wine. They wanted to discipline their
wives as they saw fit, which meant frequent beatings
and, on at least one occasion, a stabbing of a wayward wife.

Davis had his hands full. Even nose cutting was de-
fended by the more vigorous protesters. Once again,
Chihuahua led the pack. He showed up at the lieutenant's tent one morning, drunk as a lord, and had
nearly a dozen chiefs and subchiefs with him. But no
one had a chance to speak. Chihuahua was so animated, and his speech so well lubricated with a batch
of Huera's brew, that words spilled from him in an
endless torrent. Only Loco tried to intercede, but Chihuahua cut him off, complained about Davis, about
Crook, and especially about the new agent.

Wilcox had resigned, and his replacement, a man
named C. D. Ford, had been handpicked by the Tucson ring, a loosely-knit band of thieves with political
connections based in the Territory. Nearly two years
of peace had seriously interfered with their accumu-
lation of capital, and when Wilcox left, they saw
their chance.

Ford made himself a nuisance almost from the first.
He insisted on the right to control police on the reser-
vation, ignoring Crook's mandate of total authority.
He appointed a new chief of Apache police, the first
since Cibicu Charley Colvig had gone to his reward.
Ford seemed hell-bent on destroying the delicate bal-
ance on the reservation. When Davis or Emmett
Crawford, who had complete police authority from

General Crook, arrested someone, Ford's man would cut the offender loose. Ford had other Apaches arrested for no reason, and kept them in continuous confinement, despite protests from Davis, Crawford, and Crook. Appeals to Washington did nothing, since the War Department and the Bureau of Indian Affairs were no longer cooperating.

Nothing seemed to satisfy the new agent. He appointed a chief farmer, who was given the authority to interfere with the Chiricahuas' tentative essay at horticulture. Crawford had taught them to build irrigation canals, tapping the few sources of decent water to tease some corn and melons out of the reluctant earth. But that wasn't good enough for Ford's man, Jason Rawley, appointed as head farmer for the agency, over Crawford's objection. And Rawley, almost as if it had been his reason for living, proceeded to undo months of Crawford's work.

A new administration was taking shape in Washington, and the attendant turmoil only added fuel to the fire. Despite an urgent appeal from General Crook, the War Department decided Ford should have his way. Davis saw the clouds gathering, but felt powerless to stop the impending storm. Crawford, after months of frustration, asked to be relieved of his duties, and Crook grudgingly reassigned the captain to New Mexico.

The Apaches, tired of walking on the edge of a sword, soon threw up their hands. The malcontents had been handed all the ammunition they needed. And Davis couldn't argue whenever they complained that there was no point in attempting to learn to farm when everything they tried was destroyed before the plants had had the chance to do anything more than sprout.

And Huera's arrival was the catalyst, the spark that blew it all sky-high.

Less than a month after her appearance on the scene, Chihuahua, Geronimo, Mangus, and several of the other chiefs showed up at Davis's tent.

"Where is Nantan Lupan?" Geronimo asked while Davis was still halfway out of the tent.

"He is in Prescott, at Fort Whipple," Davis told him.

"Has he left us, like Colonel Beaumont and Captain Crawford and Agent Wilcox?"

"No. He is still in command of the reservation."

"Why do we not see him? Why has he not come to Turkey Creek in so long?"

Davis sensed that the Apaches were worried. He knew that Crook was more than a general to Geronimo and some of the others. They respected the general as a worthy adversary. No one had ever had the courage to chase them into the very heart of their Sierra Madre sanctuary. Not only had Crook done it, he had defeated them there. That alone made him the object of a respect that bordered on veneration. The Apaches seemed to see in the general a kindred spirit, a man they could understand and who understood them. But just as Crook was the man who defeated them, he was the man who protected them. The Apaches knew of the thievery and the manipulation of the Tucson ring, if not the way it worked, at least of its effects. Crook had put a stop to the worst excesses and tried to shield them from repeated attempts to restore the outright piracy. The general had resisted attempts to strip the best land from the reservation and repelled repeated incursions by miners. Perhaps most important to Geronimo, Crook had kept his word, despite repeated attempts to bring some of the renegades to trial in civilian courts, where the outcome would never be in doubt.

Davis tried to reassure Geronimo, but suspected that the Apaches did not believe him. Nodding, but saying nothing after his fourth attempt to learn whether Crook was, indeed, still in charge of his fate, Geronimo yielded to Chihuahua, who was in an ugly mood, obviously drunk again.

"Last night," Chihuahua said, "I drank much *tizwin*. So did Nana and Zele, Geronimo and Mangus. This is forbidden. We know this. We want to know what you are going to do about it. Are you going to put us all in jail?" He stuck his chin out and Davis caught of blast of the *tizwin*-soaked breath that had Chihuahua weaving in place.

"That's not up to me," Davis said.

"Then who is it up to?"

"It is up to Nantan Lupan."

"Then ask him. Tell him we drank much *tizwin* and want to know if we will be put in jail."

Davis started to answer, but Chihuahua waved angrily and left the clearing. The others watched him go, almost as if they wanted to know whether Davis would try to stop him, and when the lieutenant did nothing, they, too, turned and left.

Davis was in a quandary. He had to tell General Crook as soon as possible, but protocol, and the complex reality of the telegraph network, required him to wire Captain Frank Pierce, who had replaced Emmett Crawford as head of the reservation police at San Carlos. Pierce would then forward the communication through channels, which sent the message down to Willcox, from where it was relayed back up to Whipple barracks. Crook's reply would have to take the same circuitous route.

Mounting in a hurry, Davis rode in to Fort Apache and scribbled three drafts of his message before he was satisfied. Instructions were to confine any telegram to bare essentials, because the newspapers, most of which were still thundering their disapproval of Crook and his policies, had pipelines to the military wire. Davis never knew whether the operators were bribed or the line was tapped somehow, but he had to make sure Crook knew his concern but in language that could not be construed as inflammatory, even by a journalist predisposed to seeing a bloodthirsty Apache under every bed.

Frank Pierce got the message. Inexperienced as he was, he consulted with Al Sieber on almost every decision. When the wire came in, he went looking for the chief of scouts and found him sleeping off a long night full of whiskey.

Handing him the telegram, he waited while Sieber, his head bobbing unsteadily, read it over twice. "What do you think?" Pierce asked.

"I think it's no big deal. Apaches have been drinking *tizwin* for hundreds of years. Davis is seeing fire where there ain't even any smoke."

Pierce looked dubious. "You sure, Al?"

But Sieber was already snoring. With a shrug Pierce pocketed the telegram, walked back to his office, and pigeonholed it.

Davis waited for a reply. When none had come the following morning, he thought about retransmitting the same message. But if Crook had received the first, he might be annoyed that Davis was pushing him too hard. So he waited. The day after, he realized the Apaches were watching him closely, as if wondering what Crook had told him, and when he would tell them.

On the third day he considered resending the message once more. Reluctant to resend when nothing had changed, he waited.

The next day Geronimo was gone.

June 1885—Sonora, Mexico

Britton Davis sat on the crest of a hill. Ahead and behind him, more than two hundred Apache scouts and a substantial pack train straggled through the Bavispe River valley. Captain Emmett Crawford, hastily reassigned, had a second detachment of Apache scouts. In both scout units were men who had been pursued by Crawford the last time Apaches had broken out of the reservation. Davis, at least, was aware of the irony. If it had occurred to the captain, he had not commented on it.

Somewhere ahead, Geronimo led his force of one hundred and forty-four Apaches. But only thirty-five were seasoned warriors. Eight were tagged boys, young Apaches just old enough to carry weapons, and the rest were women and young children.

The trail had been the usual one, although the speed with which they had broken for the border had limited the number of casualties in Arizona Territory. But all the usual signs were there—a half-dozen dead cavalrymen, several burned ranches, pillaged farms, and the carcasses of stolen horses and cattle.

But Davis had the feeling that this pursuit was dif-

ferent. Geronimo had several prominent warriors—
Chihuahua, Nana, Perico, Nachite, Mangus, the latter
two sons of two of the greatest Apache chiefs—but
the reckless abandon of previous breakouts was
missing. Haste, almost desperation, seemed to mark
the flight. Davis and his scouts had even found the
bodies of two newborn infants, either stillborn or
simply abandoned in order not to slow down the escape. But there still had been no sign of Charlie Mc-
Comas.

It was tempting to feel that the pursuit would not
take long, that Geronimo was making one last desperate bid for freedom. But Geronimo was a special
man. Davis knew that perhaps better than any other
white man. And a desperate Apache was even more
formidable than usual.

Trailing down along the Bavispe, the scouts had repeatedly encountered signs of recent passage. Twice
they stumbled on cook fires still burning, meat still
roasting over the flames, still edible, so recently had
it been abandoned. In village after village they found
the Mexicans, mostly farmers and small ranchers,
armed and scared to death. The ragtag arsenals usually included farm implements and ancient single-
shot rifles. The few modern weapons were firing re-
loaded cartridges, probably with faulty charges.

Over and over, in town after town, the citizens
turned out to greet them. The scouts were in some
danger, since the frightened farmers could not be expected to tell the difference between a hostile
Apache and one drawing U.S. Army pay. Let an
Apache get close enough to tell the difference, and
if you guessed wrong, nothing could save you.

Several scouts had been wounded by random gun-

fire, usually fired from ambush, the gunman leaving
cartridge casings behind in his hasty footprints. The
general mood among the scouts was almost too care-
free. On any given day several would be drunk on
mescal provided by grateful Mexicanos. That day
and the following, they were all but useless, a greater
danger to themselves and their companions than to
Geronimo and his.

The temperature seemed to climb a notch or two
higher every passing day. One day the troop surgeon
measured one hundred and twenty-five degrees in
the shade. After that, Davis told him to keep his thermometer to himself.

By the last week of June there still had been no contact with the renegades. Davis was beginning to
worry about supplies. One of the scouts informed him
that they were tracking back over the route north
taken by General Crook back in 1883. Even that irony
provoked no more than a slight nod from Emmett
Crawford.

Then, on June 23, they had their first contact. Nearing the small town of Oputo, Crawford learned that
three of the renegades had been into the town the day
before. Stripping his command down to bare bones
for a fast pursuit, Crawford dispatched Chatto and
thirty scouts to follow the trail left by the hostiles. Al
Sieber and Davis wanted to go with Chatto and his
men, but Crawford denied the request. "You'll just
slow them down," he said.

"But . . ."

Crawford shook his head. "No, Lieutenant. Positively not."

Crawford and Davis pushed on, leading the rest of
the scouts and the pack train, but they were too heav-

ily burdened to keep pace. Two days of dreadful rain slowed them even more. The morning of the third day Chatto's detachment returned. He had fifteen prisoners with him, all women, and reported one renegade warrior had been killed.

And so it went for the next three months. It had become a war of attrition. The command divided repeatedly into small units, splitting itself as regularly as a reproducing amoeba. Reports from Mexican towns filtered in, hostiles sighted here, sighted there. A unit would be dispatched with three days' rations. More often than not, subsequent contact was limited to a fleeting glimpse of a hostile warrior from a mile or two, a moccasin print in two-day-old mud, a butchered cattle carcass, stripped to the charred bones, the ashes beneath it cold.

Davis was impatient, Crawford stoic. By the end of September, after getting separated from his unit, Britton Davis marched north to El Paso, his boots long gone, and makeshift moccasins worn to the thinness of paper.

Emmett Crawford was out of supplies and he, too, headed north. It was beginning to look like Geronimo's pitifully small force was a blessing in disguise for the Apache chief.

January 1886—Sonora, Mexico

Captain Crawford had refitted. Stunned and disappointed by the resignation of Britton Davis, who had left the army to take a job managing a large Mexican ranch, he felt almost isolated from his own army. Virtually all of the men he had known and fought beside were leaving or had already left. General Crook was still in command of the Department of Arizona, but Crook was hundreds of miles away, at Whipple barracks. Lieutenant Charles Gatewood had been reassigned to Arizona after Crook himself had requested Gatewood to return. Everyone else was gone.

Even most of the Apache scouts were new. Their term of enlistment ended, the original contingent had returned to the reservation and it had been necessary to recruit a new company. Some, like Chatto, had remained, but most were rookies. Al Sieber and Mickey Free were still with the command, but Crawford's reserve had never allowed him to get close to regular army men, let alone a free spirit like Sieber or an enigma like Mickey.

But the biggest surprise was the enlistment of Ka-ya-ten-nae. Paroled from Alcatraz, the young warrior had returned to Arizona a changed man. His surliness was gone. He seemed now to realize that the White Eyes were impossible to defeat. On Crook's orders he had been allowed to spend much of his confinement off the island. The young Apache now could not stop speaking of the wonders of San Francisco. He told everyone who would listen, and many who wouldn't, about the size of the city, the height of the buildings and, most significantly, the swarms of White Eyes, among whom he had been received with a mixture of warmth and curiosity.

Ka-ya-ten-nae now seemed to be a man with a mission. Crawford had been initially dubious of the wisdom of employing so notorious a malcontent and asked to see him before agreeing to accept his enlistment.

When Ka-ya-ten-nae showed up at his door, Crawford invited him in, then sat back in his chair, his customary aloofness increased to an almost arctic coolness. He watched Ka-ya-ten-nae for a long time in absolute silence. If he expected the Apache to fidget, he was disappointed. Ka-ya-ten-nae stared back at him with perfect calm.

"Why do you want to do this?" Crawford finally asked.

Ka-ya-ten-nae, who had learned English during his eighteen months in California, paused only briefly to frame his reply. "Because I care about my people."

"So you want to fight them?"

"No. I want to fight *for* them. I want to convince them that it is better to learn to live with the white man. They are fighting a war they cannot win. That makes me fear for them."

"You think Geronimo is a reasonable man, do you? You think he can be persuaded to see things your way?"

"Geronimo is a great warrior. I think he does the only thing he can, because the white man has not been fair to the Apache. But the time for the Apache warrior has gone. I think Geronimo knows that. I think he will surrender, if he can be convinced that he will be treated fairly."

"And you think you can do that?"

Ka-ya-ten-nae paused again, then he nodded. "I think I have no choice. It is the only way for Geronimo, and for the Apache."

Crawford stroked his chin for several moments. He didn't doubt that Ka-ya-ten-nae was telling the truth. And the young warrior was doing nothing more than saying what the captain himself believed.

"All right," he said. "All right."

The agreement had been reached, but neither man smiled. Each for his own reasons sensed that there was nothing to smile about.

Chapter 24 ═══════

January 1886—Sonora, Mexico

THE COUNTRY SEEMED to wrinkle itself like a drying grape, the skin of the earth puckering ever more deeply. Canyons grew more sharply etched, the ridges ever more knifelike as they slashed through the mountains. Nacori was the nearest town, but it was a world away. Crawford's scouts had the scent, but the going was so rough that even the battle-hardened Apache scouts who were used to the mountains had been abraded by the terrain, which was an enemy at least as forbidding as Geronimo's band.

Near Nacori, they had picked up a trail that was fairly recent. Geronimo had led his people so deep into the mountains that the parklike serenity of the old sanctuary was little more than a distant memory. The Apaches were in a desperate situation. Reduced in numbers, cut off from assistance, their supplies barely subsistence level, they were running for their lives.

On the morning of the ninth, two advance scouts stumbled on Geronimo's camp. Crawford, anxious to bring hostilities to an end, decided to risk a night approach. If his unit were spotted during daylight hours, it would just prolong the arduous pursuit. It had to end, and the sooner the better.

Leaving their pack train behind, Crawford and his men began a dangerous approach, winding through canyons and up the sheer face of one rock wall after another. The trails were narrow, and there was no moon. Men stumbled and fell, barking shins and putting bones at risk. Four men had to be left behind as, one after another, they sustained injuries that made further progress impossible.

At eight or nine thousand feet, the canyons and occasional valleys were full of fog. The temperature was below freezing, and the men struggled to keep their limbs flexible and their hands warm. Crawford watched his breath crystallize with every exhale, drift away like a tiny cloud, and slowly slide down into the pitch-black abyss to his left.

A few hundred feet overhead, tendrils of fog swirled against a backdrop of a gauzy overcast that seemed slowly to descend. If the ceiling lowered much further, the fog would enshroud them, and they'd be trapped on the precipitous trails until the morning sun burned off the haze.

With less than a mile to go, Crawford found himself aware of his own heartbeat. At first he had mistaken the distant pounding in his ears for drumbeats, and only slowly realized where the sound came from. His breathing was shallow, and despite the moisture all around him in the air, his throat was dry and he coughed frequently.

Inching ahead, he found Lieutenant Marion Maus, Britton Davis's successor, doubled over, his hands clasped over his leg just below the knee.

"You all right, Marion?" he whispered, his voice an alien croak in his own ears.

Maus nodded. Through clenched teeth, he said, "Nearly broke my shinbone. It'll be all right in a minute."

"Not much further, if Ka-ya-ten-nae is right."

"Ka-ya-ten-nae is always right. Damn Apache must be able to see in the dark, too."

"Can you walk?"

Maus nodded, a movement barely discernible in the heavy mist drifting past and glazing the already treacherous trail with ice.

"Less than a mile now. Then we'll wait for sunrise."

"The damned sun might not even come up in this godforsaken hole. This is what Dante's hell is like, where Satan hangs upside down through the ice."

"Don't get educated on me, Marion. I'm not used to it anymore."

Maus laughed softly, trying to maintain the strict silence enjoined on them all. "Damn it, Emmett, a man's got to have some place to hide. Books is where I go."

Crawford clapped him on the shoulder and squeezed past, the narrow trail causing him to scrape against the sheer rock face above him.

It took nearly two hours to move the last mile. Ka-ya-ten-nae buttonholed Crawford as he eased off the trail and onto a broad platform that gave some relief from the tension of inching along the rock face.

"We should wait here, Captain Crawford. Geronimo is not far. We wait for the sun to come."

Crawford nodded. "All right. Now, you're sure it's Geronimo and his people?"

"Sí, I am sure."

"All right. Why don't you and your men get some rest. We have a couple of hours before sunup."

Ka-ya-ten-nae shook his head. "Not good to sleep now. It makes you careless. Better to stay awake, stay ready."

"You know best," Crawford said. Looking around, he picked out a dozen or fifteen shapes he knew to be scouts in the swirling fog. He knew there were many more Apache scouts within a stone's throw, but the mist made it impossible to see them. The fog dampened the least sound, and the Apaches, adept at silent movement even in the dark, made no noise. The eerie silence seemed to wrap around him like a damp blanket.

Crawford huddled against a stone wall and sank to his haunches, trying to ward off the numbing cold. A fire was out of the question, even if fuel could have been found to build one. His teeth chattered and he hugged himself in his own arms, succeeding only in becoming aware of just how cold he was.

He yanked his pocket watch out from under his coat, but it was just too dark to read its face. For a moment he held it to his ear, listening to the steady tick as if to reassure himself that time was actually moving. The thought of being frozen in time in the fog and the cold, trapped forever in darkness, made him shudder.

As the metallic click, click, click of the watch continued, he consoled himself with the thought that the sun would come up again, and life would go on.

The hours dragged on, and the brightening of the sky with the approach of dawn was so painfully slow, it was well advanced before he became conscious of it. But the next time he felt compelled to look at his watch, he could read the time. It was nearly 5:30. The fog was, if anything, even more dense, but a diffuse light from the invisible approach of the sun made it look milky and less oppressive. Soon, Crawford knew, the sun would begin to burn off the haze, and then, almost abruptly, it would be gone, and the blinding brilliance of the white light would melt the ice around him, and the canyons would fill with the steady thunder of water dripping from every rock and branch.

The scouts were ready. They looked alert and anxious, not with fear but eager anticipation. Marion Maus approached, materializing out of a thick fog bank. "Are you ready, sir?"

Crawford thought it best to move as soon as possible, using the last shreds of fog to conceal their final approach. He nodded. "Ready as I'll get, I suppose."

Maus gave the order, and the scouts moved out.

Crawford started down the last leg of the trail. It would be a precipitous descent. At its bottom a narrow opening led into a bowllike valley where the Chiricahuas had made their camp. An hour's worth of luck is all they needed.

Picking his way down the rock wall, the trail widening in some places to nearly five feet, shrinking in others to less than two, he crossed his fingers without realizing it and became aware only when he slipped on some damp moss and had to grab for the wall to keep himself from pitching backward and off the trail into the rocky canyon behind him.

He was somewhere in the middle of the column, with nearly a hundred scouts ahead and almost as many behind. The sun was working its magic now, and the mist was getting wispy and much more transparent. He still couldn't see the canyon floor except for brief glimpses as the stiff breeze whisked the shroud aside for a few moments then drew it closed again. Still nearly two hundred feet up, he found himself counting his steps. As difficult as the descent was, stretching aching muscles to their limit, the agony of waiting was worse.

Suddenly gunfire erupted off to his left. Startled, he nearly lost his footing. He felt the pressure of the men behind him as they all strained toward the canyon floor. Moving more quickly, ignoring the treacherous footing, he heard furious volleys rise and fall like the thunder of waves sweeping toward a beach.

There was little noise beside that of gunfire. An occasional shout and, once, a scream, apparently from a woman. Finally he could see the ground, less than twenty feet below. He leaned back, launched himself, and dropped to the floor of the canyon. On either side of him others were doing the same. It was raining Apaches for a few moments. Falling, he had dropped through the bottom of the fog. He could see for what seemed like the first time in months.

The gunfire was already tapering off as he charged toward the mouth of the small valley. Some of the scouts were charging through the opening, others were crouched behind rocks, firing through the open end at targets Crawford could not see.

He reached the front line, dropped to his knees behind Ka-ya-ten-nae.

"What happened?" he asked.

Ka-ya-ten-nae shook his head. "They saw us." He said something in Apache, which, from its tone,

Crawford judged to be a curse, and decided not to ask for a translation.

The gunfire stopped suddenly, a last, sporadic volley dwindling down to nothing. Cautiously, the scouts started to move into the valley. Crawford darted in after them. It was plain that a fairly large group had been camped there. Several wickiups were scattered across the floor of the small valley, campfires, newly lit, just beginning to blaze.

A quick search revealed that most of the renegade supplies had been captured. But Geronimo and all his people were gone.

Crawford sank to the ground, crushed under the sheer weight of his disappointment.

The scouts systematically assembled the abandoned supplies. The wickiups were fired, and the valley gradually filled with smoke almost as impenetrable as the night fog. Crawford watched the destruction of the *ranchería* tinged with sadness. He felt something almost like remorse, a vague sense of guilt that he had been hounding a people who simply wanted the right to live as they had always lived. He stood, his arms folded, watching the wickiups blaze.

Suddenly a shout echoed off the rocks, and he saw one of the scouts pointing toward the heights. Far above, wreathed in smoke, a figure was working its way down. It was a woman. Crawford, almost elated for some reason he could not put his finger on, rushed forward. Reaching the base of the wall, he watched the woman descend the last few yards, reaching out a hand to help her, but she snatched her hand away and jumped the last few feet.

Concepción, one of the translators, rushed forward. He spoke to the woman, who said her name was Ay-deth-le. He carried on an animated conversation, ignoring Crawford's tug on his sleeve. Finally, as the woman stopped speaking and turned her attention to Crawford, Concepción broke into a broad smile. "Geronimo sent her," he said. "He wants to surrender."

Crawford heaved a sigh. "Tell her we will talk. Tell her we will meet him down on the plains, near Nacori, where we both can feel secure."

Concepción translated, the woman nodded, and started back up the wall. A moment later, she disappeared through the bottom of the pall of smoke filling the valley.

Emmett Crawford dismounted. From the crest of the hill he looked back at the straggling caravan. Nearly a hundred Apache scouts in the vanguard, thirty-three Apache warriors, with nearly one hundred women and children stretched out across the barren flats. The cloud of dust kicked up could be seen for miles. In the heavy air it hung like a beige pall, blotting out the bright blue of the sky.

It was getting to be near sundown, time to think about camping for the night. With his binoculars Crawford scanned the terrain ahead. They were a long way from the border, and he was getting nervous. The hostiles were fidgety, and already some of the more volatile among them were beginning to show signs of regret. Geronimo himself was inscrutable at the best of times, and there was no way Crawford could read the chief's mind.

As soon as Ka-ya-ten-nae got back it might be a good time to hold a parley. San Carlos was still several hundred miles away, and although the hostiles had surrendered, there was a twenty-year-old well of resentment bubbling out of the Arizona sands. And there was a chance that the caravan might run across another unit. Crawford knew that there were at least three columns out searching for Geronimo's band. If shooting started, no matter how accidentally, Geronimo would turn tail and head back into the Sierra Madre Mountains. And if that happened, he'd never come out.

Crook had already sent word to the chief that this was his last chance for a peaceful resolution. "Surrender or be hunted to the last man, like wolves," Crook had told him in 1883. It hadn't set well, but the wily war chief knew Crook was a man of his word, and he knew, too, that Crook was the best Indian fighter in the American army. The general's message had reminded Geronimo that Crook could, and would, make good his threat, just as he would honor his promise.

Crawford turned the glasses toward the border, a hundred and fifty miles away. They had some of the most barren terrain in all of Chihuahua to cross. The men were tired, the animals near the edge of exhaustion. Even the pack mules were worn-out. Crawford was torn between laying over for a day or two and pushing headlong for the border. Crook was supposed to meet them at Canyon de Los Embudos to accept the formal surrender.

Bringing the glasses closer, sweeping the valley directly ahead, he saw two horsemen running flat out. They were charging across the flat bottom, thin trails of dust roiling just above the ground behind them.

The men were too far away for Crawford to see their faces, even through the binoculars. He thought he recognized the little pinto Ka-ya-ten-nae favored, but he couldn't be sure.

The horsemen were heading to the right, planning to swing around the mountain and into the valley behind it. Crawford swung back into the saddle, the hair standing up on the back of his neck. Kicking his mount, he headed across the ridge, starting to angle down as soon as he reached a slope gentle enough to permit descent.

He wanted to get the attention of the horsemen, but a gunshot was out of the question. He couldn't risk it. All hell could break loose at the first crack of a pistol. He was charging ahead, leaning low over the horse's neck to keep his seat in the saddle. He crossed his fingers, hoping the horse didn't stumble. If the horse fell, they would both roll a long way before stopping. And by then one or both of them would be dead.

He neared the valley floor and sawed on the reins to push his mount parallel to the foot of the mountain. One of the horsemen must have seen him, because they both changed direction without breaking stride. They closed on him quickly. He was sure it was Ka-ya-ten-nae now, and the other would be Chatto. He had sent them ahead to scout the next twenty miles or so. The last thing he wanted was a surprise.

Kicking his horse once more to spur the last ounce of speed from the tired animal, he charged ahead, finally reining in less than a hundred yards from the galloping horsemen.

While he waited in the saddle Crawford patted the horse on its foam-flecked shoulders to calm it. Ka-ya-ten-nae pulled up alongside him. His uniform shirt was covered with trail dust. His face was taut under a mask of tan grime.

"Trouble?" Crawford asked.

The scout nodded. "Mexican cavalry. Three, four hundred."

"Where?"

Ka-ya-ten-nae turned in the saddle and pointed back toward the border. "Toward the border. Not far."

Crawford cursed. "Maybe four hundred, you say?"

Ka-ya-ten-nae nodded. Crawford took a deep breath. Shaking his head, he looked back up the slope. He could still see the straggling caravan in his mind's eye, horses, mules and men strung out over several miles. "What the hell . . ." He shrugged. "Let's go. We have to tell Geronimo."

"He won't like it," Ka-ya-ten-nae cautioned.

"Hell, I don't like it either. But I have to tell him. I don't want him getting wind of it someplace else. He'll think we sold him out."

Crawford rubbed a dirty hand across his chin and mouth. His lips were dry and cracked, a three-day growth like sandpaper scraping against the skin of his fingers.

Shaking his head once more, he moved past Ka-ya-ten-nae. Chatto, who hadn't said a thing, reached out to grab Crawford by the arm. "We could attack them before they know we're here," he said.

Crawford ran a hand across the back of his neck. Now he knew why the hair had been standing on end. "No, we can't," he finally said. "We're here by sufferance of the Mexican government. If we attack their army, we'll never get their cooperation again. We might even start a war."

Chatto looked doubtful. "They'll run," he said. "If they think it's just Apaches, they'll run and there will be no trouble. No one will get hurt."

"I can't allow it, Chatto. I know you mean well, but I just can't take the risk. The general would have my head if I did anything like that."

"The general doesn't have to know."

"Yes, he would have to. And I would have to tell him myself."

Chatto let his hand drop. He disagreed. That was clear. But he understood. It was one reason he liked Crawford. One reason he trusted him. It was, too, he knew, the reason Geronimo and Nachite and Chihuahua trusted him. A man who would break his word to one, no matter what the press of circumstances might be, would deceive all, if he felt it necessary. Only a man who never lied could be trusted, and you still had to watch him, if he was white.

Crawford led the way around the base of the mountain. He opened up a lead on the two scouts, letting his fresher mount run hard all the way. He reached the first cluster of scouts and yelled for them to follow him as he blew by them. He found Geronimo well back in the middle of the Apache band. Nachite and Chihuahua were with him.

"We have to talk," Crawford told him, then asked Geronimo to follow him.

Glancing back over his shoulder, he saw that Ka-ya-ten-nae and Chatto had reached the front ranks of the scouts. He should have told them to say nothing, he thought, then realized it wouldn't have made much difference. In twenty minutes, every man, woman, and child in the caravan was going to know about the Mexican troops. What mattered was getting to Geronimo first and convincing him not to bolt.

Crawford moved well away from the caravan, Geronimo and his henchmen following in a tight knot eighty or ninety yards behind him. When he was well clear of the advancing horde, he reined in and dismounted.

Geronimo approached at a canter, Nachite alongside, and three or four others right behind.

Crawford's Spanish wasn't fluent, but he had enough to tell the war leader they had a problem. Geronimo stayed on his horse, and Crawford asked Chihuahua to find Concepción. He wasn't about to trust so explosive a message to his faulty command of a foreign tongue. He watched Chihuahua ride back toward the main column, conscious of Geronimo's eye burning into his back.

Nachite watched him, too. The son of the great Cochise was reckless and as likely as Geronimo himself to go off half-cocked. That was one reason he had never achieved the prominence of his father, despite being chief by election in the Apache way, rather than hereditary right. The democracy of the Apaches allowed him to take a backseat to others, more eager or more able, and he had chosen to let that happen. He had seen what happened to his brother Taza. The pressure was more than Taza could stand, and he had died far too young. Some said it was because he had gotten too close to the White Eyes. Whatever the reason, Nachite was content to raise hell from a backseat.

When Chihuahua returned, Concepción trailing in his wake, Crawford asked all of the Apaches to join him on the ground. Concepción had passable English and his Spanish and Apache were perfect. Crook suspected that Mickey Free sometimes shaved words, not intentionally toying with the truth but accidentally losing some of it in his pursuit of economy. Unwilling to allow that, Crawford said, "Concepción, I want you to translate every word. Tell Geronimo *exactly* what I say. Understand?"

Concepción nodded. Crawford paused long enough to frame his opening, then swallowed hard. "Tell him to wait until he hears everything I have to say before he makes a decision."

Concepción talked, and Geronimo listened with one ear, never taking his eyes off Crawford's face.

Concepción listened to the chief's reply, translated for Crawford, taking time to phrase his English carefully. "He wants to know why you are worried about him making a decision. He says making decisions is something he does well, and like any man who does it well, he waits for all the facts."

Crawford nodded. "Good. Tell him I respect that, but I have something very important to say, and I want him to understand it fully."

Concepción relayed the statement, then Geronimo's reply. "Geronimo says he will listen."

Crawford took a deep breath. He nodded at the Apaches, then said, "Tell him there are Mexican troops up ahead. Maybe as many as four hundred." He saw Concepción stiffen. The Apaches saw it, too, and they reacted by moving closer together, then closing in around Crawford. "Go on, Concepción, tell him!"

Geronimo listened closely, tilting his head up a little, but keeping his composure, and the granite mask stayed in place.

"He wants to know why this is a problem," Concepción said.

"Tell him it's a problem because he has not surrendered to Mexico. He and his people are still at war with the Mexicans."

Geronimo acknowledged the truth of the statement but, in Spanish, said, "I trust the American army to protect my people."

Crawford understood, but waited for Concepción to translate anyway, buying time to phrase his reply.

"I don't know if we can," he finally said. "They outnumber us and they have supplies. We are almost out of ammunition, our horses and mules are tired, and there may be more Mexican soldiers not far away. We don't know where the nearest American soldiers are, but in any case they are farther away than the Mexicans. And we have the women and children to worry about."

Nachite started to say something, but Geronimo grabbed his arm, half turning to look at his nominal superior, but never quite taking his eyes off Crawford. It seemed to the captain that the Apache wanted to maintain the connection for fear that something would get past him.

"We can attack the Mexicans first. If they don't know we are here, we have the advantage," Geronimo suggested.

"We don't have the ammunition," Crawford said.

Geronimo laughed. "They are Mexicans," he said, again in Spanish. "We don't need bullets. Apaches kill Mexicans with stones, because bullets are too expensive." The others laughed then, and seemed to relax a little.

"No," Crawford said. "I can't allow that. I am here as a guest of the Mexican government."

"And the Mexicans are here as guests of the Apache," Geronimo said.

"No. I must forbid it," Crawford said.

Chihuahua brushed past Geronimo, a Colt in his hand. "You do not forbid us to do anything. We are free men."

Crawford ignored the angry warrior, keeping his unwavering gaze fixed on Geronimo. "I must forbid it. And I do," he said, reaching out to brush the Colt aside.

Without warning, the Mexican cavalry burst over the hill and opened fire. Crawford ran toward them, shouting in English to stop. The Mexicans ignored him, pressing their assault. In no-man's-land, between the scouts and the Mexicans, Emmett Crawford fell to the ground, a bullet in his brain. The scouts returned the fire while the renegades, either stunned or amused, watched the pitched battle. It took several minutes for Lieutenant Maus to get the attention of the Mexican commander. Finally the shooting stopped, but not before twenty Mexican soldiers had been killed by the scouts.

Emmett Crawford was the only casualty on the American side. The company surgeon could do nothing for him. He lingered on for four days, but regained consciousness only a minute or two before his death.

Chapter 25 ═══════

**March 1886—Canyon de los Embudos,
Sonora, Mexico**

GENERAL CROOK SAT on a rock under a cottonwood.
He was in a natural amphitheater, and gentle slopes
surrounded him on three sides. Bourke and Maus and
Gatewood sat behind him, curling their legs under
them as they lowered themselves to the ground. Concepción sat slightly to the left, and in front of Crook,
also on the ground.

Arrayed in a semicircle, the Apaches—Chihuahua,
Nana, Nachite, and several others—faced the general. Geronimo wasn't there and Crook looked to Nachite. It was not necessary to ask the question.

"He will come soon," Nachite said.

Crook nodded. "Good. There is no point in talking
unless all men of influence in your group are present."

"Geronimo wants to know if there is reason to talk
at all," Nachite said.

"There is every reason. Your people are surrounded by enemies on every side. It is time for the
killing to stop."

Nachite smiled. "Old words," he said.

Crook raised his voice. "You know me. I keep my
word. I know you have been told many things in the

past that were not true. But this time I will see to it that promises are kept. On both sides."

Nachite narrowed his eyes. He knew the general by reputation, but he was, after all, a White Eyes. He knew that Crook was honest, a man who could be trusted. But he knew that the Americans often sent a man to make promises, then took him away and sent someone else who didn't worry about keeping those promises. They had taken Crook away once, and here they were once more talking about surrender. It was a long and very old road. Nachite had been down that road before. But their band was small and growing smaller. They were not safe in the Mexican mountains anymore. Maybe it was indeed time for the war to end.

Getting to his feet, Nachite was even more imposing—over six feet tall, his powerful trunk and broad shoulders testifying to his physical strength. The hard, bright eyes and the firm chin testified to another kind of strength. He nodded slowly. "He will come. He will talk. That is all I can say."

"That is good enough," Crook told him.

Nachite stepped through the semicircle, tapped Ulzana on the shoulder, and pulled him aside. Crook affected indifference while the two Apaches whispered their conversation. After a minute Ulzana started up the hill across from the general. Nachite returned to his place and sat down again.

Neither leader spoke for a long time. Crook knew he was in a war of nerves. But he also knew that history was on his side. He could afford to wait. The Apaches could not. Over the crest of the little valley the peaks of the northern reaches of the Sierra Madres jabbed their purple teeth skyward. It looked almost as if a giant mouth were chewing at the sky. The weather was almost perfect. Despite the spring heat they were high enough that a cool breeze rippled through the cottonwood leaves.

Turning to Maus, Crook said, "Lieutenant, why don't you make arrangements for some food? I have a feeling this will take some time."

Davis got up and went to his horse. Nachite watched him closely, the tendons in his neck taut as iron bars. Crook sensed his apprehension. "I have sent Lieutenant Maus to make arrangements for a meal. I'd like you to join us."

Nachite said nothing, but he seemed to relax a little. Even so, his eyes followed Maus until he was out of sight. Rather than make small talk, Crook preferred to let the silence continue. He knew that Geronimo was not a chief, but as the Apache forces had dwindled away to virtually nothing, it was Geronimo who had marshaled the resistance around him. He was first among equals, at the very least. If a final truce were to be negotiated, it would be worthless without Geronimo's endorsement.

Ulzana appeared at the ridge line then and started down the slope. Only then did Geronimo make his appearance. There was nothing theatrical about it, but there was no mistaking the man's presence. All eyes turned to him, white and Apache alike. As he passed over the top of the hill and started down, a Colt jutting from his waistband and twin bandoliers crisscrossed over his chest, the gathering fell totally quiet. He was shorter than Nachite and broader, but he was unmistakably the focus of Apache energy. Every eye, white and Apache alike, followed him down. He carried a Winchester carbine in his right hand. Every meeting of dry grass and moccasin seemed to echo across the mountains. Crook got to his feet and took a couple of steps forward.

Geronimo, his broad face betraying no emotion, laid down the Winchester, stepped through the arc of his followers, and stood in front of the general. He said nothing. Crook waited, wondering whether the first word should be his or the Apache's. Finally, determined to prove his goodwill, he extended a hand. Geronimo looked at the open palm, nodded, and sat down. He braced the carbine across his knees.

"I am ready to listen," Crook said. He waited for Concepción to translate. Geronimo listened impassively. He didn't react at all. It was as if he had turned to stone when he sat down.

"I am ready to talk, Nantan Lupan."

"There is much to talk about, but you have talked before, and you have not lived up to your promises."

Geronimo shook his head. "No. There is only one thing to talk about."

"And what is that?"

"The war between the Apache and the Americans."

"I believe it is time for that war to end. But I have believed that in the past. And in the past you have assured me that it was over. Yet here we are again, in another canyon, talking again about the same things we have talked about before."

Geronimo looked bored. His face made it plain that he had heard all this before. At first it appeared as if he were about to get up, but he stopped and leaned forward. "For a long time there was no trouble between us. But then your people started to kill Apaches. Without reason. Then the Chiricahua went to the reservation. I lived there trying to be good. I tried to farm, but then your people wanted to arrest me, to take me away and hang me. You told me that would not happen. Who are these men who want to hang me? Who are these men who want to hang other Apaches? Why? For two years I lived on the reservation and I did no harm."

"You have killed many whites. It is natural that some white men would wish you harm. But they cannot hurt you on the reservation. You know that. You know, too, that *tizwin* is the cause of much trouble, but you insist on drinking *tizwin*," Crook said, raising his voice.

"A long time ago it was an American, James Johnson, who killed Juan José. Pretended to be his friend. Even when Juan José could have killed the lying American, he couldn't bring himself to believe that his friend would lie to him, so he waited. And James Johnson shot him in the face. Then Johnson had a cannon fired into a crowd of women and children. In this cannon were nails, pieces of chain, scrap metal, to make sure as many as possible were killed. That is one reason there is war between us. That is one reason why I could not stay at the reservation. If a White Eyes could kill an Apache he called friend, could not an enemy White Eyes hang Geronimo?"

"You are making excuses. It was wrong what happened to Juan José. I know the story, and the man Johnson was no better than an animal. But, as you said, that was a long time ago. And I am not Johnson."

"Always, the Americans talk about us this way. They say we are cruel. But we are different. We have different ways. We don't try to make Americans like us. Why do Americans try to change Apaches, make them like white men? It doesn't have to be that way. There is plenty of room. But always you want our land. You find metals, and you want to mine them. You find coal, and you want to mine it. If there are Apaches there, your leaders say, then we will move them someplace else. If it is our land, then it is our coal and our metal. But you just move us, and keep what is in the land for yourselves."

"I know this has happened in the past, Geronimo. But it doesn't have to be like that."

"You want me to change, but I think it is you who should change before there is peace. Why should I believe that things will not be the same as they have always been?"

"Because I promise you that they will not. I have orders from the Great Father in Washington. I have been assured that the abuses will stop, that the Apache reservation will not be violated by anyone, white or Indian. You will be sent away for a short time, no more than two years, then you can return to the reservation. Your families may come with you, so you will be together with them. When you return to the reservation, you will be given food and taught to use the land. You will learn to support yourselves without raiding and taking what belongs to others. You will have good lives for yourselves and your children, and there will be no more killing of Apaches by white men. You know these things are true because it has been so on the reservation for two years and more."

"I know about the food we will be given. I know there are bugs in the flour. I know the corn is rotten. I know the meat is less than it is supposed to be. I

have seen this. It was not that way when the Agent
Wilcox was there, but the Agent Wilcox is gone now.
And it is already like that again. I know this from people who are on the reservation. They say things have
changed back to the way they used to be. I know why
you are here, too. You are afraid that if we are not
all on the reservation, then soon none of us will be
on the reservation. You are afraid that we are right,
and that if the other Apaches learn of it, they will join
us."

"I am afraid of nothing, Geronimo. If you know
anything at all about me, then you know that. You
have to choose. You can surrender now. Or you can
be hunted to the last man. There is no third choice."

Geronimo grunted. There was a long pause, during
which the two men stared at one another. Before either man broke the silence, Maus returned. With him
he had half a dozen scouts, who lugged steaks from
a newly slaughtered cow, and a variety of chickens,
still feathered, vegetables, and several coffeepots.
Geronimo looked at Maus for a moment, then back
at Crook. One eyebrow was arched, and there was
the hint of a smile tugging at one corner of his mouth.

"Is that a Mexican cow?" he asked.

Crook laughed. "Probably," he said.

"Good," the Apache said. "Then we will eat." The
Apaches laughed, and when Concepción had finished translating, the Americans joined in.

The gathering broke up as the Apaches, hostiles
and scouts alike, mingled. Many of the men had relatives on both sides, and they took advantage of the
opportunity to catch up on recent developments in
their families.

Geronimo kept to himself, still keeping an eye on

Crook. Old Nana, who was rumored to be anywhere from sixty-five to ninety-five, and who possibly did not himself know how old he actually was, sat down beside the general. Crook knew him by reputation, and knew that within the past year the old Apache had ridden more than ninety miles in a single day, despite the effects of advanced rheumatism, which made every mile in the saddle near torture.

"You are a very brave man, Nantan Lupan," the old Apache said.

"No more than you, Nana."

"It is easy for me. I am an Apache, and I have no choice. But white men have choices. They don't have to be brave, and no one will care."

"Will you come in, Nana?"

The Indian shrugged. "I am one man."

"But you are an influential man."

"Maybe I am."

"Will you use your influence? It will save many lives. Apache lives."

"There is much hatred to overcome. I think maybe too much."

"It has to end somewhere. Why not here? Why not now? Maybe two old men can make a difference."

Nana laughed. He slapped a thick palm on one thigh and tried to get up. Crook, noticing the difficulty he was having, got to his own feet and reached down for Nana's hand. When the old man was on his feet, he started to remove his hand, but Crook held on, and Nana looked first at Crook's face, then at their two hands, together nearly a century and a half old. He understood what Crook meant and nodded.

"I will talk to him," he said.

"That's all I ask."

He watched the old man hobble to one side, passing Geronimo on the way and bending slightly to whisper in his ear. Geronimo got up and followed Nana off into the cottonwoods. Crook turned away, feeling as if he were spying on something he had no right to see. He walked off by himself, listening to the wind in the cottonwood leaves and trying to block out the sound of conversation behind him. He thought of all the sacrifices on both sides, all the suffering. He thought of the good men, men like Emmett Crawford, who had come here to tame the savage Indian and found that both more difficult, and more painful, than they had expected. And, most of all, he thought of how fragile a thing was peace.

He turned then to look toward the two great Apaches, still whispering together among the trees. Geronimo happened to turn at that moment. The war chief's face was drawn, dignified, but profoundly sad.

And Crook knew it was over.

Afterword

GENERAL CROOK WASN'T quite correct. A short time after the final conference with Geronimo, he left for Fort Bowie, leaving Lieutenant Maus to accompany the Apaches north. But a short way below the Mexican border, when they had camped for the night, Maus and his caravan were visited by a man named Tribollet, who sold the Apaches, both hostiles and scouts alike, mescal. Tribollet told Geronimo that he was to be returned to San Carlos to be hanged, and Geronimo bolted one last time, accompanied by a small band of warriors and women, many of whom returned on their own in a day or two. Tribollet is a rather mysterious character, but it seems fairly clear that neither his presence nor its effects were accidental.

In the meantime General Crook, tired of the back and forth between the War Department and the Indian Bureau, and particularly annoyed that he could not get clear acceptance of the terms he had offered to Geronimo in exchange for his surrender, asked to be relieved of his command, and his request was granted.

General Nelson A. Miles succeeded Crook, and ac-

cepted the final surrender of Geronimo, actually negotiated by Lieutenant Charles Gatewood, at
Skeleton Canyon in southern Arizona in September
of 1886, thus ending for all time the Apache wars and,
except for the disgrace of Wounded Knee, the wars
of extermination against the Indians. But, in essence,
Crook was correct. Geronimo's surrender at Canyon
de los Embudos effectively ended actual armed conflict between the Apaches and the U.S. Army. Charlie
McComas was never found.

In writing this book, I have tried to remain faithful
to the essence of real events, while occasionally devi-
ating for the sake of compression or dramatic en-
hancement. There is a great deal of superb
scholarship available to anyone who wishes to get
a fuller picture of the events than a novel can provide.
Foremost among this scholarship is the work of Dan
Thrapp and that of Eve Ball. A number of memoirs
of the Apache wars were published over the years
by the participants—largely, of course, on the white
side. Among the most informative of these are the
works of Lieutenant Britton Davis, Lieutenant
Thomas Cruse, Captain John G. Bourke, and General
George Crook. Geronimo did dictate a kind of "auto-
biography" during the years of his confinement at
Fort Sill, Oklahoma, where he died February 17, 1909.

The history of governmental duplicity, double-
dealing, and outright barbarity to Native Americans
is long and shameful, but among its more deplorable
cruelties is the treatment accorded the Chiricahua
Apaches who served as scouts for the army during
the Apache wars. They, too, were sent to Florida pris-
ons, principally Fort Marion in St. Augustine and Fort
Pickens, near Pensacola, despite their years of faith-

ful service. It took years of effort from a wide variety of groups and individuals, not the least significant of whom was General Crook himself, to enable these men and their families to return to their native territory, circumscribed and bastardized as it was.

Finally, anyone who cares about the history of the American West owes a debt to a handful of university presses, which have over the years retained in, or restored to, print many of the best works of scholarship and memoir concerned with the people and events that make that history such a rich, complex and, often, painful one.

HarperPaperbacks *By Mail*

To complete your Zane Grey collection, check off the titles you're missing and order today!

- ❑ Arizona Ames (0-06-100171-6)............................ $3.99
- ❑ The Arizona Clan (0-06-100457-X)....................... $3.99
- ❑ Betty Zane (0-06-100523-1)................................ $3.99
- ❑ Black Mesa (0-06-100291-7)............................... $3.99
- ❑ Blue Feather and Other Stories (0-06-100581-9)....... $3.99
- ❑ The Border Legion (0-06-100083-3)...................... $3.95
- ❑ Boulder Dam (0-06-100111-2).............................. $3.99
- ❑ The Call of the Canyon (0-06-100342-5)................ $3.99
- ❑ Captives of the Desert (0-06-100292-5)................ $3.99
- ❑ Code of the West (0-06-1001173-2)...................... $3.99
- ❑ The Deer Stalker (0-06-100147-3)........................ $3.99
- ❑ Desert Gold (0-06-100454-5)............................... $3.99
- ❑ The Drift Fence (0-06-100455-3).......................... $3.99
- ❑ The Dude Ranger (0-06-100055-8)........................ $3.99
- ❑ Fighting Caravans (0-06-100456-1)....................... $3.99
- ❑ Forlorn River (0-06-100391-3)............................. $3.99
- ❑ The Fugitive Trail (0-06-100442-1)....................... $3.99
- ❑ The Hash Knife Outfit (0-06-100452-9).................. $3.99
- ❑ The Heritage of the Desert (0-06-100451-0)........... $3.99
- ❑ Knights of the Range (0-06-100436-7)................... $3.99
- ❑ The Last Trail (0-06-100583-5)............................ $3.99
- ❑ The Light of Western Stars (0-06-100339-5)........... $3.99
- ❑ The Lone Star Ranger (0-06-100450-2)................... $3.99
- ❑ The Lost Wagon Train (0-06-100064-7)................. $3.99
- ❑ Majesty's Rancho (0-06-100341-7)....................... $3.99
- ❑ The Maverick Queen (0-06-100392-1)..................... $3.99
- ❑ The Mysterious Rider (0-06-100132-5)................... $3.99
- ❑ Raiders of Spanish Peaks (0-06-100393-X)............. $3.99
- ❑ The Ranger and Other Stories (0-06-100587-8)... $3.99
- ❑ The Reef Girl (0-06-100498-7)............................. $3.99
- ❑ Riders of the Purple Sage (0-06-100469-3)........... $3.99

- ❏ Robbers' Roost (0-06-100280-1)............................ $3.99
- ❏ Shadow on the Trail (0-06-100443-X).................... $3.99
- ❏ The Shepherd of Guadaloupe (0-06-100500-2)..... $3.99
- ❏ The Spirit of the Border (0-06-100293-3)................ $3.99
- ❏ Stairs of Sand (0-06-100468-5)............................. $3.99
- ❏ Stranger From the Tonto (0-06-100174-0)............. $3.99
- ❏ Sunset Pass (0-06-100084-1)................................ $3.99
- ❏ Tappan's Burro (0-06-100588-6)............................ $3.99
- ❏ 30,000 on the Hoof (0-06-100085-X)..................... $3.99
- ❏ Thunder Mountain (0-06-100216-X)....................... $3.99
- ❏ The Thundering Herd (0-06-100217-8)................... $3.99
- ❏ The Trail Driver (0-06-100154-6)........................... $3.99
- ❏ Twin Sombreros (0-06-100101-5)........................... $3.99
- ❏ Under the Tonto Rim (0-06-100294-1).................... $3.99
- ❏ The Vanishing American (0-06-100295-X).............. $3.99
- ❏ Wanderer of the Wasteland (0-06-100092-2)........ $3.99
- ❏ West of the Pecos (0-06-100467-7)....................... $3.99
- ❏ Wilderness Trek (0-06-100260-7).......................... $3.99
- ❏ Wild Horse Mesa (0-06-100338-7)......................... $3.99
- ❏ Wildfire (0-06-100081-7)....................................... $3.99
- ❏ Wyoming (0-06-100340-9)..................................... $3.99

MAIL TO:
HarperCollins Publishers
P.O. Box 588 Dunmore, PA 18512-0588
OR CALL: (800) 331-3761 (Visa/MasterCard)

For Fastest Service
Visa & MasterCard Holders Call
1-800-331-3761

Subtotal...$_____
Postage and Handling...$ 2.00*
Sales Tax (Add applicable sales tax).................................$_____
TOTAL:...$_____

*(Order 4 or more titles and postage and handling is free! Orders of less than 4 books, please include $2.00 p/h. Remit in US funds, do not send cash.)

Name_____

Address_____

_____

City_____ State_____ Zip_____

(Valid only in US & Canada)   Allow up to 6 weeks delivery.
                                Prices subject to change.   H0805

NOVELS RIPPED STRAIGHT FROM THE PAGES OF AMERICAN HISTORY

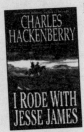

I RODE WITH JESSE JAMES
by Charles Hackenberry
Spur Award-Winning Author

Despite his promise to bring him to justice, ex-con Willie Goodwin is drawn to the charasmatic Jesse James, the clan's reckless lifestyle . . . and James's beautiful cousin. As the pressure of the law closes in, Goodwin gallops to an inevitable showdown where only the lucky will survive.

• Also available . . . **FRIENDS**

RIDE FOR RIMFIRE
by Hank Edwards

Only Rimfire's foreman, Shell Harper, can save the famous ranch and pass its title to the true heir, Emmy Gunnison. To do so he must stand alone against the infamous Billy Bishop gang, as the last hope for Rimfire.

• Also available . . . **APACHE SUNDOWN**

MOUNTAIN CAPTIVE
by John Legg

The winter of 1834-35 is nearly over, and Jim Blackwood and his partners are preparing to leave Cache Valley for the spring hunt. Just before they strike camp, the warlike Blackfeet sweep over them, capturing Blackwood's wife. Now he wants revenge, and he'll fight to the death to get it.   (Available in December)

• Also available . . . **BUCKSKIN VENGEANCE** and **SOUTHWEST THUNDER**

BLOOD OF TEXAS
by Will Camp

As a Mexican living in San Antonio in 1835, Rubio Portillo despised the heartless Mexican rule, and wants to fight instead for the freedom of Texas. When troops attack the Alamo, Rubio will have to struggle to gain acceptance as a loyal Texan while battling his own friends and family.

AN ORDINARY MAN
by J.R. McFarland

A drifting lawman with a knack for killing, MacLane was a lonely man—until an odd twist changed his fate. Only then did he have the chance to change the course of his life and become an ordinary man with an extraordinary message to deliver.